GUILTY AS SIN

THE ACCIDENTAL EXORCIST

JENNIFER CHANCE

OHB

CONTENT NOTE

This dark paranormal romance contains demonic possession and loss of bodily autonomy, body horror, complex consent dynamics, graphic violence, and explicit sexual content. Intended for mature readers (18+) who aren't afraid of the dark. Mostly.

CHAPTER

ONE

Dawn was always my favorite time of day—the hope of a fresh new beginning, a page turned, the flash of unspooling light chasing away anything dark and foul.

Too bad the sun never reached the demon realm.

At least my current home, the Palidor Hotel, remained quiet, the breakfast room still holding its breath for the day's visitors to arrive. Vases of orchids were centered on dark wood tables, gleaming china poised in hopeful expectation, while freshly rolled silverware lay tucked into linen napkins. Brass thermoses winked and gleamed at me, tempting me with the darkly sensual coffee that had been conjured up in the Palidor's back rooms. But I was meeting my office manager and official exorcism assistant, Claire, up in River North this morning, and she'd have coffee.

Or at least, she'd better have coffee. A 6 a.m. breakfast meeting that required a train trip was the stuff of horrors. There was no point in making it worse.

The staff murmured their discreet hellos to me, their bright smiles taking in my crisp silk T-shirt and light sweater, my

1

creased trousers, perfect for meeting someone who was hurting, but not possessed. Also perfect for covering the few remaining bruises and scabs that clung to my body like barnacles, waiting for fresh trauma to feed upon.

I nodded back, thinking for the twentieth time that I really needed to find permanent housing. My side of the duplex that had been my home for nearly twenty-five years had been burned out three weeks ago in an attack meant for me. It was still months away from being habitable. Maybe it was time to move on. Living in the Palidor for these past several days had distanced my real life into something I could poke at like a strange new kid in class, something that interested me but wasn't really my problem, not yet.

I popped in my earbuds and turned left out of the hotel, heading for the 'L' station at Fullerton. At least I wouldn't have to deal with transfers for this meeting.

It only took a few blocks for my feet to slow, my gaze roaming wistfully over Ash Street's old, intriguing housefronts with their walls and gates, the hints of wild foliage spilling over the edges of their metal and stone barricades. Of all the streets I walked around the Palidor, this had become my favorite.

And today one set of gates along the quiet lane was open, making my stomach tighten as I strained to take it all in with one hurried, non-stalkery glance.

This place was a *masterpiece*.

The house sat far back from the street, barely visible through dark wrought iron patterned like the companion piece to Rodin's Gates of Hell. A slender concrete drive disappeared into a tunnel of overgrown lilacs and wild privet, branches heavy with blooms. What little I could see of the structure struck me as expensive but worn—Victorian gingerbread trim gone dusky with neglect, tall windows reflecting nothing but shadow, a turret that felt like it'd been boarded up years ago.

The place wasn't possessed, I didn't think, but it seriously looked like it wanted to be. *Mansion seeks demon. Only serious ghosts need apply.*

I rolled my eyes, forcing myself to keep walking. At this distance, I wouldn't be able to recognize a home possession, no matter what its form. Making assumptions was stupid and unprofessional, and I'd been cornering the market on both those characteristics these past few weeks.

Worse, a whole lot of people had started making assumptions about me, either overestimating or underestimating me, by turns. And some of them weren't doing all that well anymore because of that.

I pulled out my phone, checking it for the fifty-seventh time. Still nothing from Lucian Gray, my business associate, recent-and-maybe-future bed partner, *and* the demon who'd invaded my body for fifteen years before I kicked him to the curb and then started working with him.

No twisted psychological issues there, clearly.

I pressed my lips together, gazing back at the house. Would Lucian know if this beautiful old pile was possessed? Was my intuition waning more as time passed since I'd evicted him from my brain?

No. I'd been special before a demon possessed me, I reminded myself. Even at ten, Rabbi Mordechai had seen that—had known he could use it, use me.

Of course, now Mordechai was dead. So was a middle-aged, stubborn, family-loving detective whose only crime was that he'd pulled my case. Both because of me?

I turned my gaze away from the elegant wreck and pulled up the Dark Streets podcast on my phone, shoving the device back into my bag as Sue Willows purred through her opening sponsorship plugs. Last night's pod had been an update on her regrettably popular 'Death from the Sky' episode, rushed out with impressive speed less than forty-eight hours after Detective Marcus Walsh had fallen from the twenty-first floor of the Prometheus Building. He'd been goaded by a vicious fifth-level demon from the Court of Ruin, the most powerful representation of the horde in the Windy City.

She didn't know that part, but she sure was getting close.

I grimaced as Sue rolled out my baby company's name with dark insinuation. "Thompson & Associates may be a new business tucked into its sweet little building in Oak Park, but we're thinking they're a company to watch on these dark streets..."

A movement on the other side of the lane drew my attention, and I glanced up, startled to see a man walking a smallish dog of pure mutt pedigree. The dog was a cute beagle mix and appropriately spry, tail wagging briskly as he tugged on his bright red leash, but the guy—lightweight jacket, brown pants, sturdy shoes—felt wrong somehow. He didn't look at me but focused on his dog. The man was slender and obviously healthy enough to be walking said dog, but he didn't seem to be flourishing. I couldn't quite reason out why. He was narrow-shouldered, his skin pale under sandy blond hair, and he murmured something to the dog that made the pup's tail wag harder, so he couldn't be that much of an asshole.

So why did he make my guts twist?

He lifted his head as Sue's podcast cut out, and I caught a snatch of the song he was humming, a simple, tuneless melody that sent a cold wash of uneasiness through me. *What the hell?*

Stabbing my phone back on, I picked up my pace in time to Sue's brisk account of Detective Walsh's death and coming burial, the statement by Prometheus Solutions detailing their grief and accountability for not keeping him safe. A statement carefully prepared for their CEO—the detective's *nephew,* in a cruel twist of fate—called it all a tragic accident. Never mind that Detective Walsh unloaded his gun into a wall-sized window...then threw his entire body against it to make it blow out the side of the high-rise.

And Prometheus Solutions was to blame. There was no doubt about that.

So was I.

I reached the Fullerton station entrance practically at a jog, taking in the blue-and-red CTA logo on weathered concrete, the remarkably clean stairs. I clattered down into familiar smells of brake dust, old coffee, and metal, and blinked to realize the guy across the street hadn't had a smell. I hadn't been able to sense his emotions, his history. Had he been too far away?

Was I losing my touch?

I pulled out my phone again and tapped it against the Ventra card reader at the turnstile, weirdly grateful for the green beep as the barriers swung open, as if I'd been accepted, approved. As if at least the turnstiles were cutting me a break.

So much therapy in my future.

It only took a few more steps to reach the platform. Fluorescent lights hummed overhead, and the 5:30 a.m. commuter set grimly watched their electronic overlord announcing the next train's arrival: RED LINE TO 95th–3 MIN.

I sheltered in place near a support pillar, away from the edge of the platform, automatically checking for messages. There were plenty, but not from Lucian.

Avoiding any contact with real humans, I doomscrolled through posts of actual doom—Dark Streets' YouTube and Insta posts, links to "Spooky Places in Chicago," and—

I stopped. Blinked. Then scrolled back four or five pictures —then seven. Where was...?

There. A Victorian house hunched at the end of a concrete drive, but not my Victorian. Totally different part of town. It had just looked so *similar*. A pan forward took me to another image, this one making me smile.

"Hotel Palidor: Chicago's Chicest Haunted Hotel?"

Haunted. Of course it was. Maybe Lucian had gotten me in there at a discount.

Unable to keep myself aloof anymore, I opened our text stream, complete with my last terse *Where are you?* text. Never mind the *Probably should talk* from last week. He'd disappeared after the mess at Prometheus Solutions, and he apparently wasn't ready to come home yet. I was going to need to chip him like a dog if I wanted to track him.

Strangely cheered by that, I typed out a quick message. *Meeting Grace with Claire in twenty. Kind of a weird morning. Let me know you're okay.*

No response, of course. And demons apparently weren't keen on read receipts.

I looked up at the approaching train, letting the vibration pound the unease out of me. An odd, tuneless song played in the back of my mind for the barest second, then was gone.

The doors hissed open, and I boarded, not bothering to try to find a seat. I was too agitated to sit, and there were plenty of workers and kids who needed them more than I did. I only had three stops.

The train rumbled and rolled through the city, coming up surprisingly fast on North/Clybourn, easing into the station almost like an apology. I looked up into the crowd of exhausted-looking commuters—and blinked.

At the back of the crowd was Jacket Guy. Same brown pants. And though the red leash was slung over his shoulders now like an errant scarf, there was no dog in sight. How in the hell had he gotten the dog back into his house and then made it all the way here so fast—and why was he still carrying the leash? He would have had to sprint the whole way, but he wasn't out of breath or sweaty—just cool and calm in his cream-colored windbreaker, watching the train.

Watching me.

Our eyes met, his like flat pebbles at this distance, and a swirl of aromas thick enough to taste swept over me. Before, he'd been too far away for me to sense anything—or maybe he'd been blocking me. But here on the platform, close enough to lock eyes, the scent hit me like a fist. Decayed fruit, wet cardboard, thick and jittering *want*.

My knees threatened to give way. They didn't. Instead, our gazes held as his lips curled into a smile, his hand lifting slowly, deliberately as the train gasped and groaned out of the station, lurching me to safety. Just a guy recognizing a fellow commuter? Could he have made that trek all the way to this station...?

Maybe?

I frowned as we rumbled through the tunnels, hunching into my sweater. That was what happened when you got people killed. You start seeing evil everywhere.

When we pulled into Clark/Division, I kept my eyes on my phone, allowing the passengers to disgorge onto the platform, which only had a few new riders willing to take their place. I shifted to the right, peering down the long aisle, into the next train, then back out onto the platform.

He was there. Standing in the crowd, cream-colored jacket, pale skin, thin lips. Except he hadn't ever gotten on the train. Not at Fullerton, not at North/Clybourn.

No human could have covered that distance on foot.

The train doors closed with him still on the platform. He hadn't gotten on the train.

Unreasoning fear clawed up my throat, along with the soft murmur of a song I didn't know—but maybe had heard. The song the guy had been humming? Had to be. I shook it off, muttering one of Mordechai's endless litanies of prayers instead.

By the time we got to the Chicago station, I was staring out the window like my life depended on it, but there was no man on the platform, no jacket, no half-smile. The doors opened, and we all disgorged, but a quick sweep around showed me it all stayed clear.

Then I looked back to the train—*inside* the train—as the doors closed.

Jacket Guy sat by the window, watching me. He'd been inside the car with me, not three rows away. Same clothes, same smile, making no move to exit the train. His hand lifted in a wave as the train started to move—the perfect mirror of my first sight of him—but I couldn't look at him anymore. I couldn't stay here!

I lunged off the platform and ran toward the stairs, taking them two at a time. At the first landing, my phone pinged with a text from Claire, but I didn't look at it, didn't respond until I reached the sunshine, bursting into the busy streets of River North like a whale breaching the water's surface. My heart was pounding, my hands shaking as I stabbed out a response to Claire, then checked my map app. Grace's house was only three streets away.

Still nothing from Lucian, and a glance over my shoulder showed—thank God—that Jacket Guy wasn't following me.

But who was Jacket Guy—and why did I keep seeing him? More to the point, why didn't Lucian respond? And why did my heart hurt so much at being alone?

I shoved all that down as I turned the corner onto Grace's street and saw Claire standing there with—yes!—a coffee tray in hand. With the allure of promised caffeine snaking around me, all thoughts of Jacket Guy receded. I peered at the second beautiful home of the day...this one far more welcoming.

Tucked into one of the quieter blocks of the neighborhood, Grace's house was all clean lines and warm wood, a modern prairie-style delight that was probably featured in architecture magazines. Floor-to-ceiling windows, a front door painted a cheerful yellow, with matching planters overflowing with peonies. The lawn looked professionally maintained, the driveway held a Tesla, and solar panels gleamed on the roof. Everything about it screamed success, safety, normalcy—the kind of house where bad things weren't supposed to happen.

My nerves started to prickle.

Claire swung toward me as I approached, her shiny blonde hair looking newly conditioned, her smile bright. In her crisp salmon-colored twinset and linen pants, her exorcism-ready leather tote slung over one shoulder, she smelled of apricot scrub and business plans, and I tensed despite myself.

She picked up on it immediately. "What's wrong?" she demanded as she handed over the coffee.

"Nothing's wrong. Just a weird commute." It was way too early to talk hallucinations, and we had Grace to focus on. "Anything new at the office?"

"Well, I'm so glad you asked. I was there this morning getting a few things before coming over, and it was like at 5 a.m., right? I got a door buzz out of nowhere. Thought maybe it was our intrepid mafia bodyguard coming to make sure we were okay, but it wasn't. It was Sue *Willows*."

I stopped short. "The podcaster from Dark Streets? I would've preferred Sergei."

"Well, so would I." Claire dimpled as she shrugged her tote higher on her shoulder. "And as long as Nikolai keeps paying for him to look in on us, I'll take it. Though he wasn't there this morning when Sue showed up, now that I think about it. I mean—it was early."

"Yeah." I took another long drink of coffee, wondering about Volkov's bodyguard. Why had Nikolai assigned him to us? Was the demon-dealing club owner watching out for us—

or just watching? "So, anyway—she buzzed, you let her in, and...what? Did she film our office with a lapel camera?"

"No!" Claire gestured emphatically. "She was actually really *nice*. No camera, no mic, just her. Professional, interested, very direct without being pushy. Not creepy at all. She left her card and wanted to tell 'our side of the story.'"

"Our side of the story about a dead cop who maybe got that way because of us?" I squinted at her.

"About what we actually *do*," she said. "The exorcisms, helping people. She seemed genuinely interested in the super-natural aspect, of course, but she wasn't, like I said, creepy. Just interested."

"Uh-huh." I took a long drink of soul-curing coffee. "We're not talking to her."

"What do you mean?" she protested. "I mean, I didn't say we would, but it's not the worst idea in the world, and the *publicity*—"

"Claire."

"I'm serious! People need to know we're legitimate, and if we don't control the narrative, it's going to control us."

I peered at her. "Did you hear that on another podcast?"

"I did not, I'll have you know. I read it in a real article." She looked at me more closely. "Seriously, though, what's up with you? You look like you've seen a—"

"Don't say it." I held up the coffee like a ward. "Seriously, don't."

She fell silent as we walked up the perfect stone path to Grace's house. Even the doorbell rang out hopefully when Claire pressed it, and I turned to see her glancing at me, her perfectly tweezed brows arched in amusement.

"Kind of like they're trying too hard?"

I snorted, but her suggestion did the heavy lifting of more effectively clearing away Jacket Guy, Lucian's silence, Sue

Willows—and even Marcus Walsh, may he rest in eternal peace.

Footsteps approached from inside the house, and the door swung open. Grace stood there, her red hair catching the morning light, pearl drop earrings swaying gently as she turned her head. At 23 years old, she was pretty and wholesome looking in a Northwestern University sweatshirt, jeans, and bare feet. But the image was marred by the fact that her eyes swam with tears, fear radiating off her in waves.

"*Grace*," Claire said immediately. "What's wrong? What's happened?"

Grace looked from her to me, fixing on me. Her hands lifted slightly, and they shook right along with her voice.

"It happened again," she whispered. "And it's all my fault."

"It's not your fault, Grace," I said with conviction borne of rich dark coffee. "Whatever happened, we'll figure it out together. That's what we do. You want us to come inside? Or should we go for a walk?"

"I mean, I—"

She looked up as a new sound broke across the morning, the soft, smooth purr of a roadster, easing up to the curb, parking directly in front of a fire hydrant. Inside me, my heart didn't just do a shimmy; it unleashed a thirty-person maraca band. The amount of relief surging through me would have been embarrassing if anyone knew about it. I was embarrassed, for sure—but also deeply, desperately glad that Lucian was here, he was safe, he hadn't abandoned me.

Yet.

The thought made my nerves prickle again.

"Who's that?" Grace whispered, her eyes widening. She took half a step back, one hand lifting to her throat. An instinctive retreat from a predator.

I didn't turn with her and Claire to watch Lucian Gray get out of the car. Instead, I watched Grace's reaction.

Normal human fear. Not possession. Not infection. Just a prey animal recognizing a predator.

She was safe...

But for how long?

Finally, I turned to see the demon strolling up Grace's perfectly manicured sidewalk, looking like he was ready to eat us all alive and enjoy every last, lingering bite.

His gaze met mine, held it. "Hello, Delia," he murmured, and I could tell by the flare in his eyes that he knew something had followed me today.

He *knew*.

TWO

"Grace, this is our associate, Lucian Gray. I thought his insights might prove useful today—if you don't mind?"

Grace's gaze jolted from Lucian to me, then back to Lucian, wide eyes the color of sea glass struggling to find purchase on reality again. I understood the feeling. This morning Lucian was dressed in a pair of dark pants with a vivid blue button-down shirt, open at the neck. It was the kind of shirt that looked like it would slide sensually under a jacket, giving him both the air of professionalism and the casual offhandedness of a man willing to get down to business. Platinum glinted at his wrist and neck, and I frowned at that detail. When had he started wearing jewelry?

It's not like he needed it. Though I knew his form was a demonic shedim, appearing human while not actually being human...it more than did the job. Tall and lean at six-foot-two inches of long, muscled legs and arms, Lucian might seem gorgeous at first glance, but he had the body and face of a predator. Black hair swept off his forehead and fanned over his ears—looking longer than I remembered it as well, nearly reaching his collar. His skin was faintly bronzed, his cheekbones cut from the sighs of angels, and his smile soft and sensual as he watched me watching him. His eyes, so dark they were nearly black, flared with just a hint of red flame as I broke eye contact with him and met Grace's swiveling gaze again.

"Oh!" she managed. "I mean, of course. Steve told me a bit about your practice, how you all worked together. I feel kind of foolish asking for help, but he said that you looked into all sorts of situations, not just...you know."

"Absolutely," I agreed, seeing her mind drift as her worries settled back onto her like a familiar but overwarm sweater. She smelled like lip gloss, lemonade, and lurking fear. It wasn't a good combination. "You remember Claire too?"

"You have a lovely home," Claire enthused, which made Grace blink and come back to herself.

"Well, thank you, but I can't take credit for it. Please, come in."

She led us into a wide hallway that opened into a sunny sitting room, tall windows taking advantage of the morning sun. She'd set up a carafe of water and six glasses and gestured awkwardly to them. "I didn't know if you'd want anything to drink."

"This is perfect—and we have coffee," Claire said brightly, moving into the room and scanning the couches and chairs. "We could sit here?"

Without waiting for Grace, she settled herself on the couch, setting her tote on the floor, and looked at me meaningfully. I hung back as Grace took the chair next to Claire. Lucian passed the water glasses without picking up any, then deposited himself on the opposite chair across the long coffee table.

"You said it happened again?" I prompted as everyone got settled. "What happened?"

"What?" Grace blinked, lifting a hand to tuck her hair

behind her ear, making the antique-looking pearl earring sway. "I..." She frowned. "You know, I'm not sure why I said that. I had this terrible feeling come over me this morning, and it built and built, really upsetting me, but—well, you're here safely. Nothing's happened."

I stared at her, trying not to betray my own lurching heart as I thought about the guy on the train. Was Grace just picking up on nearby darkness? "You just—sensed that maybe something bad was happening?"

"Yeah..." She huffed a quiet laugh. "I'm pretty overstimmed these days. But I totally did think something bad was about to go down, you know? It just came over me."

She reached for a glass of water as Lucian leaned forward. "How long have you lived here?" he asked, his warm, interested tone instantly seeming to settle Grace's nerves.

"Ah—gosh, my whole life, I guess." She smiled as she studied the room, looking like the young woman she was once again, red hair gleaming in the sun. "My parents aren't here right now. They wanted to give me some space, I think." She leaned forward to pick up her own glass, and her hand was back to trembling. "They didn't know, you know, what was going on until I finally lost it the other night. Now I think they're afraid of me."

"I'm sure that's not true," Claire murmured, with the kind of soft reassurance that suddenly reminded me of Mordechai. I winced at the unexpected memory, but he'd always been the one to get the client talking, not me. Certainly not Lucian, though here he was sitting in the middle of this woman's morning room looking like he was about to sell her fitness drinks.

"When did everything start happening?" I asked before Grace could fall into a reverie again. My tone was nowhere near as gentle as Claire's, but Grace only flinched, color warming her cheeks.

"I mean, I guess the first thing was my professor—Dr. Martin, psychology. I love that class, I really do! And I want so much to do well. But he's just a complete asshole, and when I turned in a paper that didn't worship at the altar of Jung a thousand percent, he totally trashed my grade. I remember I got really angry—like, unreasonably angry, because not only do I need this class, I was right, you know? And what's college for, if not for debate and developing your own unique perspective? It was just so unfair!"

I watched her as her color changed from delicate embarrassment to something harder, sharper, and a few other things about the room struck me. It was pretty, without question—flowers on the white wicker table by the glass carafe, light-colored furniture, a soft pile rug over warm wooden floors, yellow cheery walls with bits of greenery everywhere. But the room looked staged, holding its breath as Grace recounted her outrage at her professor. Uneasy.

"It sounds kind of ridiculous, but I just wanted something bad to happen to him," Grace continued, drawing my attention back. She stared at her glass now. "I wanted his life messed up enough that he realized that he couldn't just rule people's lives from his safe little chair in his safe little office—I wanted him to *pay attention*. Two days later, he ran a red light and was T-boned by a truck. He ended up in the hospital for, like, weeks."

"But you weren't there," I said, matter-of-factly.

She swiveled her eyes toward me, tracking me across the room. "No," she agreed. "But I was there with my boyfriend—ex-boyfriend. Jim Boggs. Boggs! What a name, I should have known." She grimaced and waved her glass, settling back in her chair. "I thought he was kind of too friendly with—well, it doesn't matter. A girl we both knew, she's in choir with him.

Anyway, they seemed kind of closer than they should be, right? But we were at a party at the end of school three weeks ago—gosh, it feels like forever—and I said something about us going to the shore this summer and he laughed at me like we'd had this conversation a hundred times and said he'd be singing his way through Europe with *her*."

"You hadn't talked about it?"

"I mean..." She lifted her glass in frustration. "Maybe? But it didn't connect until that moment that it wasn't just him and this big old choir performing together, it was him and her and —all of it. I got so angry! All those people there with their sad, knowing eyes, some of them with eyes that were just knowing —not sad at all. Mean. Vindictive. And I sort of snapped. I snarled at him to, well, break a leg and...I didn't even sound like myself. His eyes got really big and he shouted after me, but I ran out and..."

She put her glass down carefully on the table.

"And he did," Lucian said, from where he sat relaxed in his chair, one leg elegantly crossed over the other. "He broke his leg."

She gave him a wobbly smile. "The next night. He fell down the stairs at his parents' home, compound fracture, pins, surgery, the whole thing. He said he'd been drinking, that he had no reason even to have gone upstairs, but—he did and he fell. Because I *cursed* him."

The photos in the room weren't right either, I thought, my mind only half on her recitation. There weren't enough of them —not recent ones. A happy collection of the family with Grace as a young girl, maybe five years old. Two other kids too: a boy and a girl that could maybe have been twins, older than her. Everyone with smiles in their eyes. Beach vacation, Christmas morning. But then the photos shifted when Grace hit her teens. She was awkward, sure, all braces, glasses, and frizzy hair, but it wasn't just her stiffness that came through. It was her family's tension.

"I know it feels that way," Claire put in. "But if you can, tell us about your roommate too. That's what happened most recently?"

"Yeah." Grace shuddered out a heavy breath. "This is so dumb. But given the other things...and I haven't told anyone this but Steve."

I pulled my gaze away from Grace's high school graduation picture. No siblings, parents looking frozen beneath the glass, their eyes strained, their smiles painted on. Grace looked happy at least, but...what had happened here?

"Madison was one of those people who takes without thinking about it. She gives too, don't get me wrong, but if something's in her space, she thinks she has a right to it. It kind of made me mad, but she's a pretty solid roommate otherwise, and I like having her around. I spent most of college in a solo room for one reason or another, but with grad school and living in an apartment, I—this was better. Except for her stealing food."

Claire blinked. "She steals your food?"

"All the time," Grace said, a hint of bitterness creeping into her tone. "Cookies, protein bars, whatever. And I know it sounds petty, but, whatever, a week ago, I finally told her off. That it had gotten to be too much. And she was really sorry—I mean, she's always sorry—and I said forget about it, but I couldn't forget about it. I really was mad. The next morning, she ate spoiled food that was dying in the back of the fridge. She knew it was bad—she told me that later, that she knew. But she ate it anyway, like she couldn't stop herself. She got...really sick. Hospital sick."

Claire looked green herself. "Gross," she muttered, and Grace laughed.

"Yeah." She glanced up, her eyes moving from me to Lucian. "What if my complaining had done that to her? What if I made her do it somehow?"

"You didn't," Lucian said, with all the authority a demon could muster, and Grace smiled a bit grimly. "From your lips…" she began, then broke off awkwardly and took a long drink of water. When Claire glanced at me, it was my turn to give her the meaningful eyeball. She stood and poured more water into Grace's glass, then moved toward me casually. Her gaze transferred to the photos as I gestured, and her brows came together. She could tell something was off too, but I didn't know if she had picked up on the nuance yet.

I moved over to where Grace sat and took a seat on the couch. I could feel Lucian's focus on me, his gaze like a human touch. Awkward, since he wasn't.

"You have two siblings?" I asked, and she blinked at me, something flaring in her eyes that definitely wasn't possession, but could easily have passed for resentment.

"Yeah," she humphed. "Twins, four years older than me. They left the moment they could—both of them went out of state for college. I stayed. I didn't want to stay, but I stayed. First Northwestern for undergrad, then IUC for grad school. And now, my parents are gone a lot too—my mom traveling with my dad more often than ever. They're in Belgium now, back in a few weeks. The fact that they're coming home at all is kind of a miracle, though I'm sure they'll leave again soon."

Over at the frozen family pictures, Claire stiffened, and I could practically sense her mind making connections. What had moved this happy group of people to the "girl with everything" left behind, even by those who supposedly loved her most?

"Grace," I said quietly, and she looked at me—full on looked at me the way nobody possessed ever did, her eyes wide and as open as the sea, her tear-stained face ethereally beautiful. I leaned forward. Down at the end of the couch, Lucian leaned forward too, but there was nothing in Grace Mercer that gave off anything more than fear, despair, and guilt. She now smelled like vinegar and rust, the copper of fear crackling beneath, but there was no smell of burning sulfur, no rot—no anything that I could pick up on.

Which...should have been good news. Was good news.

But also not.

Because if Grace wasn't possessed...

Lucian's quiet words jolted me. "Grace. When did you first know things were different?" he murmured.

She turned, but not fully. "What do you mean?" she asked, and my gaze snapped to her. The voice was different. Not a lot, but enough. Still, there was nothing inside her!

"I mean, when did you feel like—you didn't have as much control?"

"I..." She frowned, but her body language lightened. She physically lifted, straightened, squaring her shoulders, brushing back her hair. "I know this sounds totally rude, but, um—never?"

She turned my way, smiling without meeting my gaze, her manner as light and easy as spring. "I've been lucky, legitimately, my whole life. Everyone says so, and they're right. That's why all of this is so weird. I mean, yes—it sucks that Jim cheated on me, no doubt. It sucks that I got a bad grade on my paper. It was even borderline infuriating that Madison kept eating my Golden Grahams. But these are not actual problems, you know?" She waved her hands. "It's just the weirdest thing."

"It's weird, and it's not fair to you," I said, surprising everyone—even myself—with my calm, steady tone. This time, when Grace half turned, it wasn't Lucian she couldn't look at directly, it was me. It took her a full ten seconds to meet my gaze with her guileless eyes. "I'm so glad your parents are coming back soon. Would you mind if I talked to them directly? You could be with me when I do."

She screwed up her face. "You know, I already take therapy —which they still pay for, thank God. Maybe you should talk to my shrink first?"

"We can absolutely do that as well," I agreed. "But your parents too. I'm sure they're distressed."

"Distressed," she scoffed, laughing. The sound didn't start out as much more than a chuckle, bitter and knowing in a way that made me sad for her, but it grew and shivered into something lower, rougher—a second voice threading underneath hers like a harmony sung in a minor key. The laugh stretched too long, too loud, jangling the glasses and filling up the room with an earthy, throaty subvocal that smelled like desolation and scraping claws, and life squeezed out of a thumping, pumping heart.

And, finally, the barest whiff of burning sulfur.

Then she snapped her mouth shut and blinked around at us, the three of us frozen in our seats, staring back at her with nothing to say. Even Lucian.

Grace's smile split her face with beatific joy. "That would be fine," she said.

THREE

Silence swelled through the room for another half-moment, until Claire finally broke it with a bright, cheerful, "Well!"

"Thank you, Grace," Lucian said, surprising me as he stood. We weren't done here. We barely had begun, but he gestured expansively to me and Claire. We dutifully stood, and Grace did as well. "There are a few things we'll need to research now that we have a better understanding, but you've been incredibly helpful."

"I have?" she asked wryly. She reached up to fiddle with one of her earrings, a nervous, unconscious gesture I suspected she did a dozen times a day. "What—ah...so what happens next?"

"First off, if there's anything you feel like talking about, or anything you think we should know, just call," Claire said. She moved forward with a crisp-looking card, which she pressed into Grace's hands. "Otherwise, we'll be in touch, what—" she glanced at me. "In a few days?"

"Maximum," I said emphatically, and I meant it, never mind Lucian's tense stare. "I do want to check a few things, but you should try to get some rest and sunshine, spend time doing the things you love. Are you taking classes right now?"

"Not really." She shook her head, glossy red hair moving easily. "I have an online course I'm taking more for prep than anything, but it's no big deal. I can read, though—go on walks? If that's okay?"

"That's perfect. Truly." A working theory was rumbling around my mind, skirting the edges of my thoughts, but I felt out of my depth, standing here with Grace. She'd seemed possessed for half a second there, but now it was gone again, and I smelled a new mix of scents, sweet pea body lotion and anxiety. But no burning sulfur, no rot.

Did that mean no demon? From Lucian's glower, I didn't think so, but with Claire's gushing compliments filling the space around us, we moved easily to the front door and out onto the porch. Then stopped.

Lucian's car was gone, replaced by a large, aggressive-looking SUV. A quick glance up the street confirmed that Claire's Lexus had vanished too. Could you hotwire a Lexus?

"Hey." Claire jolted, her protest cut off by Lucian's hand on her shoulder. I think it might have been the first time he'd ever touched her, and I watched with amusement as her eyes nearly crossed.

"Thank you again, Grace," he said, guiding Claire down the stairs as Grace turned to me.

"Thank you," she said emphatically, her sea-glass gaze meeting mine. Nothing stared back at me from inside her, though. Nothing lurked behind those eyes, waiting to pounce.

Grace Mercer *wasn't* possessed. So what was happening here?

I trotted down the steps after Lucian and Claire, taking in the black Range Rover that clearly waited for us. It loomed at the curb, sleek and expensive in a way that didn't advertise itself—until you noticed the reinforced panels along the doors, the way it sat lower on custom springs designed to handle extra weight. Armor, I thought. This wasn't a luxury vehicle; it was a mobile fortress with heated seats.

No one popped out to open doors, so Lucian did the honors, ushering first Claire and then me into the dark interior. The space smelled like expensive leather and gun oil, and I wasn't surprised to see Volkov's bodyguard at the wheel.

"Where's my car?" Claire demanded as Lucian closed the door, then moved to the front passenger side.

Sergei Barbu met her gaze in the rearview mirror, his deep-set eyes intent and not at all deferent—but not hostile either. I was pretty sure he had a thing for Claire, and judging from her sudden blush, I was pretty sure she reciprocated. Though she and our first client, Max Graham, remained friendly enough, text relationships didn't really rank when you had six-foot-four inches worth of bulging muscles and square jaw hanging around, dedicated to your protection.

"It is safe," he told her gruffly, as Lucian slid in beside him.

"We needed to ensure it hasn't been compromised," he said, turning halfway in the seat as Sergei started the car.

"Compromised—are you serious?" Claire protested. "Since when do we rate that level of attention?"

"You were confronted this morning at the office by a podcaster well before business hours," Lucian pointed out, and Sergei's gaze was back on Claire, more accusing now, I thought.

"I didn't think it would be a problem to go in early!" Her gaze shifted to meet his. "I didn't want to disturb—"

"Disturb me," Sergei cut her off. "It's my job."

"But—how did you start the car?" She frowned. "Never mind. Whatever. If you find anything in there, though, you need to tell me."

There was no response to that, and I shifted my attention to Lucian.

"Where are we going?"

He turned back forward. "There's something you need to see, and our conversation with Ms. Mercer plays into it."

"And you couldn't tell me that over text?" I didn't mean for my voice to sound quite so needy, but Claire huffed beside me.

"She felt weird, but not, like, possessed weird. Was I the only one picking up on that?"

I sat back in the luxurious seat, glaring at the back of Lucian's head. "I don't know," I said honestly. "I think I might be losing my touch."

"You're not," he countered, his words clipped and assured. "There are many ways that evil can adhere to a soul, and she's definitely been touched by evil. She's not a Hallow. She's being damaged—has been damaged over a long stretch of time. But —I couldn't get a fix on the exact nature of her affliction, either." He glanced over his shoulder. "That is usually your skill set."

"Well, I couldn't see a damned thing—pun absolutely intended. It was almost there, though, during the laugh..."

"Oh, it was definitely there then." Claire snorted. "But then it was gone again, you know? Just like that."

"Yeah." I pressed my lips together and stared out the window, noting that Lucian offered no further thoughts on the matter. If anything, he seemed preoccupied, which did nothing to improve my mood. What was he worried about? Claire pulled out her laptop and asked Sergei for the in-car Wi-Fi, but I couldn't settle enough to care about what she was surfing. As I gradually recognized familiar streets, my sense of dread coalesced into a hard lump in my gut.

"Why are we going to Holy Angels?" I asked, making Claire look up.

"The cemetery?" She peered down the street, then frowned as Sergei pulled to the sidewalk before the entrance. "They let you drive inside," she pointed out.

"They do," Lucian agreed. "But you can remain here. Delia and I won't be long."

He opened the door before she could protest, and I was right there with him. I didn't mind him sidelining Claire for this visit, but it only made my sense of dread peak. "What happened here?" I asked quietly as we strode through the cemetery, angling for the Jewish sector.

"I didn't want to tell you this over the phone, but there's been a…disturbance here. I have a cleanup team assigned to address it, but I wanted you to see it first."

I frowned. "What sort of…" My words petered out as we reached the small section of gravesites that included Mordechai's. Only, unlike the tidy, faded gravestones surrounding his, Mordechai's plot had been—well, desecrated was the only word for it.

My heart plummeted into my stomach. I hadn't come to visit his grave—I hadn't honored or protected him. "Who *did* this?" I hissed, shame blasting through me, followed by rage. "Who would *dare*?"

The gravestone itself had been splashed with crudely painted sigils and pentagrams, and more symbols were cut into the soil, the freshly laid sod and flowers torn out by the roots, leaving the grave with the impression of being naked and open to the elements.

"Delia…" Lucian began.

"No, seriously. Who did this?" I whirled on him. "And why? Demons don't have hands, Lucian, other than you. And desecrating a grave is a felony. This cemetery will have cameras everywhere—they'll know who did this. When did it happen?"

"I was notified of its existence early this morning. The

cameras caught the disturbance, yes, which occurred between 3:45 a.m. and 4 a.m.—multiple perpetrators. From their appearance, they were likely from the homeless encampments a few blocks away."

"Unhoused people did this?" I gestured angrily at the symbols cut into the ground. "What the hell is this even saying?"

"It's mostly gibberish, which tells you that it's a lower-order demon's work, third level. Possessor demons most likely taking over minds that were already broken. Mordechai has—had—a long history of rousting demons in this area. You know that."

"I know that he did work in the food kitchens and shelters, sure. But what the hell point is there in defiling the man's grave? He's not here to give a shit about it, and Ethan doesn't live anywhere near here. What's the point?"

The answer to my question hit me almost immediately. "They did this for me? To hurt *me*?" I gaped at him. "But to what end? They have to know they're just going to piss me off."

He shifted uncomfortably. "They're third-level gluttony demons—"

"I don't care if they're demon dandruff," I snapped. "They did this for a reason. I just came off an attack where I saw the people I cared most about explode on the pavement and get sucked underwater to their deaths. This is what? A message that nothing is sacred? That they're stronger than I think they are? What is it they've written here—and here? And don't give me that bullshit that it's gibberish. If it was gibberish, you wouldn't care if I saw it."

Lucian grimaced. "It's a message that it's not over—that Mordechai's death doesn't erase the debt he owes."

"Owes who?" I demanded, my mind instantly jumping to Nikolai Volkov. The Eastern European club owner had served a debt to the demon Pithius, which had resulted in his complicit possession, but he was a criminal. "Mordechai was a rabbi—"

"Ex-rabbi—"

"And he consulted with the Vatican on exorcisms, for Christ's sake."

Lucian's lips twitched. "Well, probably not—"

"You know what I mean!" I stormed. "He would no sooner owe a debt to one of these sacks of shit than he would dance naked in the street. So I'm not—"

"You've been summoned to the tribunal alongside me, Delia," Lucian interrupted me. "That's also what is written here. It's Friday, four days from now, and all seven courts will be in attendance. I killed a demon outright, and you..." He waved at the ground. "You're going to be held accountable for the sins of your master."

I rolled my eyes at the overturned dirt. "Held accountable by a bunch of demon scum. Oo. Scary."

"You should be scared," Lucian said quietly. "Mordechai didn't confront demons in their own den. No exorcist should. But he was powerful, and you were his assistant, and you've already proven yourself to be...unusual. The Court of Ruin thrives on picking apart the unusual. Mirr knew that, knew Asmodaea would want you. Planned to offer you up to her on a platter."

I stared at him. "That's why you killed him."

He shrugged. "I thought destroying him would help cut short that thread of knowledge, but rumors had already started twisting in an inexorable weave. Now your name is on the tip of the tongue of every member of the horde with a grudge against Mordechai, and if I am not here to protect you...you'll be hunted down. Killed, eventually."

"Why wouldn't you be there? They can't kill you."

"They could, but they won't," he said matter-of-factly. "But they could weaken me, attempt to strip my powers, cause me harm; that part I'm not worried about. But I am worried about you."

I blinked at him. "It's literally my job to handle demons, Lucian. And if you know they're coming…"

His chuckle was low and soft, and he lifted a hand to drift it over my hair. "So fierce," he murmured. "So certain. If I were Asmodaea, I'd want to take you apart too."

My lip curled. "If you're hitting on me, your approach needs work."

"Oh no, sweet Delia." His hand trailed down my cheek, along my jaw, and I shivered. Had he been warmer before? Now the cool touch of his fingers sent whorls of wrongness through me, as if my body was recognizing the otherness of him more strongly. Lucian's smirk told me he knew how I was reacting. The glint of red flame in the black depths of his eyes told me further, he didn't care. "The more you pull away from me, losing my imprint from your body, the more we are intractably intertwined."

A strange note of—longing? Need?—quivered just beneath his words, enough to make me feel an echoing pang deep within me. I stared at Mordechai's damaged grave, its rebuke laying me bare. "Unless maybe I'm the problem," I muttered. "First Mordechai, then Marcus…I'm killing anyone who gets too close to me, Lucian. I might be more dangerous to you than you think."

"No," he said again. His finger firmed on my chin, tucking beneath it, turning me toward him. There was no denying the fire in his eyes. "You're not going to lose me, Delia. I won't let that happen."

I let myself hold his gaze for longer than I should, his internal fire promising me a heat both blessed and damned. "Yeah, well, you can't promise that."

Those deep, banked flames flickered. "Watch me."

He leaned toward me then, the barest inch, and his cool breath skated over my lips, making the sensitive skin twitch. "There are many things I can do that I haven't yet, sweet Delia. But not here, I think. Not yet. Soon."

I swallowed, forcing myself to smile. "If you're lucky, maybe."

The spell broken, Lucian reached for me and pulled me away from Mordechai's grave, raising a hand as if in greeting. When I blinked up, I saw a van I hadn't seen before idling at the edge of this end of the cemetery, its side emblazoned with an innocuous-sounding landscape company.

I frowned at it. "You guys have your own gardeners?"

"I want you and Claire at Descent tonight, 9 p.m.," he said as we walked back to the SUV. "Sergei can drive you. Dress for moving quickly. Nothing you like too much."

I made a face at him. "When are we getting Claire's car back? You're not going to find anything there."

"Perhaps, perhaps not." He stopped at the gates of the cemetery. "I'll leave you to Sergei. You're going back to the office?"

"Yeah." I shivered against a sudden chill breeze and glanced around quickly. "I need to look through Mordechai's files." I thought briefly about telling him about Jacket Guy but didn't. He was already getting heavy-handed with the security detail. Demonic hallucinations weren't going to make me stabby, but being smothered by Lucian would.

Claire watched me with curious eyes as we got back into the SUV and nodded when I told Sergei to take us back to the office, but she quickly returned her focus to her laptop. Sergei watched us both when he wasn't focused on the road, but none of us spoke. None of us needed to.

I stared out the window and let the anxiety wash through

me. A client who may—or may not—be commanding evil to do her bidding without ever realizing it. A hallucination-throwing entity leering from the shadows. A horde with a weirdly intense vendetta over a soup-loving exorcist who brandished a shofar, not a battle ax. And my own dark, beautiful demon, whose ash-tipped wings were going to be ripped straight off him unless I got out ahead of this fucked-up jury of his peers in five days.

I needed to read Mordechai's files.

Sergei deposited us at the back door entry to our building, not bothering to park the SUV in the lot. He rumbled off, muttering something about checking the surrounding quadrant, while Claire and I stared after him.

"He takes his job very seriously, doesn't he?" I asked as we keyed our way in. For a wellness center, this place was big on security unless there was an active scheduled class on the books, and those usually happened in the evenings. Lucian's impromptu subbing for a Vinyasa class last week had sent a bit of attention our way, but since he hadn't shown up since, his yogi notoriety was fading—and the metaphysical community wasn't a crowd who followed the news. We'd gotten more attention since the Prometheus Solutions case, but not from inside the building, at least.

"I'd like to say we're a boring assignment, but he doesn't make it feel that way," Claire agreed. "I've never seen anyone more plugged into electronic surveillance, police activity, even special events happening across the city. I have to think we're only one part of his overall detail, but every time I turn around, he's here. At least he's hot."

"Yeah?" I glanced at her, sensing my opening to get caught up on her personal life in the least intrusive way possible. Though I'd clocked her appreciation for our bulky bodyguard, she had also seemed to have an interest in Maxwell Graham, a young lawyer whose family we'd messily liberated from their own demon affliction. I didn't care who Claire hooked up with, but I found myself, once again, feeling strangely responsible for her. It was just too bad that the only guys I knew happened to be demon-adjacent. "So, you and Max aren't really a thing?"

She sighed. "Max and I would absolutely be a thing if Max had the brain space for anything besides his family and getting his career back on track. I think he was surprised to realize how much he'd let everything slip in the wake of, you know, his entire extended family being possessed to varying degrees by demons summoned up through a Ouija board. It's like he's lost entire years and doesn't exactly know where he placed them. We've agreed to just do our own thing for right now."

"Well, that sounds very responsible of you," I pointed out as we trudged up the stairs. It was not yet noon, but it already felt like deep into the evening.

She snorted. "It's not like we had a super healthy basis for a relationship, you know? Granted, he wasn't *my* client, he was strictly working with you, but it's still a heck of a first date to meet someone at a church when your new best friend and future business partner is bleeding out the next pew over."

"I mean, fair." Her words bounced around my head as we clicked down the long hallway toward office 212, the gleaming metal placard of Thompson & Associates mocking me as I unlocked the door and stepped inside—hopping a bit to avoid stepping on a small scatter of business cards on the floor.

"Oh, cool!" Claire announced, swooping down for them. "I'm making a diagram—ugh, we *got* it, Centered Yoga. This is your fifth card this week. Let it *go*. Lucian's not for sale."

I snorted as she dropped the offending card in the trash but carried the others to her desk like found treasure. True to her word, she had a poster-sized layout of the building—which she'd gotten from Sergei, I had no doubt—posted on a corkboard behind her desk. She pulled it out and settled it on her desktop, ready to add to her collection.

Meanwhile, I flipped on the lights, though the day was bright and sunny, and took in the office's carefully curated sense of calm. Other than the electronics bristling from both Claire's and Steve's desks—dual monitors and backup towers in addition to laptop docks—the place projected the serene welcome so important to the wellness center's ownership. Creamy furniture, tones of gray and taupe, and comfortable textiles softened the edges of the space, with an inviting seating area where the possessed or possessed-adjacent could take a load off, and a door into my inner sanctum that blocked the view to the barely controlled chaos.

Finishing her art project, Claire pulled out her laptop and nudged her chair away from her desk to set up her command center. "You know, I've been thinking about Grace ever since we left her house—and I've got some ideas."

"Yeah?" I moved to my own office door, eased it open, and flipped on the light. Part of me held my breath that I'd see Lucian stretched out at my desk, but I didn't really expect him there. I was still disappointed, sure, but that was on me.

"Absolutely," she said crisply as I turned back to her. "So, the whole reason why you decided we could take this job is because she wasn't possessed. And then we get to her house, and, creep central. Well, what if she's not possessed in the traditional sense? In other words, what if it's something around her that's possessed?"

I leaned against the door frame. "I'm listening."

"Okay, so those pearl earrings, did you notice them?"

I nodded. "They were pretty."

"Pretty and *old*," she said with emphasis. "Like heirloom old. And Grace was wearing them in the last photo I saw where she looked anywhere close to being normal, and she looked like she was right around age twelve in that snap. What if she got those earrings, they were cursed, and ever since, something bad has been attached to her? That would explain why you couldn't see the demon, right? Because it's not inside her, it's in the jewelry."

I made a face. "I think I would've still picked up on a sense of wrongness, though." I wanted to believe that anyway.

"Oh, honey, you totally picked up on a sense of wrongness." Claire waved that off. Your hackles went up the moment we stepped into that morning room. You were the one who noticed the photos, and you barely sat down the entire time we were there. It was hink-central, and you knew it."

I smiled, knowing she was saying all of this in part to make me feel better, but okay with it all the same. "Fine, it's possible. What else do you have?"

"Variation on the same theme," she said crisply. "What if she did experience some trauma around the age of twelve, and it's so severe that she's projecting demonic-level energy, like a psychic manifestation of rage or something. In other words, she's not possessed, but she is manifesting significant anger. Didn't Steve say that she's been in therapy since she was twelve, with an emphasis on woo-woo stuff, to find her joy or whatever? What if her joy is coming out in ways that she's not expecting? Her anger is literally manifesting and, I don't know, attacking people. What do you think?"

She bounced nervously in her seat, as if giving this particular theory space to live out loud made her realize how insane it sounded. And it did sound insane, but that didn't make it not true.

I blew out a breath. "So, it's possible, but that really isn't how this works. At least, it's not how demons work. I don't know about manifestation. I've never read those books. But demons are intangible entities. As a result, they don't have tangible power over humans. They can disturb the energy of lower-level objects, yes. They can even shove things toward a human, and the human can then react to the thing and, say, slip and fall, or they can freak out a human to the point where the human does something from a place of emotional distress, but demons can't literally shove a perfectly good human off a ledge. At least not in my experience. And, frankly, if they started having that ability, we'd be in way bigger trouble."

"Fair, but if it's not demonic but, you know, straight up supernatural, she could have that kind of influence? She could have made the professor go through the red light, her roommate eat spoiled food, or..." She frowned. "Except she wasn't there when any of that was happening. That doesn't feel right."

"No, but again, I'm not an expert on manifesting energy. There are a lot of stories out there about manipulating darkness through rites and rituals, so yes, it's possible. But I think she would need to be doing it willfully. So, either she's the world's best actress, or she's not the catalyst. What was your third option?"

"Well, this one is kind of also weird, too, but maybe less weird than Grace secretly being a voodoo priestess. She's kind of guileless, right? Open, trusting—it's as if she doesn't have any psychological defenses. What if she's simply a handy skin suit for wandering demons looking for a good time?"

I blinked. "An empty vessel?"

"Yeah—they slip in when she's stressed and use her body to create their influence on another person, plant a demonic seed that will flower later, or whatever, and then slip out when they're done. She doesn't know it's happening because she's not fighting it. There's no resistance or even awareness."

She threw up her hands. "It's either that, or her family's cursed. I mean, something had to have happened to these people to cause their photos to fall apart."

I blew out a breath. "Any of those are possible," I admitted. "I've seen cursed objects, for sure. And non-demonic projection is totally outside of my experience, but also seems super reasonable. Grace being an unwitting vessel would for sure explain why Lucian could sense something wrong with her, but I couldn't see it for myself. Either way, we'll need more of her history—and we're going to want to talk to her parents and her therapist too, if that's possible. Can you see if you can get any more information out of Steve?"

"Definitely." Claire pulled her phone out. "He's working today, but I know he'll want to see what we think. And now that we've met Grace, you know, in her own house, we can ask her about maybe what happened at twelve, though I don't think he's known her that long."

"Worth a shot." I gestured toward my office. "I'm going to look for anything in Mordechai's files. Grace's family has been here a long time, I think. Maybe he worked with them before?"

We turned toward our respective tasks, but when I stepped into my back office, I breathed out a sigh of relief I hadn't realized I'd been holding. My office felt...good. Right. Despite Lucian's redecorating job to make it sleek and functional, I had plants on the windowsill now, and soft throws and pillows on the chairs. Even my desk felt more homey, with its stacks of journals and open boxes all around.

I wove my way through those boxes and to my desk, realizing that Grace at twelve years old would have been right around the time of me at thirteen, three years after I'd begun helping Mordechai. I'd been working my way through his old journals, and I'd finally started showing up in his notes—some of them cribbed and cryptic, but I was there.

D—id. Z in less than 5 mins.

D—scratch marks. Not eating.

D—id. multiples—they were as surprised as me.

That last one made me laugh, but though I remembered rituals and lessons, and of course an endless litany of psalms, I didn't recall specific cases the way I thought I should. Names ran together, blurring, and my memories were indistinct. Still, I noticed that a cluster of cases kept taking Mordechai back to the North Side of the city, and I remembered that, vaguely. Same city streets, similar houses and parks. There'd been a lot of parks with those cases, only not pretty or well-tended ones. More like the scene behind the gates at the house I'd walked by this morning.

Had that just been this morning?

I turned the page, and my gaze jittered over a name in Mordechai's list of clients—one name in dozens, with no other reference, but something about it...

I frowned. "Thomas Keegan," I murmured aloud, trying on the sound. It didn't ring any bells, but I glanced around at the unopened boxes. Mordechai's nephew had sent me case files dating back fifty years, but nothing was labeled. I'd unboxed about half of them and gotten them on shelves, files from way before my time, and then another set of files from the most recent cases we'd shared. But in between there was a vast wasteland of empty shelves and overly full boxes that needed to be sorted, each heavier than the last.

Claire drifted in and out over the next few hours, bringing both more coffee and eventually lunch, and even helping me stack the files in sections as I got them sorted. It still took until nearly three o'clock before I found Thomas Keegan's file.

And when I fanned it open, I froze. Jacket Guy—looking not

a day younger than he had on the street today—stared out at me from the middle of a news clipping about the opening of the Near North soup kitchen. Same sandy blond hair, same pale face, same thin build. Unbidden, a tune started up in the back of my brain; his tune, I realized now. Four notes in a cascading rhythm of no discernible pattern—up, down, steady, down, up—each held a different length of time. As quickly as it appeared, it slithered away, leaving me peering at the photo.

Keegan was part of the staff at the soup kitchen, it appeared, unsmiling and remote-looking. Honestly, he looked kind of terrible. Was this before Mordechai exorcised him, or after?

I carried the file back to my desk and set it beside Mordechai's journal. From the date, I would have been fourteen, and I screwed up my face. I remembered the man's face and body from this morning, but why couldn't I recall a single detail from the exorcism? The notes below the name weren't all that helpful either.

Hallucinations. Schiz. Violent.

D—identified Z.

Rec. psy followup. Dr. JB-S. V-D?

The last two letters had been heavily underscored, and space had been left beneath the entry, as if Mordechai had expected to come back to the page. But no additional notes were listed, and as I paged through the file, there was nothing else interesting on Thomas Keegan, other than he'd worked at a soup kitchen where a whole bunch of people seemed a bit broken, from my read. There was even a couple of deaths listed, a Wendy Simms and Barry Stone, though not Keegan's. Mordechai's notes on the guy were written less than ten years ago—would Keegan be alive, still? Living in the city, working at the soup kitchen? It was worth a shot.

I reached for my laptop, then hesitated. Even if he was still alive, why was he showing up out of nowhere to harass me? Him or something looking like him? I'd been roaming the streets of Chicago for a full decade since Mordechai had exorcised Keegan's demon. Why was he only surfacing now?

The answer was obvious, of course: things had changed. I was no longer possessed, and the imprint of the demon who'd lurked inside me was fading by the day. Mordechai was also dead.

I was alone. Unprotected. An easy mark.

"Fuck that," I muttered, and I pulled out my phone, photographing everything in case I needed it later—especially the photo of Keegan. I went through the folder again, and there were a few more clippings—more deaths of unhoused souls. George Roberts, David Chen, and Luke Wilkins. George had jumped off a bridge, while David and Luke had died of heart failure, months apart, no suspicious circumstances. I glanced back at the others. Wendy had overdosed, while Barry had walked into traffic. *Jesus.*

This wasn't an easy life for the sick, the unprotected. Mordechai had clearly felt guilty that he couldn't help them all.

I was just finishing when Claire poked her head in.

"So, we should probably go get cleaned up if we're supposed to—whoa. What's wrong? What's going on?"

I scowled at the file, then at Claire, surprised by the flare of annoyance. Irritation spiked not because of her concern, but because I needed to be concerned for her. She was my responsibility, whereas before, I'd only needed to take care of myself.

But if I was going to allow her around me, she needed to understand how dangerous things could get.

"This morning, I saw someone on the train, a man who looked like this." I scrolled to the photo of the newspaper clipping and showed it to her. "He appeared on the platform at my first stop, and then on the train at the third—when I got off the train. He never got on the train, but he was there."

She looked up at me, understanding stark in her eyes. "Demon?" she asked. She'd come a long way in just a few weeks.

"Maybe. Except, I didn't recognize him when I saw him—only when I found this Thomas Keegan in Mordechai's files. Someone he helped, it looks like, but there's not much information on him."

That made her tilt her head. "So, an ex-demon from an exorcised client. Sort of."

"I...I honestly don't know. But if you see him—and you probably won't, he's probably focused on me—I wanted you to be aware. I apparently was around for his exorcism, but I don't remember it."

"Lucian would, don't you think?" She jolted as her watch buzzed and started scrolling.

"It's Steve." She bit her lip as she read. "He says Grace's therapist is Dr. Brennan. Office in Lincoln Park. He's texted her about getting a release form signed." She scrolled. "Oh. And Grace's parents aren't calling him back. They're apparently really, really busy. All the time."

"Convenient," I muttered.

"He's worried about her," Claire added, still reading. "Says she seemed really shaken up when she called this morning. Kept apologizing."

"She needs to quit that. Tell him we're on it, and we'll call the therapist tomorrow. It's getting late in the day to hit her up now."

She nodded as she thumbed through the message. "Speaking of which, we've got to get ready. I have more clothes for you back at my place—something that'll work. We can grab food on the way..." She broke off, and her face now reflected irritation. "Except I've got no wheels."

I glanced out the window, which offered me a vantage point of the parking lot. Sure enough, Sergei's SUV was there, though the big man wasn't visible through the tinted windows. "Then I guess we get to be chauffeured." I sighed.

It was another four hours before we finally made it to the Descent. Claire had opted for bootcut leggings and a sleek black bodysuit with a loose, silky overshirt that made her look ready for either a nightclub or a Pilates class, paired with heeled ankle booties that added three inches to her height. She also carried her sleek leather exorcist tote, which she never seemed to go anywhere without.

She'd taken it upon herself to outfit me too, since neither one of us had wanted to swing by the Palidor. The dark-wash skinny jeans she'd recently had delivered were so new they still had that stiff denim feel, and the crimson fitted tank was tags-off-an-hour-ago fresh, but I'd given a hard pass to the ridiculous sequined surplice wrap top she'd offered. I'd browbeaten her into digging through her impressive closet until she'd found a several-year-old leather jacket that had seen better days. So had I, and I immediately appropriated it. Paired with my already beat-up-looking boots, it almost made sense.

I'd been to the Descent before, but my first visit to the nightclub had been much later in the evening. 9 p.m. Descent was decidedly more civilized.

The club occupied a converted brick warehouse in the West Loop, the kind of place that had probably churned out steel or widgets a century ago before being gutted and reborn many times over, depending on the vices being served. There was no signage—if you knew, you knew. If you didn't, the line of beautiful people in expensive clothes waiting behind a velvet rope would have been your first clue that this wasn't the kind of place you stumbled into by accident.

Sergei pulled into a VIP spot like he owned it, which, knowing Volkov, he probably did. He circled the SUV to open our doors with the kind of old-world courtesy that felt weirdly out of place, given we were headed into what was essentially a demon bar. The bouncer—a wall of tattooed muscle with an earpiece—gave Sergei a nod that was equal parts recognition and respect. The velvet rope lifted without a word.

The people in line watched us pass with the kind of envious curiosity usually reserved for minor celebrities. Claire hunched her shoulders like she could feel their stares, but I kept my eyes forward. I had bigger problems than whether I looked the part.

The moment we stepped inside, the bass hit me like a physical blow, thumping through my chest and into my bones. The music was dark, electronic, hypnotic—even now, well before the witching hour, it sounded nothing like the mindless club pop you'd hear at a normal bar. This was the kind of music that made you want to do stupid things. Descent felt different because it *was* different.

Underneath the expensive alcohol and designer perfumes, beneath the sweat and pheromones of bodies pressed too close together, I caught the telltale whiff of burning sulfur. Demons. Plural. I sorted through the scents automatically: cinnamon and musk, copper and oil, an ozone-sharp tang from somewhere in the VIP section. I didn't know enough about individual demon courts to pick out their creatures by scent, but I suspected there was a healthy mix of every evil that was any evil in the city here tonight. Still, people danced, laughed, drank, and were generally unmolested. Volkov's territory meant Volkov's rules, and apparently, those rules included not eating the guests.

Sergei cut through the crowd like he carried a disease, but he didn't head for the back rooms where I'd found Volkov the first night I'd crashed his party. Instead, he angled toward a guarded staircase. The bouncer there took one look at him and stepped aside, and Sergei took the first step up.

That was when Claire's hand locked around my arm, her grip tight enough to bruise.

"Delia. *Delia.*" Her voice was barely a whisper, all the blood draining from her face as her gaze locked on the nearest heavily stocked bar. "Oh my god, I can't believe he's here."

FIVE

Claire gripped my sleeve like a trauma victim, and I turned to where she was looking, fully expecting to see Jacket Guy. But it wasn't.

The man standing behind the bar was male, late 20s, cute in a preppy sort of way, with light blond hair and a clean-cut appearance that seemed out of place in the industrial-chic Descent. He appeared to be good at his job, mixing drinks while carrying on a lively banter with his clients, and he certainly didn't notice Claire watching him from across the room.

"What's wrong?" I asked her, as quietly as possible, though nobody was paying attention to us.

"That's Jay Butler," she said as if that meant anything to me. "Lily's boyfriend. From high school."

I stared at her another second before the dots got close enough to each other for me to make the connection. "The mean girl from high school? The one you, ah, handled?" Even though Claire's transgression was twelve years in the past, I didn't want to be indiscreet. She believed she might still be held accountable for staging a lab accident to take out the two high school bullies who were extorting her for homework support, and just generally because they were nasty asshats. I refocused on the bartender, trying to imagine him as a bully, but it was a stretch. Still, he was a bartender at Descent; he probably had something wrong with him.

Sergei turned back to us, his hooded eyes flicking from Claire to the bar. "Problem?" he asked gruffly.

"No! No," Claire said, clearly forcing herself to pull her gaze away from Jay to focus on the bulky bodyguard. "I recognize him from my high school, if you can believe that. I just didn't expect to see him here."

I quickly filled in the gaps for him. "He and his girlfriend made Claire's life hell."

Sergei's gaze sharpened as he turned from Claire to take in Jay more thoroughly. More professionally, I realized with a start. "You want me to trouble him?"

It took Claire a second to understand what he meant. "What? No. God no. I mean, he was a dick, yes, but I mean, he's just a bartender now. I can get over it."

Sergei snorted. "No one is just a bartender at Descent. He's probably clearing six figures, easy."

"Seriously?" Her lips twisted into a wry smile. "Well, I guess he landed on his feet okay then. And if he left Lily behind, then that was maybe his first right step."

Sergei humphed. "I will look into him, make sure that I know his details." He lifted a hand to forestall Claire's protest. "He will not bother you again."

He turned back and continued up the stairs, saying nothing as we entered the narrow, dim hallway, barely illuminated by soft red lighting. He knocked briefly on a door labeled only with the number nine, then opened it without waiting for a response.

Volkov's observation room took itself very seriously. In addition to a floor-to-ceiling two-way mirror that overlooked the main dance floor, providing anyone in this room a sweeping view of the writhing crowd, it also boasted easily twenty different monitors, queued to security feeds. There was a sleek black central conference table with chairs around it, and two larger-than-life males who sat like predators in two of those chairs, eyeing us both with naked interest.

I took a moment to savor the impact of their sheer beauty. Nikolai Volkov wore a tailored charcoal gray suit and a black silk eye patch over one eye. His remaining ice blue eye swept over me with a palpable touch before taking in Claire. His defined, angular face with its high cheekbones and sharp jaw drew the eye, but his full, sensual mouth made it hard to shift my gaze away. It curved into a smile as I studied it. "Miss Thompson," he practically purred. "Miss Bickwell. A pleasure to welcome you here."

In contrast, Lucian's vibe was closer to Sergei's. He wore black jeans and a tight-fitting black shirt. His platinum watch glinted at his wrist, and his dark eyes fairly gleamed as he trapped my gaze fresh off its perusal of Volkov.

The two alphas couldn't be more different. Where Volkov was all deceptive polish, brutality, and black ice, elegant and controlled, Lucian wore his emotions like fine cologne. Dark, sensual passion swirled around him, somehow radiating heat even though the temperature was markedly low in the room, whether due to the air conditioning or his demonic presence. Volkov was dangerous because you'd never see him coming, but Lucian was the guy who'd broadcast exactly what he wanted. And then take it.

"Please, sit," Volkov ordered, but while Claire complied immediately, I was too keyed up. Instead, I moved to the window, staring out at the undulating crowd. Sergei took up position by the door, watching everything from the monitors, to the conference table, to the dance floor.

"Why did we need to meet here if Lucian has a target on his back?" I asked. "Descent is public."

"It's also a Ravening Court way station, and a key intersection between the city and the demonic plane," Volkov said. "Add to that, it's where the tribunal will take place in four days, and it's under my jurisdiction. That provides you some protection."

He glanced at Lucian. "But only some. Lucian asked me to give you the details of the tribunal, and I am happy to do that. But if you show up that day to defend him before you are summoned, I will detain you."

"Uh-huh." I folded my arms. "Judge Judy is really gonna be that scary?"

Claire snorted. No one else did. Volkov continued. "Because Lucian's crime is against the House of Wrath, their general or his proxy will preside over the tribunal. Four courts must be in attendance, and my money is on Wrath, Envy, and Pride, as well as the Ravening Court, of course, with a representative that Belial appoints—or the general himself." His gaze flicked again to Lucian. "Belial would be the best choice. Even if you've angered him, if he assigns a minion, that would sway the others into believing you don't have his attention or protection."

I expected Lucian to interject a smart comment at that, but he remained silent, and Volkov continued while I stared out at the dance floor. "The crime will be stated, evidence presented. Lucian will have the opportunity to state his case as well." He regarded Lucian with a raised brow. "Though perhaps you would be better served as Palemerious?"

That did elicit a response, if only a dry chuckle, though I didn't understand the humor.

"What's the downside of presenting that way?" Claire asked, clearly as confused as I was. "I mean, you were a higher-level demon before, right?"

Lucian inclined his head. "I am still a higher-level demon, no matter the form I am currently taking. But I will retain the name Lucian for this, I think. That's who killed Mirr." His lips curled with satisfaction. "And no one should doubt that I will kill again."

I winced but didn't say anything. Claire didn't have the same reticence.

"Seriously? Isn't that the whole reason why you're in trouble?"

"Not exactly," Volkov put in, his own amusement drawing my attention. "Demons *can* kill one another under the right conditions. They simply don't. And not every demon is up to the task even if it was sanctioned. Mirr was an unsanctioned kill. That is the violation. The four courts that make up the tribunal will all make their statements, and then there will be a vote. The Ravening Court does not get a vote, of course, but it does get to oversee the punishment if any is ordered."

I made a face. "And what would those punishments be?"

Volkov waved a negligent hand. "Demotion, exile, execution."

"Execution?" My heart lurched sideways in my chest. "Permanent execution?"

He shrugged. "It's rare, but possible. Mirr was Asmodaea's prized pet. She had skilled him up over centuries to get him to a place where he could handle the assignments she meted out. Now she is left with nothing but a bunch of chaos demons more apt to smash heads than understand the nuance of her structured thinking. It will take some time for her to recover. She wants blood."

"Uh-huh." I turned to Lucian. "And your defense?"

He smiled at me, all teeth, and the red flames danced in his gaze. "I don't need a defense. I also wanted blood. And I had an asset to protect. You."

My lip curled as I realized what he was saying, drawing the parallels to Volkov's description of Mirr. "I'm not your pet."

He didn't have anything to say to that, and Volkov took up the narrative again as I resolutely returned my gaze to the dance floor. Almost idly, I picked up someone who looked dead-on Jacket Guy wandering through the crowd. Same slender frame, same sandy blond hair. Same sense of feeling out of place, though I couldn't get a direct fix on his clothes. Something in my stance got Claire out of her chair, and she came over to me while Lucian and Volkov devolved into a conversation about defenses at Descent.

"Where?" she asked quietly, and I pointed.

"Back of the room, near the bar. Right by the group of bach-elorettes. You see him?"

She leaned in. "I totally don't see anyone like the guy in the clipping. I see the girls and the lady in the red dress, those guys dancing. But not Keegan."

Almost as if the sound of his name had pull, Keegan suddenly turned and stared up at the window where we stood. Just as he had on the train platform, he tilted his head slightly, the angle not quite human. He lifted his hand and smiled.

A breath later, low, staccato alarms erupted across the room, and Claire and I turned as Volkov pushed away from the table and strode over to the main bank of monitors, where discreet red lights flashed in urgent lines. "What is it?" Claire demanded as Volkov silenced the alarms. "What's happening?"

"Unsanctioned entry." Volkov leaned forward. "Level three only, yes?"

Beside him, Sergei grunted, but Lucian stood and stepped toward me. "You saw something just now." I jerked my gaze up to meet his eyes as they flared red. "What was it?"

"I—I don't know," I managed, which was more truthful than I wanted it to be. "What I see, Claire can't see, so maybe it's some sort of hallucination, but it's been happening to me all day. It's also maybe possibly tied to an exorcism that Mordechai enacted a dozen years ago, but I only discovered that later, and —" I glanced back over the dance floor, still in full swing. Whatever Volkov's unsanctioned entry was, it hadn't interrupted the vibe here. "Now he's not there anymore."

"Which exorcism?"

"Breach contained, but there is a mess of screaming third-level scum with nowhere to go in the back rooms," Volkov interrupted. He flicked his gaze to Lucian. "Sloth, looks like. Leviathan stirring up trouble? He knows you're here."

Lucian's lips twisted. "Then he knows any unsanctioned breaches are cause for sanctioned kills. How many?"

"Fifty-seven separate entities. They will escape if you go in."

"Where's Sarial?" The name sounded like a stain on his lips, and my brows went up. I hadn't heard this name before, but it carried definite demon taint.

Volkov shrugged. "Typically here, though I haven't seen him in the past week. We don't talk."

"He's not summoned for breaches? Descent is Ravening territory."

I had to fight to keep myself from gaping at the two of them. They were discussing demonic courts like they were mafia syndicates and Chicago as the site of a major turf war. Was it like this place everywhere, or just in the bigger cities?

"Leviathan's also as lazy as everyone else in his court," Volkov said with a sneer. "He's not doing this on his own."

If anything, that seemed to amp Lucian up more. "Asmodaea?"

"That would track," Volkov nodded. "Perhaps she didn't want to wait for the tribunal. Perhaps she wanted to see how strong you still are."

He gestured to the screen. "They'll push into the crowd in

another few minutes, tops. It'll end up as a rave, but with Sloth...a messy one."

"It won't." Lucian looked at me, then pointed. "You, stay here with Claire and Volkov. Don't leave."

"But—"

"New breach," Volkov announced, this time with palpable irritation, as a new trill of alarms chirped from the monitors. "This one—fucking Asmodaea. Has to be."

As he devolved into a series of Russian-sounding invectives, a chill swept through me. The shifting light in the room beneath ours drew my attention back to the mirror, and I watched as a ripple of darkness swept over the room once, twice. The dancers jittered when it passed them, some of them falling, some seeming frozen in place. Even the music stuttered as the DJ's hands lifted off his machine.

The faintest whiff of brimstone rose from the room below.

Then everything snapped back into place, the crowd re-finding their groove, the music blaring out louder now, more angrily. And there, at the edge of the dancers, Thomas Keegan stood once more, looking up at me as if he could pick me out behind the two-way mirror.

"There!" I blurted, pointing to the window and half-turning back to Lucian—

Only Lucian was gone.

"He's already on the floor," Volkov told me before I could ask. "He's heading for the back rooms first. Asmodaea is in the mix now. She'll pay for that—but she's the party favor, not the party."

I tried to process that as I watched Lucian cut through the crowd, the dancers falling away from him like he was a fell wind. Occasionally, he brushed his hands over hair, clothing, and their dancing changed into a languorous tangle of bodies and movement, seductive and impassioned.

Ravening Court, I thought. The Court of Lust. Just what kind of influence did Lucian have on humans when he was channeling his court's energy?

And had he used it on me?

"What's he doing?" I murmured, and Volkov sighed, rubbing his forehead like a parent of feuding kids.

"Marking his territory," he said. "Showing Asmodaea she can't take what's his. And no, he's not as strong as he used to be, Delia. You should know that. But he's not as weak as they believe him to be, either."

Claire shifted beside me. "What's happening there?" she asked, pointing.

The monitors showing the private salons of the back rooms jittered another second more and then went black as Volkov leaned forward, his hands on the keys. For the first time, Volkov looked genuinely surprised—and dismayed.

"Security team's not responding," Sergei murmured, his hand on his earpiece. "There's more than third-level in that mix."

"Leviathan, you slimy fuck..." Volkov grimaced, then looked at me, his one working eye flashing with irritation.

"This is too planned," he said tersely. "The moment Lucian goes into the back rooms, you may see what a real party looks like. One they're throwing just for you."

"Yeah?" I frowned. "What exactly will that—"

The entire club plunged into darkness, even as the music soared to a crashing, thunderous roar.

"Here we go," Volkov sighed.

CHAPTER
SIX

LUCIAN

Lucian moved through the main dance floor of Descent like the wraith that he was, shedding his shedim form the moment he blended into the first knot of sweaty, tangled humans. The surge of relief and power drove him forward another twenty paces in a blink, which was good— even if he would rather have stopped to savor the moment, the freedom.

He'd grown used to his shedim form, valued it for the access it afforded him to the human world, but its constraints were never more obvious than when he returned to the realm of mist and shadow. He stared around the room as he moved, reveling in the heat of humans, their fiery emotions making them spark and pop within their shadowy, translucent forms. Fear played out in flares of yellow, lust in crimson heat, despair in washes of blue and dull silver, like cobwebs over a stream. But as glimmering and shimmering as the humans were, the demonic entities that graced Descent shone like beacons, incandescent with strength. The higher their level, the brighter their hue—at least if they weren't careful.

Lucian was very careful.

He eased through the crowd, cataloging the other demons present: the moldy, stagnant rot of the Court of Indolence, the ash and brimstone of Ruin, the jasmine and musk of the Ravening Court. These were all lower-level demons, third through fifth, which gave them easy access to the common rooms of Descent. Volkov would know that they weren't here to possess his patrons—not overtly, and not for very long. They came to touch, to taste, to slip a finger along a trembling soul, quivering with promise.

Except for the third-level Sloth desecration in the back rooms, of course. They came to feed.

He followed the trail through the dance floor, his own bloodless heart thumping with the energy of the humans around him—speed marking terror, sensual thuds marking lust, shivering patter marking nerves or self-doubt. Humans were so often given to self-doubt. As the music pounded, demon voices overlaid the sound, their dual-toned howls creating an overlapping frequency that mortals could feel, even if they couldn't understand it. He thought he heard screams too —probably did. But they weren't coming from the back rooms. Not yet.

The crowd fell away as he slipped through them with the precision of a murderer's blade, and one dancer's wild fall of hair brushed against his shadowed form. The woman's reaction was instantaneous, her heat signature flaring, arousal warring with need. He grazed another dancer, and the man wrapped his arms around his partner's shoulders, tangled and hot.

Power surged within Lucian, quick and true. Anyone watching would see it. He was here, and he was claiming his territory. This floor, these humans. This club.

An unexpected bolt of need followed on the heels of that power surge, the demonic compulsion to touch, to taste of this human feast. But he pushed it down ruthlessly. First, he needed to—

A heat signature flared at the back of the room—too bright to be human, but still remarkably closer to human than not, sort of how Lucian himself felt. And yet...

He narrowed his eyes as the entity shifted toward him, finding more familiarity. This was a fourth-level Sloth shedim, but he wasn't visible to the humans here. Still, he was agitated, excited—an unusual state for a Sloth demon. Warring scents of rot and spoiled fruit wafted across the room, and then the crowd shifted momentarily, giving Lucian a clear view.

Hunger. Need. The creature ducked in deference to Lucian's station, not pressing, not pushing, but despite his lowered chin and hunched shoulders, he was quivering with barely controlled—what? Curiosity? Want? Well, he would find plenty to sample here in this room, Lucian thought. Any fourth-level creature knew better than to interfere with a seventh-level's hunt.

Lucian pushed on through the crowd until he reached the heavy door signaling the entrance to the back rooms. In addition to the two beefy humans who barely registered to him in his current form, three second-level Sloth demons had slipped through from the room beyond, jittering in a long, sticky stain that bled down the doorway. They peeled away from the surface as he approached as if to stop him, then confirmed that intent by coalescing into a single serpentine form.

He would have smiled if he weren't worried about the humans catching the scent of his excitement. Instead, he grabbed the slithering twist of demons and squeezed their collective neck, reveling in the sheer pleasure of sending them back to the primordial ooze from which they came. It took less than thirty seconds but did little more than whet Lucian's appetite for what might lie behind the door. He laid a hand on the human guard, causing the man to turn and open the door with a jolt of sheer, undiluted panic, then he was through.

The pressure change between the common area of Descent and its back rooms was immediate, the air thickening to soup and colors deepening to dark crimson and black. And he was *solid* now—flesh and bone made real on demon terms, corporeal in ways the infernal realm demanded.

He could still hear the pulsing music in the background, but it was drowned out by the screeching terror of whatever was happening in cell number two. Human terror, he realized distantly, amusement flickering through him. Someone had been back here after all for the third-level demons to assault.

They probably wouldn't recover quickly from that.

Other sounds spiraled up over the human screams—hoots of pleasure and vice, garbled snuffling of demons feeding on the emotion so willingly spilled out for them. He opened the door to cell number two and was struck with another wave of stench as the feeding demons sucked up terror with greedy maws, draining human will, though they couldn't be seen, couldn't be felt except for the rushing, freezing wind. Adding to the stench of rot and decay was despair, hollowness, grief.

The demons turned as one at his arrival, recognizing him, then howled in outrage at the intrusion.

All of them but one.

In the center of the room, visible now that the demons had stopped gorging on the dozen or so humans who lay strewn about the room in various states of staggering fear, stood a dark crimson demon as bright as blood. Her eyes raked across his face, and he knew her as Delia had taught him to know her, taught him to see. Pruflas, fifth-level demon of Leviathan's Court of Indolence, presenting as a lushly formed human with long, flowing red hair and sun-bronzed skin, an earth goddess from wild, untamed lands. Her body shimmered with golden heat, her hooded eyes gleamed, and her full, pouting lips stretched into a languorous sigh.

"*Palemerious*," she murmured, somehow audible above the screeching. "Or should I say Lucian Gray? I wondered if you'd come. Such a shame to waste the energy otherwise."

"You're trespassing on Ravening territory," he said, but his own voice was as soft and sinuous as a lover's caress. Pruflas vibrated with power and importance. She wouldn't suffer under his hand. But she would die, knocked back down to the slimy pool of whatever corner of hell from which she'd originated. Leviathan may have given her Lucian's name, but he hadn't fully briefed her on his capabilities.

She turned and drew a long hand along the skin of some screaming sycophant, her red hair hanging in knots and twists around her body, somehow both ragged and lustrous at once. Her half-lidded eyes drifted over him again, and she smiled, smelling of honey and sickness. "Leviathan thinks you weak."

"Does he?"

Lucian spread his hands into spiky claws, casually ripping his way through the mindless, milling horde. There were fifty-seven third-level demons in this room, but they fell as quickly as they attacked him, their rot-soft flesh pierced and sliced by his claws, their own battering defenses weak and pitiful. With each death, pools of despair opened in the space around him, pulling at him, dragging him down. Why fight? Why struggle? Why try?

The humans' screams turned into shuddering sobs, and that, to Lucian's surprise, proved harder to resist, his demon-heavy gaze unable to see their eyes, their faces. He wouldn't know anyone here, he told himself. No friend of Delia's would be that stupid, not anymore. But still, it slowed his progress, and he set his jaw, turned toward the waiting Pruflas—

And faltered.

Suddenly, Delia stood before him, blocking the way between him and the Sloth demon, her gaze on the far wall, her body lax, listless as demons sucked on her fingers and scurried over her feet. She looked completely empty, hollowed out, and he called her name sharply—but though she turned her head in his general direction, she didn't respond with any sort of urgency or even awareness. She didn't care. She couldn't care. And even as he watched, she was fading—fading—

"Ah!" Lucian jerked to the side as a slash of brutal, soul-jerking pain electrified him, a Sloth demon's teeth so deeply embedded in his limb that it took him three punches with his claw-tipped fist to knock it free. He obliterated the demon into a gooey mass and reoriented on Pruflas, understanding ripping along his senses.

She—a pitiful fifth-level demon, a Sloth demon at that— had bested him. Distracted him. Used his connection to a human to—

A second vision smote him, this one far more visceral and real.

Delia lay on the floor in front of him now, sprawled like a discarded doll, eyes staring, mouth slack. Squeezed out and ruined, the purest incarnation of despair he had ever seen. He knew it was lies, a trick of Pruflas and her slimy horde, but... there was truth in it as well. The Court of Indolence was known for taking its victim down to their greatest weakness, their soft and vulnerable core.

Was this Delia's weakness?

Would she allow despair to take her the way it had her weak and craven mother, drowning herself in alcohol or simply fading into a hollow shell, translucent as dust?

Rage consumed him, and as quick as a breath, he strode through the illusion of Delia, shattering it, and reached for Pruflas.

She met him more than halfway. Her hair now raged around her like striking snakes and coils of red-gold smoke, lashing toward him. He felt them rip through his spectral form—deeper than they should have.

Pruflas laughed. "You're weaker than I expected, Palemerious," she cooed as they circled each other. "Belial's pet general, reduced to this? Pathetic."

As she spoke, he struck, arms out, claws extended, and though she blocked him with a deflection of twisting shadow, their claws entangled. Sharp, searing pain ripped through him again, surprising him. For a fifth-level demon, she was good.

They grappled, claws locked, circling. She twisted her wrists, and her shadow-deflection solidified into writhing tendrils that wrapped around his forearms like living smoke. The tendrils burned—not with fire, but cold, the kind of cold that sapped strength and will. Sloth made manifest.

He snarled and wrenched free, but she was already moving, impossibly fluid for someone who should embody lethargy. Her hair lashed out again—those red-gold coils he'd dismissed as merely decorative—and he felt them slice across his shoulder, his ribs. Each strike left trails of numbing cold.

"Leviathan taught me well," she purred, dancing back out of reach. "He said you'd be rusty. Soft from playing human."

Lucian lunged, faster than her eyes could track—or should have been. She twisted aside at the last second, laughing, and her nails raked down his back. Four burning lines of pain. He whirled, catching her wrist, and *squeezed*. Bone ground against bone. Her smile finally flickered.

"Not that soft," he growled.

She yanked free—flesh tearing, her own blood now mixing

with his—and stumbled back, breathing hard for the first time. *Good*. Let her feel it. Let her understand what she'd underestimated.

Or was he simply out of practice?

The smoke raged around him, screaming third-level demons wailing in fear and confusion. Defilement they understood, draining life and wallowing in the fear of humans. But this was heat and action, this was death.

Suddenly, an image of Delia appeared in Lucian's mind—his mind, not before him, thrown to the floor in some lewd pose of Pruflas's choosing. And in his mind, she once again looked hollow, empty. In his mind she'd given up, and been lost and left to the side like an abandoned—

"No!" he roared, charging forward and ripping great handfuls of hair from Pruflas's head. She jerked back, scrambling, but he bore down on her, and her eyes were finally alight with awareness, her legs churning as she ripped her hands away and clawed his chest, freeing thick, gouting bursts of blood to mix with her filthy skin. He wrapped his fingers around her throat, even as she gasped.

"Wait!" she demanded. "Leviathan will—"

"Leviathan can collect your ashes," Lucian snarled, and with a vicious twist, he wrenched her head to the side, all the energy evaporating from Pruflas in one breath, leaving a withered husk behind—and then nothing at all.

For one heart-stopping moment, silence reigned—

And then the demon horde screamed in deep, soul-frying hysteria.

They surged around him, knocking him to the ground, but they were no longer trying to attack him or even obstruct him. Instead, they fled, sightlessly, mindlessly, howling around the room until Lucian finally reached the door and yanked it open, dimly aware of the deep gouges he'd sustained from Pruflas's claws. How had she been able to hurt him that badly? How had she—

A sudden pain erupted along his side, ripping deep, and a plume of Lucian's own ash-tinged blood gushed forth anew, down his demonic form, a river of muddy red oil. He roared and turned, only to see the fourth-level shedim demon—another piece-of-shit Slother, but a fucking fourth-level!—dance back, grinning and feral.

Their eyes met, and something deep and familiar sang in Lucian's mind, a memory, a moment, then his gaze refocused on the demonic wretch in front of him. Decayed flesh barely adhered to a gray-green skull, mold-ravaged shoulders and belly, eyes filmed over with milky-white fluid. Ordinarily, even a Sloth demon would have more self-respect, but Zagan had used all his energy to get close, to strike, and now his claws gleamed with the evidence of his victory, stained with Lucian's blood.

"Did you think I'd miss a second time, Palemerious?" he croaked, words that made no sense. "I've been waiting so long."

Second time?

A flash—memory, not hallucination. Soup kitchen. Mordechai chanting. A demon vomiting forth from a homeless man's mouth, green and rotting, lunging toward young Delia. Palemerious roaring through her throat: *Mine.*

Zagan. It had been Zagan.

What had Mordechai done?

Blind with rage, Lucian struck out, claws extended. Zagan dodged nimbly to the side, deceptively fast despite the mold hanging off him. He circled Lucian, keeping his distance, laughing. "She'll be mine eventually. Finally. You're weak—fading. And about to be judged."

The image of Delia leapt to Lucian's mind, and he lurched at Zagan, his claws wrapping around the creature's arm. He ripped the limb from Zagan's frame—the squishy pop of the socket sickening, even to him. Zagan screamed and wrenched free, leaving his arm behind, then stumbled back into the shadows, back toward the main area of Descent, leaving a green stain behind. "Pruflas's position is mine!" he screeched with joy. "I'm closer—closer still to your precious—"

He dissolved into the shadows.

Lucian sagged against the wall, realizing with some surprise that he was no longer shadow and mist, but flesh and blood. When had he reclaimed his shedim form? And why, considering the blood pouring out of his side, soaking through his shirt?

Closer, Zagan had crowed—but what did that mean? When had that fourth-level fuck been anywhere near Delia?

A wave of dizziness swept over Lucian, and he staggered down the long hallway toward the blue light that represented the back exit out of Descent. He pushed through the door and out into the surprisingly warm night air, only to hear a sound that arrowed through him like lightning in a storm.

"Lucian!" Delia gasped, and then he was falling into her arms, his blood on her skin, his shedim heart hammering out of control. He opened his mouth to warn her, to protect her, but only the deep, rough gurgle of his kind choked out.

"Shhh..." she said. "I've got you. You're safe."

She turned her head toward other people running toward them, and she stumbled, her arms tightening in a spontaneous clutch as she struggled not to drop him. "Sergei, I—"

"We go," Lucian heard in the bodyguard's thick, heavy accent. He felt himself being lifted—and then he did something he had not done for centuries.

He blacked out.

CHAPTER

SEVEN

"Okay, here we go. Slow and easy. We've got this."

"Not too slow." Sergei grunted a short laugh from Lucian's other side, who still hadn't spoken since he'd regained consciousness in the SUV, eyes dull and staring, breathing uneven. "He may be a demon, but he bleeds red enough. He'll leave a trail."

I glanced down at Lucian's shoes, still perfectly polished, but I could practically hear the blood oozing down his legs as we quick-shuffled through the lobby of the Prometheus building, Lucian's current home. Lucian mouthed words I couldn't quite catch, and the cheerful staffers at the front desk smiled benignly toward us without quite focusing. We made it to the elevators unaccosted.

"I know what he needs. I've got it from here," I told Sergei. My tone brooked no argument, though I wasn't anywhere near as confident as I sounded that I knew what the hell to do to heal a demon from an attack of his own kind. We'd had this fight already in the SUV, settled only when Sergei had demanded approval from Volkov before leaving me the task of getting Lucian into his apartment. I'd actually been surprised when

Volkov had ordered his man to stand down after getting me to the elevator. Surprised—and leery.

What did Volkov know that I didn't?

Sergei stepped back, and the doors closed around us, the elevator controls accepting my selection of Lucian's private floor once I scanned his keycard. A second later, the carriage eased upward, smooth and controlled.

I couldn't say the same for my own heart rate. Lucian wasn't heavy, exactly, and he didn't lean fully on me, but he stood hunched over, head down, like he was drunk or half-drugged. His breathing was soft, ragged, and pain radiated off him in thick, undulating waves of blackberry wine, jasmine, and rust.

"Up we go," I murmured to him, earning me a low chuckle that did nothing to settle my nerves. Still, at least he was awake, reacting. That had to be good, right? He couldn't be as injured as he seemed. Claire had insisted on stopping for drugs on the way over, but I hadn't wanted to stop, hadn't wanted to do anything but get him out of sight, a monster retreating to his lair. "We're almost there."

"Are we?" he murmured, or I thought he did. The words were lost as the elevator opened with a regretful sigh, and I urged him forward onto the plush expanse of creamy carpet.

We'd made it only five steps before he listed sharply, staggering against me. "Where to?" I asked him, my voice straining as I gripped him tighter, my heart spiking again. "You want the kitchen floor? Couch? Shower? Claire can hook us up with drugs as strong as you need, but you've gotta tell me how this works, Lucian. I don't know how to heal a shedim."

He didn't speak—he didn't laugh. He didn't even sigh.

He struck.

Multiple ribbons of pain erupted on my back as he spun to the side, the cold feel of something unnatural gouging my skin and ripping away before I stumbled in the other direction. I landed on my ass and scrambled back, eyes wide as I tried to track him across the open living room. He'd become a dark and dripping horror of wings and talons and teeth, a horned monster shimmering in and out of existence with a thick head, hooded and elongated like a deformed alien, a cadaverously thin body with a bulbous belly, and skin that looked like it had been fried into place, gleaming with blood and bile and smelling of bloated death. He spread his hands and ten long, spiky claws protruded, sharp and unforgiving.

He was a nightmare come to life. My nightmare, I realized with a blurt of clarity through the howling fear that threatened to consume me. My nightmare. The creature I had drawn on my own walls.

"Sweet *Delia*," he hissed, the sound burbling over with laughter. "Here's how you can *help* me…"

He flew forward with a rush of heat and frenzy, catching my feet as I tried to scramble back, wrenching me forward beneath him as his crackling hot, steaming body landed on my legs. I barely got my hand up to my neck and curled my fingers around my Hamsa Hand medallion before he lowered his face to my abdomen, his tongue snaking out to lave my belly bared above my pants. The putrid stench of him swirled around me, and his tongue felt like acid as he dragged it up, up—

Then he lifted his head and I shoved the amulet into his face.

The chain snapped as he roared and fell backward, a blast of rotten eggs and char sweeping over me, but I held his eyes as I lurched up into a squat to match his own. He split his mouth into a heavily fanged grin, cruel and wide enough to turn the roots of my hair white, but I was done with being terrified by him. Between my revulsion and my fury—my deep and unquenchable outrage that this *creature* had taken over the form of someone I knew, someone I had touched and spoken to, someone I *would* fucking protect—a new energy notched into place within me, like a bullet sliding into a chamber. I could fight this creature, this evil that was so desperately trying to surge to the fore again, where it wasn't needed nor wanted. I would fight it and I would win.

"You *dare* mock me?" I hissed. "You dare defy the hand at my back?"

Then more words spilled out of me, Mordechai's words—ancient, guttural, and demanding.

"*Yakum Elohim, yafutsu oyvav,*" I breathed out. "You cocksucking mother fucker, you think I don't see you? You think I don't *know* you? It was through my agency and the will of God that your sorry ass was even released back into the world again. *Lo-ira mipachad lailah.*"

The demon in front of me hissed out his own garbled curses then, spells and exhortations from languages I didn't know. Sigils erupted across his ruined skin, flaring bright then burning out, candles guttered in a storm. The creature's body jittered, shifted, and I lifted my Hamsa Hand higher, conviction flowing through me. Every angle and curve of him was wrong, every breath and sneer and drop of blood. But I would not be overcome, I would not fear—*he* would.

Palemerious, Lucian...or whatever beast he cloaked himself with now, mindless and desperate in his pain and rage.

I leaned closer, and he did too, his eyes wild, his mouth stretching to the side in a grotesque rictus of despair, thick tongue working up green bile that crested over his cracked lips to stretch in sinewy, dripping streams over his chin. He stared at me, vibrating with chaos, the very embodiment of death and despair and wasted hope, all that was left after the ravages of lust had stripped away everything good and beautiful, and I didn't care. I wasn't done with him yet.

"*Shema Yisrael, Adonai Eloheinu, Adonai Echad,*" I whispered, grinning with almost savage joy as his gaze snapped back to mine, the faintest stain of black bleeding into their fiery, unrelenting red orbs. "You are bound to me."

His face contorted into a credibly humanesque rage, shock and fury mingling as he rocked forward on hands and knees, a predator primed to spring. "*No,*" he snarled, crawling toward me now, his face morphing as he neared. I shuffled backward, Hamsa Hand held out, secure in my power over the demon that was Lucian, but not in what was happening here, what was transforming before my eyes.

Because with every inch he slid toward me, with every clicking snap of claws, grinding of fang, rustling of scales, and creak of shattered bone, the creature in front of me was shifting back into a far more devastating form. His head contracted, drawing in cheeks and chin, wild horns smoothing into jet black hair, extruding brow evening out into chiseled beauty. His claws slid back to become long, elegant fingers slipping forward along the lush carpet. His bronzed skin fairly glowed with sigils now, archaic symbols devolving into languages I could almost decipher. They slipped and eddied over his skin, glowing brighter as they swept over the wounds he had sustained.

His torso stretched, the bulbous belly dissolving into tightly corded muscle and ridges that arrowed down in a decidedly human vee that ended in the perfectly formed cock, the narrow hips, the long, muscled legs and beautiful feet that made up the illusion of Lucian Gray that I had already wrapped my body around once, glorying in the pleasure he had given me. The pleasure and the pain.

From the feral, possessive gleam in Lucian's eyes, he remembered that pleasure, that pain as well. But his smile was brutally hard as he raked his gaze over me.

"No," he said again, this time in a slow, seductive drawl.

"You play a dangerous game, Delia. You cannot cherry-pick invocations of power to use at your whim. Eventually, you'll choose the wrong one. Or use one with implications you don't fully understand."

I didn't drop the Hamsa amulet. I didn't trust him, I didn't trust myself. "It worked, didn't it?" I challenged him right back. I liked the sound of my voice. It was low and as stony as his smile.

If anything, my rebuke seemed to satisfy him more, and a satisfied lust demon was probably not the best plan. He chuckled low in his throat, and he inclined his head, as if conceding the point.

"It did," he murmured. "But at what cost?"

He moved forward then at a speed that was nowhere close to human. In one blink, he was several feet away, in another he was on top of me, his naked body pressed against mine, his hand shackling the wrist that held the Hamsa Hand amulet far up and away from my head, pinning it to the floor. Without giving me time to speak, to counter, his mouth came down on mine—only this time he didn't smell like trash set out in the summer heat, but jasmine and coffee, vanilla and sunshine glinting off an endless ocean. My brain, scrambled from adrenaline and the heady power that had flowed through me and out over this room not a heartbeat before, straight-up fried at Lucian's hungry, demanding kisses. This wasn't the moment of healing and connection, reassurance and mutual need that had wrapped around us in the hotel during the first time he'd held me so intimately—this was need and want and fire and—

Lust.

"No!" I gasped, biting down hard enough on his lip to draw blood, and he reacted viscerally, instinctively, pulling back from me as his hands loosened on my wrists. Knowing it was my only chance, I lunged away from him, scrambling on all fours, then whirled around, my clothes hanging off my body where his talons had raked me, my lungs heaving.

Lucian, for his part, barely moved, just rolled over on one impressive hip, unabashedly naked next to his rumpled pile of blood-stained trousers and shirt he'd worn to Volkov's club. His gaze never leaving mine, he stood, stretching his arms overhead. Sigils no longer decorated his skin, but even while forcing myself not to take an exacting inventory of every square inch of him, I could see that the deep, ragged gashes torn into him at Descent were gone—the bruises and burns, vanished. Lucian's skin was smooth and unblemished.

Perfect.

"You were right," he murmured, his voice rich and full as he regarded himself. He smoothed a hand down his ribcage, and I could feel an associated twinge in my body, the touch drifting like a brand over my own skin. This was new, I thought. This was bad.

He glanced up toward me, a smile curving his beautiful, cruel lips. "That was exactly what I needed."

I stiffened, stepped away. "Good. You might want to throw out those clothes before the blood seeps into the carpet."

I turned on my heel, stuffing what was left of my shirt into the hem of my blood-stained pants, hoping like hell that the smeared mess of my clothes looked more funky girl-about-town than serial-killer survivor. Without looking back at Lucian, I stalked toward the elevator, barely slowing down long enough to scoop my discarded phone from the floor. I punched out a text to Claire, praying she and Sergei were still close.

Lucian didn't stop me. Didn't speak. I could feel his gaze tracking me across the penthouse like a physical touch, could feel the breath of his exhale against my neck, slipping down my spine. I hit the elevator call button three times before it registered I'd already pressed it.

The doors slid open. I stumbled inside and slammed my hand against the lobby button.

Only when the doors closed—only when the floors started ticking downward—did I let myself lean against the wall. My hands were shaking. My whole body was shaking—

And then I froze as a warm, sinuous pressure skated along my ribcage, over the hipbone. His hand on his ribcage, I knew. His hand on his own skin—and somehow also on mine—smoothing and touching, dipping and feeling—

"No," I gritted out, my stomach flipping as the sensation drifted lower, rounding my hip, brushing my thigh. Five floors, ten.

The phantom touch didn't fade.

Fifteen, and I was sweating now, feeling his fingers dip and curve against the vee between my legs, hearing the softest rush of laughter in my ears.

His hand. My skin. The connection pulling taut between us like a wire.

Ground floor.

The sensation snapped.

I sagged against the wall, gasping. When the doors opened onto the lobby, I lurched out on quivering legs, barely able to keep my scream contained as I stumbled blindly toward the door.

CHAPTER

EIGHT

I jolted awake at an unfamiliar sound, jerking upright and scrambling three steps before it struck me that I was in a strange place, at a strange time. Early morning sun streamed through the window, throwing Mordechai's books into bright, cheerful relief, and everything seemed brighter, fresher, and incredibly wrong.

"Hello?" I demanded as I strode forward, anger and panic bunching up in my chest, my whole body tensing for a fight.

"It's Sergei." The overloud, brusque announcement was so unexpected that I stopped short at the entry to the outer area of my office in the Oak Park building. It was quiet and empty—no electronics humming, no lights blinking—but of course it was. It was seven in the morning.

"What are you doing here?" I asked as Sergei moved over to the short table in the sitting area, depositing what looked like a heavy sack that smelled... "Wait. Is that bacon?"

"You need food," he announced, ripping open the bag to reveal carefully boxed takeout items. He shoved them out onto the table along with a sturdy cardboard drink holder that bore

75

two Styrofoam cups of coffee. He liberated one of them and stepped back, then gestured me forward. "You don't eat enough."

"Please tell me that's not all for me," I said, unable to resist the scent of coffee now overpowering the breakfast food. I moved toward the table, then stooped down to scoop up the second coffee cup. "You've got to eat something too."

"First, I watch you eat." His eyes tracked me as I sat, and I didn't have to speak Romanian to interpret his grunt of disapproval. I knew what I must look like. My body was bruised up one side and down the other, bruised in places even the demon's claws hadn't reached. I felt raw, ragged, and though I hadn't felt his hands on me since I'd fled the Prometheus building, I kept waiting for that phantom touch to occur again, the slide of his fingers along my skin.

To cover my shiver, I leaned forward and unwrapped one of the sandwiches, allowing the aroma of charred meat and cheese to ground me. "Stop standing there and eat one of these," I said, before taking a healthy bite. I set my coffee down and grabbed a fistful of napkins, glad that I didn't care if I screwed up my current outfit. Dark jeans and a lightweight, long-sleeved black henley might not be a match for the summery light filling my office and now spilling into the common space, but it was still cool outside—and my current attire made a lot more sense for an exorcist than the fancy suits Claire had me wearing.

"You didn't stay at the hotel. You came here after we dropped you off. You've been here all night." Sergei still stood by the door, and I waved him over and pointed at the opposite chair.

"You're looming," I informed him.

"It is my job to loom."

"Well, loom from a chair. And eat before it gets cold. Cold eggs are gross."

That seemed to be logic he couldn't refute, and he moved to take a seat opposite me, but he didn't stop staring at me with obvious judgment as he scooped up one of the other sandwiches.

"Volkov is worried about you," he said, before cutting the breakfast sandwich in half with one massive bite. His dark, hooded eyes remained trained on me, assessing my reaction.

I rolled my eyes. "I'm fine."

"Fine." He grunted, then finished off the sandwich, washing the food down with a hefty swig of coffee. His eyes met mine again. "Even I know you are not fine. You work with a shedim, a demon-made-flesh, and worse, one that is rightfully a seventh-level commander. That is dangerous enough. Lieutenants from other houses are flooding into the city for the tribunal of a sort that has not been held in more than a hundred years. That is more dangerous."

I blinked up at him, this catching my attention. "Yeah? Is that a problem?"

"Not yet." He shrugged. "But it will likely become a problem. Volkov wants you to know he is ready to assist you— resources, more protection, information. Whatever you need."

"Information," I echoed, the coffee finally kicking my brain into gear. "Information about what?"

Another grunt, this one of grim amusement. "About the demon you tried to heal last night, and who ended up attacking you. Volkov told me he would. And he said that warning you would do no good."

I snorted. "Well, you could've warned me. But fine." I sat back. "He did attack me, but he was injured, damaged. Lucian wouldn't hurt me."

"Perhaps, perhaps not," Sergei countered. "But Palemerious would. He is one of the most powerful commanders to ever rule the Ravening Court."

"Was," I corrected, eyeing the rest of the sandwiches and opting to stick with coffee. The others would be in soon enough, and they should enjoy this too. "He quit that job."

"No." Sergei's rejection was final. "You do not quit being a commander. He fled and got—where? Nowhere. He was found out and trapped within you."

"He wasn't trapped," I argued back. "He chose me, and Mordechai didn't fix the problem because—well, that part I don't know. Maybe Mordechai didn't have the strength, maybe he didn't want to hurt me—or risk me losing my abilities, or whatever—I don't know. But Lucian was never trapped. You said yourself, he's a big, powerful demon. I was a ten-year-old girl. Give me a break."

Another grunt, and it occurred to me Sergei probably had an entire lexicon of grunts I should start figuring out how to decipher. "When you are ready, you should talk to Volkov." He paused, his gaze turning speculative. "He looks forward to that, you should know."

I didn't want to analyze the zip of sensation that lit up my spine at that, crackling through my blood. I had enough problems without crushing on two predators at once. "Fine." I leaned forward and snagged another sandwich. There were still four more, and it'd been a hard night. "And thank you, again. I don't know why I'm so hungry."

"Mm." Still, Sergei reached for another sandwich, his dark eyes watching me with too much knowing. He gestured to the food. "There's a reason your strength is being sapped. Eat. And when you are ready, talk to Volkov."

It was another two hours before Claire and Steve showed up—Claire with coffee, and Steve instantly turning toward the remains of breakfast I'd wrapped up in ripped paper as best as I could.

"Hey!" he began and was halfway to the bag before I came out of my office. "Food! I'm hitting the micro."

He disappeared back out of the room, and Claire frowned at me. "What's with the outfit? You going on a stakeout or something?"

I frowned down at my soft, long-sleeved shirt, my loose jeans. "I'm comfortable."

"You're hurt, you mean." She handed over a fresh cup of coffee and narrowed her eyes at me. "And clearly not eating enough, if Sergei decided to bring you breakfast."

She leaned against her desk and crossed her ankles, her soft cream linen dress and pumps the literal opposite of my attire. Her gold cross necklace glinted at her throat, and gold hoops hung beneath her carefully brushed hair. I pondered my own hair as I took a sip of coffee, unsure of when I'd last looked in a mirror. "So, last night you didn't want to talk about what went down at the apartment, but you don't look much better for a full night's sleep. Unless..."

Her gaze went from me to my office door. "You've been here all night, haven't you? Why? What did he do to you?"

"He didn't do anything to me," I snapped. "I just—this isn't anything I have experience with, Claire. Lucian's a seventh-level demon in a fourth-level form, and he's not just, like, the median of that, he's the nth degree of both levels rolled up into something entirely new. Before a few weeks ago, I never thought about demons at all, other than they sucked. I didn't worry about levels or variations or hierarchy. But there's like a whole freaking ecosystem they've got set up, and Mordechai wrote down detailed descriptions of all of it. You know what he doesn't mention? That he knew Palemerious had taken up residence inside me. And that he never tried to get him out."

Claire frowned, speaking into the silence that landed like a thud between us. "Which means he let you suffer. For fifteen years."

I took another long pull of coffee. "Yeah."

"Whoa, whoa, whoa!" Steve's voice rang out down the hallway, sounding like he was shouting from the bottom of a well, and Claire had only just made it to the door when it burst open to admit three hard-striding people holding out iPhones and boom mics—none of whom were Steve.

"Excuse me, Ms. Willows?" Claire began as the three spilled into the room, clearly not recognizing the guy holding the iPhone with the shotgun mic or his sidekick filming with just a phone. But both of us recognized the woman who'd entered first. Claire had met her, and I'd been staring at her face on my own phone screen for several days now.

"Sue Willows," she confirmed crisply before I had the chance to ask. She held out her hand, her expression as confident and authoritative as her voice, her lav mic prominently clipped to her scoop-neck tee. "Dark Streets podcast. Thank you so much for agreeing to meet with us today. We're so excited to meet Chicago's newest and, some would say, most effective exorcism expert, Delia Thompson of Thompson & Associates right here in Oak Park. Our listeners have been crashing our system eager to understand exactly what happened last night at Descent, and we knew just who to ask. Can you help us out?"

Seeing Sue Willows appear literally on my doorstep after having listened to paranormal speculation after paranormal speculation had set me up for a certain type of question from her, specifically something to do with the exorcisms that I'd conducted over the past few weeks, or even something that Mordechai had done months or even years ago. My brain had slotted in answers for any of those opening salvos.

But Descent? That hadn't been on my dance card.

Claire stepped in smoothly. "It's so great to see you again, Sue," she said cheerfully, and I noticed that one of the cameras —the one with the attached mic—swung her way, but videographer number two kept his phone trained on me. "You haven't officially met Delia before now, have you? I told her about you and your interest here—"

"And I was truly delighted to learn more about the work you're doing to educate the community," I said, sounding as cheerfully polite as any corporate talking head reading from a teleprompter, and met Steve's eyes as he strolled into the room, breakfast sandwiches tucked into his arms. "Ah! Steve is here. He's the backbone of our team, but I'm sure you knew that?"

"Steve?" With as quickly as Sue Willows turned to peer at him, something shivered in the back of my brain—especially as confusion chased over her face. "You were there last night? At Descent?" she asked carefully.

Okay, then, I thought. *Someone expected to meet Lucian Gray today—but they don't know who he is. Not yet. They only have a description that Steve in no way matches.*

"Oof! Not me, not last night," he said, dropping the sandwiches on the desk. He casually reached over and fiddled with his keyboard, then turned back. "You guys hungry? We totally scored breakfast this morning."

One of the videographers muttered something and tapped his headphones as Steve continued. "For what it's worth, I didn't hear anything from my buddies about Descent," he said, leaning against the desk as he unwrapped a sandwich. "Why, what went down?"

Sue Willows swung back toward me. "We have it from a very solid source that there was a paranormal disruption yesterday at Descent—very big, very dark. You were on-site, right? Given your line of work, were you called in to stop the problem...or to cause it?"

"Cause it?" I echoed, looking credibly chagrined and trying to pay no attention to Steve as the air conditioning hissed on and he practically started bouncing on his toes with delight. "Oh, gosh, no. Absolutely not."

"I'm so glad to hear it," Sue said with impressive earnestness. "So, you were brought in to resolve it? I understand you jumped the queue waiting outside the—"

"Sue, we've got a problem here," Headphones said, frowning down at his phone, which was no longer trained on anyone. "The sound just crapped out."

"It didn't crap out," the second videographer said tightly, already adjusting dials on the receiver clipped to his belt. "Levels are spiking. Noise floor's way too high all of a sudden."

"What does that mean?" Sue demanded.

"It means," Headphones said, pulling one ear cup slightly away from his temple and then replacing it again, as if hoping the problem would reset itself, "that there's a constant broadband hiss in here. Like someone turned on a masker."

He scanned the ceiling automatically—professional reflex, I suspected—eyes catching the small, almost invisible perforated discs embedded between the light panels.

"Maybe it's the AC?" Claire put in helpfully.

"No," Headphones said. "HVAC doesn't sit at a steady eighty decibels and track under speech."

"Could we try again?" I asked, cheerful as all hell, while Sue scowled back at me.

The second guy stepped closer to me, as if proximity might fix physics. "Try talking again."

"I was saying," I began carefully, "that no, I did not cause any paranormal disruption."

From what I could see on his screen, green bars climbed and danced around, never dropping back to silence.

"See?" he muttered. "It's constant. We can't isolate dialogue with that much room tone. It'll take hours to clean."

"Can you fix it?" Sue asked, her words clipped.

He hesitated.

"Not if it stays like this."

Across the room, Steve took a cheerful bite of his sandwich, the soft hiss of the air system threading through every word like static woven into silk.

"You're doing this, aren't you?" Sue turned on me, her eyes narrowing. "You're blocking recording."

I gave her an enthusiastic smile. "Well, I'm not, but as it turns out, I'm thrilled—we've only just started talking to clients here. If no one can record our conversations, that will just give the public an added layer of security. We do want people to feel safe. Should we maybe reschedule this interview at your recording studio?"

"Or we could just go outside," Sue countered, her cheer as tightly set as her jaw.

"Well, we could, but we're kind of busy today."

"You know, we've been investigating you," she continued, narrowing her eyes at me. "Offering exorcism services with no apparent accreditation, charging vulnerable people who are clearly experiencing mental health crises. Some would call that fraud, Ms. Thompson. You wouldn't want us to tell people that, would you?"

My cell phone rang loudly in my office, making everyone jump. I ignored it.

Claire, however, had her notepad out now. "I'm sorry, are you threatening us, Ms. Willows? Is that why you wanted to speak with us?"

"Oh, it's no threat."

"I mean, it kind of sounded like a threat," Steve said around a sandwich.

The phone cut off after the third ring.

"It's not," Sue assured us, looking around. "It's just incredibly interesting to our listening public to learn about a new paranormal problem solver right under our very noses. A problem solver who apparently is riding on the coattails of a rabbi who was a stalwart figure of the community, a true hero among men. But where is Rabbi Mordechai? Oh, that's right, he's dead."

"I'm aware," I said, encouraging her to continue. "It's a shame you're going to have to re-record that whole spiel, but it does sound good."

Anger darkened her eyes and flushed her skin, and my phone started up again—then cut off a second time.

"Shouldn't you get that?" she asked silkily. "I assume it's a new client? Surely you don't have anything to hide."

The phone on Claire's desk rang, its panel lighting up. Before she could move, Headphones zipped to the side with his phone, clearly recording. "Chicago phone number," he announced, turning back to smirk at us. "Easy to track."

"Hey!" Claire protested, but Steve was already on the move.

"Okay, so, fun fact, we *also* have visual recording devices tracking all this – though no sound, because, you know, privacy." He pointed to a camera in the corner of the ceiling, mostly hidden from view. "I'm sure you won't use the number you recorded to harass our client, and I'm sure we'll be happy to answer your questions at a time and place we both agree on. But for now? Maybe you get the hell out."

Headphones had already taken the shotgun mic off his phone, tucking them both back into his jacket. "Sound is trash," he shrugged. "We got what we wanted."

"We did," Sue said with satisfaction, and I knew what she

meant. If she could trace the phone back to someone real—a new client, Grace, someone we'd already helped—she would, and she'd go after them. "We'll be in touch to set up an interview. And Delia? We're watching you."

"Ooooo, scary," Steve deadpanned.

But we didn't say anything else until after they left.

I felt him enter the building.

It wasn't a creeping sensation, or a slow build, just the sudden shock to the system like I'd been plunged into a snowbank. One second, I was staring blindly at a hoary old book of kabbalistic prayers that smelled of burnt sage and faded hope, and the next I was jerked upright in my seat, my gaze pinned to my office door as Claire and Steve murmured in the next room, oblivious to the demon flowing toward us like polished heat and prickling death.

"Knock it off," I muttered, and I heard him then, too, the soft, sinuous chuckle shivering up my spine.

I'd made it to my door just as he entered the office, forcing myself to glance up from the folders I'd grabbed from the corner of my desk as if I'd just randomly chosen this exact moment to ask Claire a burning question. But the sight of him sent another jolting shock through me, rooting me to the spot.

"Lucian!" Claire exclaimed, and she was out of her chair and hustling toward him, whether to cover for whatever expression she read on my face or because she was genuinely that excited to see him, I wasn't sure. "What are you doing here? I didn't expect you back on your feet for days, from the way you looked last night."

He spread his arms as she stopped short of him. "One of the many advantages of my dark nature," he said with a smile directed at her but meant for me. Irritation spiked deep in my gut, shoving out the uglier, more twisting need forming there.

"Is that true?" I asked, with so little edge to my voice, I deserved an Academy Award. I leaned against the doorframe casually. "Demons can heal that quickly?"

Now he did swing his gaze my way, and I was glad for the bolstering solidity of the wood pressing into my shoulder. Lucian's eyes seemed sharper now, harder, more alive than they had just yesterday, but he looked perfectly at ease, otherwise— no visible blood marred his vibrant blue suit or crisp white shirt, open at the collar. No bruising bloomed along his jaw or down his neck. Even his hair appeared healthier than it should, thick and lustrous as it flowed back from his forehead, curling around his ears. Was it longer than it had been yesterday too? Was I cursed to deal with him getting more attractive, the longer I knew him?

I couldn't tell from his smirk if he could read my thoughts, but I schooled my expression to neutral as he shook his head. "Healing is a matter of perspective, but this form allows us to show what we want to, and when. As a result, I can appear to heal as quickly as I'd like."

"But you're still hurt." Claire stepped closer, then frowned, her clinician's gaze sweeping over him. "Or...maybe not? Something's different about you."

"Yo, we've got breakfast," Steve put in, waving a sandwich from his position on the couch. "We've also got Grace incoming in fifteen, so I was gonna finish this off. Unless you want it?"

"Go ahead." Lucian's gaze tracked from Steve back to me. "You ate?"

"I ate," I acknowledged tersely. What was it with everyone being so worried about my diet? I realized I was holding the folders over my chest like some sort of armor, so I handed them off to Claire. She took them and retreated back to her desk, her gaze tracking between Lucian and me like she was afraid one of us would lash out. "We had some excitement here a bit ago. I told you about the Dark Streets podcaster? She brought camera guys in to get our take on the 'big fight' at Descent. Any idea who would've spilled that info to her?"

"Dark Streets," Lucian mused. He strolled over to Steve's desk, sat on the edge of it, his gaze sweeping first to the keyboard, then up toward the ceiling. "You employed a sound masking device to keep them from recording." He glanced toward Steve, who was now grinning broadly, already halfway through a sandwich. "Your work?"

"Who else?" Steve chortled. "They were *pissed*."

"And also very well-informed," I reiterated. "How would anyone know about the attack in the back rooms who wasn't an actual demon? Could ordinary people see any of that? Feel it?"

"No," Lucian said, frowning. "The staff would know if they'd been read into the secondary nature of the club, but I would think Volkov would be more discreet than that." He reached out long fingers to twitch at his right cuff, and I followed the movement with narrowed eyes. "Anyone who has worked with him for any length of time would realize the danger of drawing too much attention."

"You would think." Something shimmered at the edge of his jacket sleeve, just over his wrist, then was gone again, covered by the material. Ink? A brand of some sort? Unbidden, the image of glowing sigils danced through my memory, making my own skin heat. "We've got a theory on Grace, by the way. A couple of them, actually. Haunted item on her, something in the house itself—or maybe buried trauma. Dealer's choice."

"It's not the house, I don't think," Lucian said. "The energy is off there, but not demonic-entity off. Buried trauma, on the other hand…"

I jumped as Claire's computer chimed, and she swiveled to the screen. "Hello, Grace," she said brightly. "Come on up!"

"Delia," Lucian murmured, low enough only for me to hear as Claire and Steve cleared away the rest of the breakfast trash and blew through the office like they were prepping a dorm room for a parent's visit. I moved over to him but stopped a solid foot away. I didn't want to touch him, didn't want to even look at him directly, but I felt his energy ripple along my skin as I neared, the air charged with the scent of cinnamon and smoke.

His lips twitched as I resolutely watched Claire and Steve hustle around, Claire stopping to open the door wide before moving on to fluff pillows. "I would like you to render whatever assistance you would like for Grace Mercer before Thursday. I may not be available after that, and that might open you up to unnecessary risk."

I jerked my gaze to meet his, a red fire glowing at the dark rims of his irises. "Thursday," I echoed. "That's when it is? Should I be there?"

For just a second, something shifted in his gaze—something desperate and raw. It was gone as quickly. "You should not, unless and until you're summoned directly. You should be as far away from that collection of broken souls as possible. But the timing has been set, yes. I wanted you to know."

"I—"

My reply was cut off with the sudden appearance of Grace Mercer in the doorway—only I could see at a glance that this was a far different Grace than we'd seen earlier today.

"Yo, Grace, what's going on?" Steve blurted, hurrying over to her. "You okay?"

"I—oh, Steve," she practically keened, accepting his outstretched hand and going willingly into a hug. Claire and I exchanged startled glances as he helped her to the couch.

"Grace?" I asked, moving to an opposite chair as she composed herself. "Thank you for coming in to see us, but you're clearly up—"

"Could you join us?" Grace blurted in a high-pitched, little girl voice, and I blinked as she waved at Claire eagerly. "I like you. I think you're pretty."

I tried not to stare as Claire stood at her desk, coming over with an easy, measured cadence that they must have taught in pharmacy school.

"That's very kind of you, Grace," Claire said warmly, taking a seat next to her on the couch as Steve edged back from the two women. If he could have bolted from the room, I suspected he would. Lucian remained at the edge of Steve's desk, still unacknowledged by Grace. "Why don't you tell us what happened today?"

"Today? Nothing. Nothing ever happens during the day," she sighed, her voice still sounding oddly young. She reached out and took Claire's hand, holding it up to display her fingers. "Your nails are nice. You keep them nice."

She glanced toward me, frowned. "You don't."

I nodded. "I don't, you're right. You do, though."

"I do," she said happily, looking down at her own perfectly polished nails. They gleamed with a soft pink hue. "I like being pretty. I've always been pretty. Everyone says so."

Recalling the staged photos and trying to process the unnerving cadence to Grace's voice, I asked the next question quietly. "How old are you, Grace?"

"Old *enough*," she said slyly, her lips curving into a sneaky grin. "Old enough to know that you're not nice, but you are."

She squeezed Claire's hand. "And you..." she turned to Steve, tilted her head. "You're *handsome.*"

She still hadn't looked at Lucian, but when she glanced back toward me, I held her eyes for just a second, but there was nothing in there looking out at me, nothing I could latch onto. "Do you know why you came here today, Grace?" I asked.

She nodded, dropped her eyes again to Claire's pale hand. "I'm scared," she said. "Nobody ever tells me anything, but I'm scared. I'm not supposed to talk to you."

From the corner of my eye, I could see Steve flinch, but it was Claire who spoke. "Don't you trust us, sweetheart?" she asked gently.

"I do," Grace assured her quickly, looking up to meet Claire's gaze. "I do. But not everyone does, and I have to be careful and quiet. No one can see!"

"I can understand that," I said, and this time my voice was quieter too. I didn't know what exactly was wrong with Grace, but possession wasn't her only issue. "But it was super brave, you coming here yourself to let us know. You came all this way to tell us—something, right? Can you whisper it to Claire, maybe?"

To my surprise, Grace blushed to the roots of her red hair, then bit her lip and looked at Claire with adoring eyes. "You won't tell anyone?" she asked breathlessly.

"Not unless I have to, honey—"

"You can't!" Grace insisted in her little girl voice, then she tugged Claire toward her and whispered in her ear.

An abrupt knock sounded at the door, and I jerked around with a huff of surprise—only to feel my own eyes pin wide.

"Officer Hernandez!" I blurted, standing. Claire looked up too, her eyes going wide.

"You're the police!" she said guilelessly.

"I am," Hernandez nodded, her dark eyes shrewd in her

bronzed skin, her hair slicked back as ruthlessly as ever in a tight bun. She swung her gaze to me and over to Lucian, where she held it. Then her gaze shifted to the shelves behind Claire.

"Those look familiar," she said, tilting her head, but before I could explain how I'd ended up with Mordechai's treasure trove of books, she glanced back at me. "I need to speak with you, Delia, if you don't mind? And your, ah, associate here? I don't think we've met."

"I've got this," Claire put in before I could object. Grace still held her hand in a death grip, and Steve had started to look green. I suspected he'd rather take his chances with the police too versus sitting any longer next to baby-voiced Grace, but I didn't give him the chance.

"We can take a walk," I said, gesturing to the door. Hernandez's gaze pinned back on Grace for another second, then she stepped back into the hall. Lucian stood as well, his smug smile firmly fixed on his face as we joined the police officer.

"Officer Hernandez," he began, holding out a hand. "Lucian Gray. I've heard so much about you."

Charm practically cascaded from him, and Hernandez smiled back, blinking quickly. This close, she smelled like soap and sorrow, but the sorrow faded as she shook Lucian's hand. "Are you an exorcist as well?" she asked.

"Alas, merely an assistant." Lucian executed a short bow. "But one day, who knows?"

I fought to keep from rolling my eyes as Hernandez unkinked another notch. I appreciated Lucian greasing the wheels of this conversation, but I didn't want them to fall off. "Is there some way I can help you?" I asked, drawing her attention back to me as we reached the staircase and started moving down.

She blinked, and a brief flare of color warmed her cheeks.

"Kind of the opposite, really. I picked up some chatter about you that kind of struck me as off, thought you should know."

"Chatter." I lifted my hand to my brow. "If you mean the Dark Streets podcast, I don't know why she's fixating on me, truly."

"I've heard of Dark Streets." Hernandez snorted, then shook her head. "But no, I mean real chatter—like police detail. Well, unofficial police detail, just a couple of off-duty cops pulled in for some surveillance work, who were talking too loudly. Your whereabouts were noted last night at Descent. Thought you should know someone was looking at you."

I made a face. "Me specifically? Like, they used my name?"

"Not your name, no. I think the term they used was 'exorcist freak.' But that sort of narrowed it down for me." She eyed me. "You were at the club last night?"

My lips tightened. "I was."

"So, see? I was right. That's some crack policework for you. You need to be careful, Delia." She waved a hand back in the general direction of my office. "You notice I didn't exactly need to get buzzed in. Some guy walked out, and I walked in, which means your security here is shit. And that young woman in there didn't look a hundred percent stable."

"I..." I frowned, but she was right—she shouldn't have gotten up to our office unannounced. "I mean, thank you."

"Yes, thank you," Lucian said, and there was a strange timbre to his voice that made me glance his way. I blinked. He somehow appeared even more dangerously attractive in the low lights of the hallway—vibrating with an energy that I could feel. "What else did you want to tell us?"

Hernandez bit her lip. "It's the club—Descent. Of all the places for you to be seen right now, Delia, that one isn't great. Nikolai Volkov is already on our watch list, no matter how many elbows he rubs up against at cocktail hour with the mayor. He's gotten flagged by the FBI and Homeland Security, and that's just for the legal stuff he's running. You don't want to be mixed up in that."

I lifted my brows. "I didn't think I was high on your list of people to look out for anymore."

She snorted. "Believe me, I wish you weren't. I liked Marcus. He was a mess of a man and probably not the greatest husband, but he was a good partner and a good dad, and he loved his ex-wife more than he ever wanted anyone to know, especially after she moved out of the city and ditched him. We got the results back on his autopsy. When he fell out that window, he was already dead. Heart stopped cold. So, something he saw scared him so damned much he chased down his own bullets trying to get to it. Something got into his head so damned deep that he couldn't shake it off."

She eyed me. "I don't know how much *you* can shake off, is all."

As she stepped out the door, I gestured for Lucian to wait for me. I followed her into the parking lot, the two of us standing in the dappled shadows of the unseasonably cool June day.

"Thank you, Officer Hernandez."

She sighed. "You should probably call me Natalie at this point, unless I'm coming to arrest you. Which could still happen. There are a lot of unanswered questions that are all leading back to you. It's just that—the more I hear, the more I'm not sure you're the one I should be holding accountable. But..." She smiled wryly. "The day's still young, I guess."

I watched her get into her car, then scanned past it, into the trees that framed the lot. I felt...watched, observed, but there was no one else in the lot, no one driving up the short hill to reach our fenced-off enclave. As I turned back to the door, though, a movement in the corner of my eye caught me.

I turned—then froze.

Off to the side of the lot, beneath the trees, lay a coiled length of red woven rope—a dog leash. Exactly the same kind of leash that my imaginary shadow stalker had been using to walk his imaginary dog yesterday morning.

This was some *bullshit*. Anger igniting within me, I stalked across the parking lot, then swooped down to pick up the leash, fully expecting it to disappear the moment my fingers brushed it.

Except it didn't disappear. It was real.

I picked up the length of rope, turning it over in my hands. One well-worn, red dog leash and buckle, only there was no dog attached to the end of it, and no long-dead stalker attached to the other.

So where did the thing come from—and why?

And how was it *real?*

I turned back to the building and somewhere distant, barely carried to me on the breeze, I heard a low, tuneless song, four notes over and over again, up and down, fast and slow.

CHAPTER

TEN

Lucian was waiting for me, opening the door as I approached. He tilted his head, lifting an aristocratic eyebrow at the red leash that I'd managed to wrap completely around my hand five times in the short trip from the parking lot.

"You found a dog?"

I shook my head. "Not the dog, just the leash. That guy who was following me yesterday morning? I mean, he couldn't actually have been following me; it had to be a hallucination of a guy from my past—some rando Mordechai exorcised. He showed up too many places too far apart. But at the beginning, he had a dog. I noticed him walking him down the street, singing some weird little song."

"When you saw the house," Lucian put in, and I glanced sharply at him as we headed for the stairs up to the office.

"I didn't tell you about the house."

He shrugged. "You didn't need to. The connection between us is fading, without question. But anytime a human thinks about anything to do with the demonic realm, an astute demon knows. I consider myself one of the more astute demons, especially when it comes to you."

"Wait, what?" He started up the stairs as my brain struggled to put together new pieces of a puzzle whose image was only now beginning to creep in at the corners. "That house really was possessed? *That* was why I noticed it?"

He chuckled, the sound as ancient as old leaves, and I caught the scent of red wine and fine leather, warm skin and whispering silk. "Not possessed, no. It doesn't need your services. But it is a very old house. Over the centuries, it's had associations with the horde."

I made a face. "And this is why we can't have nice things." Still, I had other concerns to be thinking about than gothic deathtraps I couldn't afford. I held up the leash to Lucian again, my finger scraping along the rough edge of its metal tip. I winced at the flash of blood that welled up, but it simply proved my point even more. "This is real," I said.

"I noticed that."

"But *how* can it be real? It was around that apparition's neck when he appeared at the 'L' station. Then that same apparition then showed up inside the train without ever boarding it. I'm okay with all of that, I really am. Hallucinations gonna hallucinate. But this dog leash is real. I felt like I was being watched, I turned around, and—"

Lucian glanced at me sharply, then continued up the stairs. "You felt like you were being watched? Has that happened before?"

"Of course it hasn't happened before," I snapped. "I've gone my entire life being the person that nobody wants to look at directly. But starting with my Thomas Keegan lookalike yesterday morning, I just feel more, I don't know, seen. And not in a good way. Why? Is that a problem?"

No sooner were the words out of my mouth than I played

them back for the benefit of the thinking side of my brain. "You think this is because of the tribunal? Like, we've got a bunch of new demons in town sniffing around, and they've caught my scent?"

Lucian gestured to the doorway to our office as we crested the top of the stairs.

"There are newcomers to the city, yes, but you're also garnering attention of a very human sort. This podcaster, for example."

"Well, she's pretty fringe." I shrugged. "I mean, yeah, she's mentioning me, but this is Chicago. There are a few other things going on for people to pay attention to."

He didn't respond to that as we reached the office, stepping inside to see Claire and Steve still at their posts on the couch, talking to Grace. Claire looked up with palpable relief as we entered.

"There you are!" she said brightly. "We were just talking to Grace here about some of the therapists we have in the building. We think she would benefit from talking to one of them."

"She's scary," Grace said quietly, shrinking back on the couch. It took me only a second to realize that she was referring to me. And I was just pissed off enough about being jerked around by a dog leash that I wasn't willing to let it go.

I crossed to Claire's desk and leaned against it, knowing that Grace's gaze followed me from beneath her long, curled eyelashes. "Grace," I began steadily. "Did you think I was scary when we talked yesterday morning? Because I thought you were very nice. So smart and so capable, what with your work at the university, your plans for the future. Yesterday morning, you could do anything you wanted to. What happened? You were so strong."

Grace's chin jerked up at my opening address of her name,

her shoulders stiffening as her gaze snapped to me, fully focused for the first time since she'd walked in the door.

"Of course," she said brightly, a genuine smile crossing her face. Her cheekbones seemed sharper now, her chin firmer, her smile steady and sure. "It was lovely to have you visit, and I'm so glad that I was able to meet you here. You have a very nice office."

At her side, Steve struggled and failed to keep from gaping, barely clearing his expression when she turned to him. "You were so right to bring me here, Steve. I already feel better. What do we do next?"

"Excuse me."

The sound of Sergei's rough voice at the still-open door startled me so much I nearly fell off the edge of the desk, but the stoic Romanian wasn't addressing me. He had his glare pinned on Lucian.

"I have brought Mr. Volkov."

Before I could react to that salvo, Sergei stepped aside, giving me my first view of Nikolai Volkov outside one of his lairs.

It was a pretty good view. In an apparent nod to the summer day, never mind that it was a bit cool out, he wasn't wearing a suit but a pristine white shirt open at the neck and tucked into trousers the color of midnight. Platinum glinted at his wrist and neck, the brief glimpse of some sort of chain draped over his collarbone sending urgent spikes of panic and need through me that I couldn't fully process. His skin seemed darker, more bronzed than I remembered it, his dark hair swept back like Lucian's but with less curl, as if even his hair refused to allow itself softness. He wore a silken midnight blue eye patch that only added to his roguishness, and his jawline and cheekbones were blade sharp, his gaze intent as he swept the room.

"We need to talk," he said tightly to Lucian and me, while Grace emitted the tiniest "oh!" of feminine awareness that drew his focus.

Those hard lips suddenly curved into a devastating smile. "Forgive me, I didn't realize you had a client, Ms. Thompson."

"We were just leaving," Claire announced, her voice overloud, striking me at hard angles. She stood, and I didn't miss how Sergei stepped closer to her, his strong presence seeming to bolster her plan.

"We wanted to give Grace a tour of the building and see if maybe one of the other practitioners was in residence right now. So, this works out!"

Grace blinked up at Claire as Steve stood and reached for her hand, and while she allowed him to draw her upright, she seemed genuinely confused. "I did? I have a therapist. She's very good."

"You can never have too much therapy, isn't that what you always say?" Steve countered, smiling at her. "They do yoga on the first floor here too, but there's no class going on right now, so no point in checking that out. Still, the space is pretty cool."

"Absolutely." Claire crossed the room to her desk and plucked a few business cards off the magnetic board she had propped against the wall. "We'll just go see if anyone else is around, then make sure Grace gets home. Unless you need me?"

"I will drive you," Sergei said, and Claire's gaze, too wide, too focused, swiveled from me to him. What was going on with her? She'd met Nikolai last night—had he freaked her out that much?

"Ah, everything okay?" I asked Claire, and she waved the cards at me.

"Absolutely, I just want to make the most of Grace's visit here while we have her with us." She smiled brightly at me, and I finally got it. Frozen child Grace wasn't going to be much value to a therapist. Now that we'd knocked ordinary Grace back into focus, Claire wanted to strike while she was hot.

They were out the door in less than thirty seconds, leaving Lucian and Nikolai staring after them.

"She has been touched," Nikolai observed, earning him a sharp glance from me.

"No shit," I said, unreasonably irritated. "Any idea how? Or by whom?"

He turned his sardonic smile on me. "I should think that is your specialty."

Without waiting for me to retort to that, he focused on Lucian. "The terms for the tribunal have been set, just thirty minutes ago. I wanted you to know. With the infrastructure of the city so recently compromised, I decided a personal visit was more appropriate."

"Did you," Lucian said coolly.

"They'll use Descent as the entry point," Nikolai continued. "The energy there still holds a record of the attack last night, and your defense."

I frowned at this. "I thought he was being held accountable for what he did to Mirr. That didn't happen at Descent."

Volkov nodded. "He is. However, his current form has excited a new layer of curiosity. No seventh-level commander has ever relegated himself into a fourth-level form, and no fourth-level has ever comported themselves so effectively against a concerted demon attack by a fifth-level leader followed on the heels by a different, fourth-level antagonist." He smirked at Lucian. "You've become very popular, it would appear."

"Is that good or bad?" I asked. "I mean, if he's a badass, isn't that a good thing?"

Lucian snorted, leaning against the doorframe to my office. "It depends on whether or not I can be controlled."

"Exactly so," Nikolai agreed. "You should know that the betting is fierce that you cannot be."

That generated another hard smile. "And which way did you wager?"

Between my night at the desk, the red dog leash still wrapped around my hand and their snippy comments, my temper was starting to fray. "I feel like maybe you guys aren't taking this seriously. And if you're not taking it seriously, then that means I don't need to take it seriously, can we agree on that?"

Nikolai shook his head, his smile twisting. "Exactly the opposite. Gallows humor was, after all, invented by demons."

He slanted a glance toward Lucian. "She'll draw their attention next, if you're not there to protect her. You have to know that."

Lucian curled his lip. "And I suppose you are offering your services as my second?"

Irritation spiked. "So, hey, thanks to both of you, but I'm good. I don't need anyone's services—first, second, or anywhere in between. Unless you guys missed the memo, I'm the exorcist here. My protection, if you will, starts way above your pay grade."

I expected my rejection of Volkov's offer would at least find support from Lucian, since they clearly didn't like each other. But I was destined to be disappointed. As I spoke, Lucian turned his gaze toward me, his eyes flaring red, breath hissing through his lips. I swore I could almost see his nostrils flare, like a predator sensing nearby prey, and I fought to keep myself from shivering.

"What?" I snapped instead. "You're not going to change my mind on this. I don't need *protecting*. Not from demons. That literally is my job."

"She doesn't understand," Nikolai put in, sounding amused, but also intrigued.

"She doesn't," Lucian agreed. "A demonstration may be in order." He drew in another, savoring breath, and I smelled cloves and charred wood.

"Hello, standing right here, no need to talk about me like a couple of weirdos—"

Lucian and Nikolai struck at once.

Based on the intense smell of smoke clogging my throat, and with my memory of what had happened in his apartment so fresh, I was already on my toes expecting a sideways attack from Lucian. Volkov, however, was a totally different problem.

Lucian raced forward, shedding his shedim form, showing the demon beneath before re-solidifying his hands into claws, his mouth now a fanged snarl. But Nikolai was human, a big, meaty ballbuster of a man who knew how to fight and fight dirty. And though I hadn't been lying about protection from demonic attack, I could still get the shit beaten out of me by a human.

Which I suppose was exactly their point, but I wasn't in the mood for the nuance right now.

"No!" I snarled and pulled the ends of my dog leash tight, a sharp, fresh pain ripping along my forearm. I ignored it and met Nikolai head-on with the taut leash, clotheslining him under the chin as he lunged for me. His right eye popped wide with surprise, and his hands immediately went to his neck, giving me the space I needed to scoot around him, still holding tight. I used the man as a human shield, forcing him to take the brunt of Lucian's attack dead on.

I didn't have my props, I didn't have my words, and I fell backward on Claire's desk under the weight of Nikolai and the scrabbling demon looking like he was trying to tear through him to get to me.

Then I realized that Lucian wasn't getting through him.

Nikolai was a Hallow. Hallows couldn't be damaged by demons.

But he—a grown-assed, oxygen-breathing man—had attacked me too.

And that was the point.

"Get off me!" I snarled, lunging for the scissors Claire kept in a cup and hacking at them both. Nikolai flipped around, and Lucian stood beside him, both of them smeared with blood. Which made no sense until I looked at my own hands. The rough edge of the leash had slashed along my forearm and both men—creatures, whatever they were—now wore the dark red stain of it, their bodies shaking, their lungs heaving, their eyes wild with passion and heat.

The moment stretched between us, as brutal as barbed wire...charged, but not with fear, exactly. With danger. With need.

What the hell?

I blew out an unsteady breath. "I get it," I said tightly, forcing them to look at my eyes as I swung my gaze back and forth. I still held the scissors up like a weapon, and I was more than happy to use them. "Demons can't hurt me unless they influence a person to do so, which they sure as shit can. Demons can't hurt Nikolai. Lucian can protect me against demons. Maybe you both can. But if Lucian's not here and somebody decides to get cute and get a couple of others to pile on, God may not be enough to save me."

That last made them both wince, seeming to shake them out of their thrall. Nikolai straightened, stepped back, and Lucian took a moment to shoot his cuffs out from beneath the sleeves of his suit. As he did, his gaze swung from Volkov to me, the smile that tugged at the corner of his lips more unsettling than anything else that had happened today, and that was saying a lot.

"I think...we begin to understand each other," he said.

CHAPTER

ELEVEN

Volkov didn't bother cleaning the blood off his face before he left. That disturbed me more than I wanted it to, especially as I watched Lucian's gaze stray to it several times as we straightened the office, locked it, and exited to the back parking lot. Sergei's SUV was gone, and Volkov slid into his sleek Audi coupe with a few muttered words to Lucian. I was numb enough that when Lucian offered to drive me home, I got into his low-slung deathtrap without complaint.

The smell of fresh leather revived me but also tweaked my nerves again. I reached out and drew my hand along the armrest, sensing Lucian tense beside me. "Where do you get your money, anyway?" I asked. "For this car, your apartment— all of it. Even your clothes. Demons don't usually have physical form."

He chuckled softly as he angled us down streets that had grown familiar in the past few weeks; we were heading to my new neighborhood, home of the Palidor Hotel. "*What demons require, humans must provide,*" he purred, as if quoting from some ancient text, both profane and arcane. "And they do. They always do. Over the millennia, it became expedient for money to facilitate some of those transactions. Those investments have done well, you could say."

I curled my lip, hearing the amusement in his tone but not knowing where it sprang from. "I don't even want to know if you're joking."

He didn't answer that, and I stared out the window for another half-block, too restless to stay quiet for long. "So, what exactly does it mean to have Volkov's protection? He's already assigned Sergei to us. Anything more, and I'm going to have to start paying taxes on him."

Lucian chuckled. "The kind of protection that Volkov would be required for is twofold. If you receive human threats, he is uniquely qualified to ensure your safety. If you have the need to interact with the demonic realm, he can serve as your personal bodyguard. While the former protection is already in his purview, the latter requires him to be bound to you as I am bound."

I shifted in my seat, instantly regretting that I'd brought it up. "I know what I said in your apartment, but it wasn't true. I was trying to distract you. You're not bound to me, Lucian. That's not how any of this works."

Another soft laugh, this one darker and more twisting, poking at the places deep within me that I didn't want to explore too closely. "It is exactly how it works, sweet Delia," he murmured. "And the sooner you understand that, the stronger you will be."

He turned down the street near the 'L' station, and I straightened. "This isn't the...why are we going this way?" I scowled as he turned again onto the same street I'd walked this morning, so familiar that I craned around in all directions, as if I could somehow catch sight of my stalker hallucination again.

"Do you think the dog is still here? Do you—what are you *doing*?"

With the lazy click of his finger on a fob I hadn't noticed nestled into a cupholder on his center console, Lucian activated the gates in front of the same sprawling Victorian mansion I'd mooned over less than forty-eight hours ago.

The wrought iron barriers swung open with surprising silence, their elaborate metalwork revealing itself in full Gothic glory as we passed between them. Up close, the gates were even more spectacular—and more unsettling—than I'd imagined from the sidewalk opposite. The iron had been worked into patterns that seemed to shift and dance in my peripheral vision, vines and thorns intertwining with shapes that could have been wings or flames, faces or flowers, depending on how the light hit them.

"What are you doing?" I asked again, my voice barely above a whisper as Lucian guided the car onto the curved drive.

"Exactly what you think," he said simply. "This house would fall within one of those needs that humans have conspired to meet for us."

"But…" I fell silent as the drive curved in a graceful arc across the front of the mansion, noticing how the house grew better-tended, not less, the further back we got from the street. Flowering shrubs lined the lane and spilled into the walkways, heavy tree branches arched overhead. Despite being only seventy-five feet from the street, the house felt completely removed from the urban bustle behind us—as if we'd stepped through a portal into another century.

Lucian stopped the car and clicked the button again, and I didn't have to turn to know the gates swung shut. We were cut off, alone. Safe.

Well, maybe not safe.

I pushed open the car door and stepped outside, surprised

by the scents that converged upon me. Lilacs, cabbage roses, and a heavy, decadent musk that was equal parts decay and desire, old secrets and older crimes wrapped in rotting velvet.

The mansion itself loomed over the lane like something from a Gothic novel, three stories of weathered limestone and dark brick that seemed to absorb the late afternoon light rather than reflect it. Elaborate gingerbread trim dripped from every eave and corner, carved with intricate patterns of vines, flowers, and creatures that might have been cherubs if you squinted, or something far more sinister if you let your eyes focus properly.

"How is this even here?" I asked, craning my neck to take in the full scope of the building. "Somebody has to own this, right? Like an actual human, somewhere?"

The wraparound porch stretched across the entire front facade, supported by massive columns carved with faces that seemed to track our approach. The tall, narrow windows marched across each floor in perfect symmetry, their original wavy glass intact in sharp contrast to the distant modern Chicago high-rises visible just beyond the property's tree line.

A single corner turret rose above the roofline another floor, its conical roof crowned with wrought iron finials that twisted skyward. Even in the heart of the city, with traffic humming just yards away, the house commanded its small kingdom with absolute authority.

"You like it?" Lucian asked, as if he genuinely didn't know the answer to the question. I tried not to let my hysteria show as I followed him up the stone steps.

The front door was a massive affair of solid oak stained nearly black, set with panels of deep red glass that glowed like garnets with the light from within. He pushed the door open without fanfare. It wasn't locked.

We stepped inside, and my eyes instantly complained against the drape of darkness, helped only by the weak light

Lucian summoned to life in the overhead chandelier. The foyer was two stories tall, dominated by a staircase that curved up into the gloom, while the floor displayed an intricate parquet of ebony and cherry wood, worn smooth by more than a century of footsteps. Dark paneling chased up the walls to meet rich, burgundy wallpaper flocked with thorned roses, and oil paintings too shadowy to make out marched high along the wall.

Everything smelled like beeswax and old wood, leather and vice. And it was beautiful. "Who cleans this place? This polish is recent. And there's no dust, like, anywhere."

"If you want to meet the staff, you can. When you're ready." Lucian reached for me. "They are very discreet."

I took his hand, then once again regretted it as the touch of his skin made my heart pound in a quick, panicked staccato. Unnerved, I pulled my hand away again, gesturing around. "So, people actually live here? On the regular?"

"Do you want them to?" he asked, moving into the first room to the right, a room hung with heavy curtains that let in only the smallest sliver of light. A fire crackled in the marble fireplace, making the room almost uncomfortably warm.

"Who lit that?" I demanded, my brain finally coming back online. "And don't say demons, or I'll throw holy water on you. Does someone seriously live here?"

"Yes. You do." Lucian flicked his hand with something approaching annoyance as I gaped at him. "There's a problem with your housing. The Palidor is no longer suitable."

"It's fine," I said quickly, but he cut me off.

"It's not fine. You slept in your office last night rather than face it again. You need your strength and your sleep. You need safety. You have both, here."

"It's a Demon Airbnb, Lucian. I don't think it's going to be all that safe."

"It will be, as long as you are residing here. It will be bound to you, should you choose it."

I winced. That word again. "Demons are really big on that, sounds like."

"Bindings have their uses."

I looked around the room and sighed. "If I say yes to the house, what's the catch? You guys have some sort of lien on my soul at that point? Because that's not going to work for me."

"No," Lucian said. He strolled over to one of the couches near the fire, then sat, looking for all the world like he owned the place. Maybe because he did. "It's yours until you no longer wish it to be. Then it stands vacant again. There are enough other properties in the city for demonic use; this one can be claimed for your lifetime, as short or long as that may be."

I made a face. "Why this one?"

"Because you chose it—as you chose to recall me to your side, you chose to free Volkov from his debt, you chose to protect your housemate, and to help Claire rid herself of a parasite of a boyfriend."

I moved over to the couch opposite Lucian, but sat uneasily, leaning forward to rest my elbows on my knees. "I didn't so much choose that last one," I pointed out. "And Volkov was just in my way."

Lucian's lips twisted. "I'll wait until after the tribunal to tell him that."

"Yeah, about that." I shifted closer, staring at him. Why couldn't I see him well? The fire was plenty bright, but Lucian's features seemed to soften into shadow as I watched him. "Now that we have a date for this thing, can you tell me what happens in it? No more bullshit half-answers, either. I get that you taking Mirr off the table wasn't allowed, but what can they do to you? What's the worst-case scenario? You go back to Level 1?"

"For the offense of unsanctioned murder, that wouldn't

typically be a strong enough sentence," Lucian said, surprising me. "However, I'm a seventh-level commander. Knocking me all the way back to Level 1, with the prospect of it taking millennia for me to reach my former station, might be considered a viable sentence for the crime."

"Assuming they find you guilty," I pointed out.

He smiled. "Oh, they'll definitely find me guilty. That part isn't in question."

"Then what's the point of all of this? Why are all these demons coming here, if they have already decided that?"

"Because they want to know why I chose to do what I did—which I cannot let them know."

I tilted my head. "Well, they'll figure that one out, too, won't they? You did it because—"

He lifted a hand, effectively cutting me off. "I did it because Mirr challenged me. Because he dared to believe he was stronger than I was. That alone is enough for me to squash him like a bug, but I didn't squash him. I unshackled him from the grips of Hell and sent him hurtling into the void. For we who have given up all for Self, it is our only fear."

The silence hung between us then. "Okay, then..." I began, and Lucian's gaze flicked to me like a snake.

"The only question the tribunal needs to answer is, given my crime, can I be trusted to follow orders in the future? And if I cannot, am I worth enough to the courts to serve anyway?"

"But the answer to that has to be no, right? If you've already proven that you're going to color outside the lines when you decide it's worth it, why would they trust you?"

He spread his hands. "They would trust me if my skills were such that any one of them could use me as their executioner and know I would not fail. It's not enough, you see, to simply be willing to enact violence on another. You also have to be good enough that you cannot be beaten. If you take the weapon out of the hand of even the greatest general, that general falls. Only the strongest weapon can be used. Otherwise, it's not worth the attempt."

I pursed my lips, more of the puzzle pieces coming together. "If you can be controlled, you're a weapon to be used at the highest levels—so long as you can't be overpowered. The fact that you just survived the attack at Descent just proved that point. You survived, while your attackers got kicked down a few rungs. In all these millennia, the one thing demons couldn't do was take each other out-out. Void-level out. But with you in the mix, they can. That's valuable to them."

He smiled. It wasn't a good smile. "Now you understand."

"But if enough of them gang up on you, I mean...you could be destroyed too, right? Even if it takes legions?"

He shrugged. "It wouldn't be the first time the creatures formed by the Creator turned against their very own and struck them down. It would not be the last."

"And you're okay being an executioner."

He smiled, showing teeth. "What do you think?"

"I think there's something I'm not understanding here," I said, frustration spinning up within me. "What do you really want, Lucian?"

The question was almost unbearably simple, yet it hung between us, a shimmering thing. Lucian froze in his elegant recline across from me, and his eyes flashed with red flame. "There are certain questions that you never ask a demon, Delia," he said. "That's one of them."

I felt the breath dwindle in my throat, my heart rate going thready and weak, the blood moving slower in my veins. I'd been attacked by this creature, I'd been hunted and bitten and scraped, and yet the low quivering feral intensity of his gaze right now frightened me more than anything that had come before. This was a monster sitting opposite me. This was an entity I didn't know at all. This was thorns and daggers and scraping pain wrapped in liquid absolution and I wanted to drink deep, needed to drink deep. Was this me? Was I feeling these things? Or was this some trick of a demon-infested household preying upon my mind, my nerves?

I didn't know. I didn't care.

"Lucian," I whispered again. "What do you want?"

TWELVE

LUCIAN

To use the vernacular of humans, Lucian didn't move a muscle. In truth, the form of the shedim shouldn't allow him that ability. Within this husk, there should be no sensation of muscular tightening or tension, no spiking heat, no shivering chill skittering along his bones. But whenever he was near Delia, an entire world of new sensations spiraled up within him, threatening to break free with every gasp and sigh.

Now, here in this house, it was a thousand times worse.

A thousand times better? No. Worse.

Because here in this house lined with bindings and sigils buried in the floorboards and woven into the fabric of the walls, here in this home hung with shadow and arcane invocations that dated back to when the very ground of this holding was consecrated with dark intent, here he was both in his element *and* hers.

He moved forward as subtly as possible and in that blink was on her.

"Lucian!" Delia gasped his name, her voice barely audible, yet it crashed through his skull like the howl of a thousand devils. He didn't give her a chance to draw breath but drove down, covering her lips with his and pulling her into an embrace so tight he could feel the brand of her skin along his body, the heat igniting between them despite their clothing.

Clothing.

"Delia." He pulled himself away to hover into a crouch before her, unsurprised to see the drop of blood on her lip. Had he done that? Had she? As it had in her office, the sight of her blood, the smell of it, sang to him, a keening response blossoming deep within his shedim form, expanding out as his muscles tensed, his blood rushed, his cock hardened with a thrumming insistence between his legs.

He was not an animal, yet he was every bit that with her, savage and needy, demanding and impatient, but there was so much she didn't know and still so much she needed to remain ignorant of until he could keep her safe...

Safe.

Safe from everything but him.

"Do you trust me?" he murmured, and though he kept his voice deliberately low, he didn't miss the way she glanced around as if she could hear the words echoing back to her from the ancient furnishings of this room, a chamber that had been designed for this very purpose, hidden away from all that was right and good. This house would keep her safe too—as long as she wanted it to—but to ensure that protection, she would have to consent to its binding.

"Not one fucking bit." Delia's sharp words drew his focus back to her, and then he noticed the grip of her fingers against the cushions of the couch, the pound of her pulse in her throat, the hiss of breath against her teeth. She glared at him with eyes that sparked with fury and more than a bit of fear. "This is what you want? To make me doubt your sanity?"

He leaned forward again, his lips a secret's breath away from hers.

"Yes," he said, fanning her mouth with the word as his eyes locked on hers, feeding on her fear, her need. Feeding on the energy that crashed through her body, racketing around for any exit. "Yes, that's exactly what I want. I want you to look into my eyes and know exactly what I am, and then to fuck me anyway. I want you to give me your body and your mind, your tongue and your cunt, and when you are all twisted up inside, then I will come after your heart and maybe your soul—but I don't need that now. I may never need them, and I sure as fuck wouldn't know what to do with them. I only need you to say yes to this."

He closed the space between them, taking her mouth again, branding her with his own heat. Pushing her back against the couch, he shackled her wrists in his hard grasp and drew those fisted hands high against the plush velvet cushions, dragging his mouth along her chin and upper jaw to the sensitive lobe of her ear. He hovered there, breathing fast, relishing the trapped spirit beneath him so like a swallow beating against a windowpane.

"I want you to feel everything, Delia. And I want you to let this house *know* that you're feeling everything."

She went still beneath him, her breath hollowing out, but her brain clearly working again. "What do you mean, this house?" she asked, the words ending on a groan as he nuzzled her neck, his mouth burning a trail over her collarbone to the scoop of her shirt...

And he saw the first bruise she was hiding. He reared back, suddenly rigid with something other than need.

"You're hurt," he accused. "Why are you *hurt?*"

She wriggled out of his grasp and scooted away. "Maybe because you went full demon on me last night? Remember that?" she snapped. Without his prompting, she reached down and pulled off her long-sleeved shirt, grimacing with the effort. Then she stared at the garment in her hands.

"I don't know why I did that," she protested, the words edging toward anger as she brought her gaze up to meet his again. "Did you make me do this? Did this house make me do this?"

He didn't know the answer to that, and he didn't care. In a series of swift, economical movements, he slid his own clothes off, tossed them to the side, until he was naked on his knees before her, never mind that she still clutched her own shirt in her hands. His gaze raked over her body, the curves of her breasts, the dip of her waist, the roundness of her belly. She was still bruised, he saw, despite the sigils he'd drawn along her flesh, the spells of healing he'd spoken over her.

The scrapes where he had gored her flesh were closed over, pink and shiny against her pale white skin, but the bruises went deeper, darker. As if something buried within her had been damaged and wouldn't heal so easily as forgiving flesh, no matter how tightly they were bound.

"I was injured," he said, drifting his mouth along the worst of the bruises. "I didn't realize…"

Under the pressure of his lips, she groaned and sank back again against the cushions, and he could see the skin lightening. The human mind never failed to astound him. It was an endless marvel that these creatures, born of a power they would never understand, had so much strength within them that they were too afraid to draw upon, unless and until it was literally ripped out of them. She was healing herself because she believed she could be healed.

It was as simple and as terrible as that.

He traced the bruising down to the tip of her quivering breast, then took the nipple into his mouth, reveling in the throaty groan that escaped her lips. He tugged and licked the nervous peak until it scrunched tight, needy and hard against him.

"I asked you a question," Delia managed.

"Shh," he whispered back, moving to her other breast. His hands slipped down her body now, skimming the scars that he had inflicted upon her, smoothing the puckered skin that he had damaged. He should feel terrible for marking her this way. He did feel terrible and yet...not only terrible.

There was something else riding beneath that sensation, blossoming like a forbidden flower on a broken stem. He wanted this. He needed this—in a way no demon ever should. The connection he had with Delia was driving everything to high, unholy levels of sensation that he couldn't understand and was absolutely terrified would end before he experienced it all.

He dipped further, drawing his mouth level to her quivering upper thighs. The heat of her rose to meet him, and he nipped and licked and suckled until she writhed. At every twist and shudder, he could feel what she felt, his own body reacting, mirroring her sensations as if bound to her.

Bound.

He looked up then and saw it.

The edges of the room were shifting now, the twining, thorned-rose wallpaper shivering, undulating like a living thing. He must have breathed out a response to the sight, because Delia shifted beneath him, her face turning toward the wall, following his line of sight. When she would have frozen, he drew his tongue down along her slit, trapping her against the couch with his mouth.

She didn't shake so easily, though. "What in the..."

He lifted his head again to meet her wild gaze. "Hallucinations," he said, seeing no need to lie to her. "Your mind sees what it senses, not what's really there. But the energy of this house, this place, is reaching out to you. Taking hold."

"I don't freaking want it to... ohh!" She jerked, her foot kicking out as the nearest tendril of shadow wrapped around her ankle, sliding up her leg.

"I've got you, I've got you," he promised.

"I'm not so much worried about you," she managed, and he laughed, the sound so foreign in his own ears that the house reacted too. Seeing and experiencing through her body, through her sight and taste and touch, unnerved him to the core as the tendrils of dark vines split away from her body and coiled around his calves as well, reaching up to his thighs. He levered himself into position over Delia, unsure of whether he was choosing the movement or being pushed into it, and definitely not caring. The energy, the need, stoked high within him, and when he looked up, it was to stare deep into Delia's eyes and see something he didn't expect.

Understanding. And shared emotion.

"You're surprised too," she breathed out. "Isn't this your freakshow funhouse?"

He choked out another laugh, but the need overwhelmed him, and he could no more hold off another second than he could stop drawing the breath required in his shedim form. He slid into Delia, meeting her resistance, easing it, and then sinking his cock deep within her in another long thrust. She lifted her hips beneath him, welcoming him deeper, her eyes going wide as another tendril of shadow lifted and wrapped around her upper arm.

"Hallucinations," she repeated drily, and he smiled.

"They're very *good* hallucinations," he admitted, and she laughed again, the clenching of her low belly almost too much for him to bear. He pulled back, then plunged deep, reveling in her heat, her fire, the kind of heat he had never imagined was possible before now. The kind of heat he suspected was not only forbidden but impossible for his kind to experience.

Except he *was* feeling it. He was drowning in it, and he would never give it up. He would never give *her* up. After this night, this moment, not even the void could keep her from him. And he would do whatever it took to ensure that safety even if, *especially* if, he needed to recruit a human to his cause.

"Ah!" Delia gasped, and she arched beneath him, her mouth softening into an O of pleasure that finally overrode her focus on the shadows slipping around them. The shadows that still twined, now with even greater speed as her climax lifted her up, up, and sent her tumbling over the precipice, taking Lucian with her.

He wasn't spent, not close to it, but he gathered her against him, hauling her up, surrounding her body with his. The shadows now fully bound them both together, and something tugged at his mind at that, an anomaly that he couldn't quite grasp—not with Delia bracing herself against his chest, her eyes soft and liquid, her mouth loose and bruised, this time not from his fury but still very much from his need.

She shifted, moved higher on his body, the movement instantly sending the blood rushing to his groin again, thickening his cock inside her.

Then she stared down at him, her mouth set in a determined line. "If I can come with those things crawling around us, you sure as hell can too," she informed him.

Meeting her gaze, he felt the twinned sensations of their joining forms, not only the pressure of her against him, the sweet slick slide of her body joining his, but also the fullness of her as she grounded him inside her, and the combination of sensations that assaulted her—his heat, the salty sweetness of his lips on hers, the soft, sinuous slide of their bodies moving against each other. They were one complete unit, engaged in a give and take of a kind that he once again was sure a demon was *never* supposed to feel. But he was. He fucking was.

He grabbed her arms, sliding down until their fingers intertwined, and he pulled her hands above his ears so that her face was a mere inch from his. Staring into her eyes, he whispered words of ancient power, grace, and sacredness. Words that he had read a hundred lifetimes ago, branded into his broken soul, stitching together his shattered bones and spilling out over her as the flaring tendrils of shadow and smoke whipped around them, shrinking away, then rushing forward again to bind and tie and witness.

The explosion of Lucian's climax felt like it was wrenched from the deepest pits of hell...

And maybe it was.

THIRTEEN

"Thompson & Associates, can you hold please—Fuck!" I glanced past Steve's tall, angular form as it hovered at my open office door, grimacing as Claire's phone rang again on the heels of yet another failed attempt to put someone on hold. Her hasty, exasperated voice still managed to radiate confidence to whoever was on the other line, while her computer pinged its own chorus of notifications.

"You're telling me not all of these are legitimate?" I asked Steve, whose gaze ping-ponged back to me, the grin on his face betraying his good-natured enjoyment of Claire's fluster. Today he wore a T-shirt, jeans, and slipper-style sneakers, while Claire had breezed in wearing another million-dollar suit and a light floral perfume that probably would have cost me a month's salary at the deli. I'd stuck with a tank top, light sweater, and linen pants—all in something Claire referred to as "contrasting neutrals." Not exactly the cutting edge of exorcist fashion like my coworkers, but at least I'd be able to move when needed.

Steve split his attention between me and whoever Claire was sending to voicemail. "I mean, some of them are totally legitimate, like that lady Claire just hung up on. She's been trying to get through for about forty-five minutes."

"Not helping!" Claire called out as her phone rang again. When she segued into a renewed, sing-song cadence of professional earnestness, Steve's grin only deepened. Then he refocused on me.

"But yeah. Above and beyond the people legitimately in search of help with everything dark and nasty, we've got our share of assholes coming in. I'd say right now, we're running eighty percent legit and twenty percent assholes, but I think that percentage is going to get uglier before it gets better."

"I have a bad feeling you're right." I shook my head. "You got somebody monitoring the podcast? I can't force myself to listen to it anymore, but somebody should."

"All over it. Anya and Rook are tag teaming, and they're cross-referencing comments on some of the other pods as well to make sure that we don't have a pile-on situation. Mei is doing a sweep of other categories and covering the less active social platforms. Dark Streets is by far the most successful show in Chicago, but if we offered an exclusive, maybe to one of the other pods, especially if they weren't dicks about it, that could be an interesting strategy."

I made a face, though I was definitely grateful that Steve's gamer team was up for research duty. "I can't imagine that many people out there are interested in what we're doing. Mordechai lasted his entire career without going viral."

"Well, Mordechai wasn't witness to a cop jumping out a window either." Steve and I both flinched at his harsh words, but before he could apologize, I waved him off. He wasn't wrong.

"Still, just because I didn't give that woman an exclusive interview doesn't give her the right to harass me. Though I guess from her perspective, there's no greater outrage than somebody telling her no."

"Pretty much." Steve's mouth kicked up into a lopsided grin. "I mean, you could sic demons on her, but I think she'd be one of those people who'd record her mother's face being eaten if she thought it would get ratings."

"That's...disturbing."

"But not untrue. Anyway, we should have better data soon. I've got an app halfway coded that will help us track where our inbound traffic is coming from, and another one collecting data on any particularly problematic content, though I'm gonna try and keep that last bit on the down-low. Sergei has already poked his head in to let us know he's got a full team ready to protect our reputation as well as our bodily assets." He made a face. "Not gonna lie, that guy scares me."

"I think that's in his job description."

Steve ducked out and shut the door behind him, which didn't do a perfect job of drowning out the chaos in the front office, but it helped. Faced with the alternative of fielding some of these calls myself, I resolutely returned my focus to the pile of journals in front of me.

I'd narrowed down my search to journals and records that started about three months after I'd begun working with Mordechai and ended about five years ago. For whatever reason, he'd stopped taking notes about me shortly after my mother had died. I wasn't one hundred percent sure that there was a direct correlation there, but even the occasional mention of me didn't just dwindle down at that time. It completely disappeared. Something about that bothered me, especially given Mordechai's obsessive need to record everything, but whether he simply found me increasingly boring or he'd gotten spooked by something I'd done or said in the wake of my mom's death, any mention of me was off his playlist.

That said, what I could find was interesting. The time around the Thomas Keegan case, in particular, had spawned a significant uptick in info-dumping, always in Mordechai's strange shorthand. There had been a flurry of demon activity that summer, which I didn't recall at all. But I barely recalled Thomas Keegan either.

I'd been about fifteen then, a late bloomer by any account, but I didn't think that the increase in activity had anything to do with me personally. Knowing what I knew now, I wondered if there'd been another tribunal at that time, some other reason to bring a bunch of demons into the city. But I wasn't ready to have that conversation with Lucian, and I didn't think he'd necessarily even know. When he'd been buried in my guts, it was as if his world had shrunk to Delia-sized proportions, and he didn't really track what would have been going on outside of that. Then again, that's simply what he told me. Was it true?

I grimaced as I reached for another notebook, seeing the long bruise along the edge of my forearm. Distractedly, I pulled down the light sweater to hide it more fully. For all the bruising that Lucian had seemed to ease on my body during our frenzied encounter yesterday, he'd left me with a dozen new marks. Scraped skin, bruised muscles. Those hadn't faded. We'd collapsed onto the couch in the Victorian house, and I slept like the dead for fifteen straight hours—which had to be a record. When I awoke, he'd been gone, of course, leaving me completely alone. I hadn't even felt the weird phantom touch I'd experienced after I'd left his apartment. Hell, maybe I'd imagined that sensation; I'd been pretty strung out by then.

When I'd finally made it out the front door of the Victorian, I'd found Sergei and his SUV waiting for me in the front drive.

The bulky Romanian had taken me back to the Palidor with instructions for me to pack up, that Volkov had learned of my assignment to this house and fully supported it. Although I chafed a bit at the idea of needing anyone's protection, there was something important about the house. Something I needed to understand, and I did need some place to stay. Plus, I liked the place. I hadn't seen much of it beyond the drawing room and the bathroom I'd found just down the hallway, but it felt like a treasure box that had been set out for me to open.

Thinking of Sergei, I glanced out the window to the back parking lot, surprised not to see his meaty SUV but a bright red Mini Cooper convertible drive up the short hill and into the lot, parking crookedly in one of the spaces. The car was piled high with boxes, textiles, and mismatched throw pillows, and the driver flung herself out of the vehicle as if she'd been burned, then twirled around in a wildly printed dress, lifted one of the boxes and swung toward the door, only for the bottom of the box to collapse under the weight of whatever was inside it, and the whole multi-colored mess crashed to the concrete.

Balls, I suddenly realized. The woman had an entire collection of colored bouncing balls.

She stood frozen, her corkscrew hair flying, her caftan slipping off one shoulder, as she stared in horror at the chaos she'd just caused. Across the lot, Sergei opened his door and bounded out, clearly intent on helping her, and she dropped the box as well, her arms going out wide as she laughed with absolute delight.

She shouted something I couldn't make out, but I smiled and turned back to Mordechai's journals, determined to make some headway. If she could track down two dozen bouncing balls, I could find one thread of relevant information in all his scribbling.

"Excuse me!" Not two minutes later, Claire's professional-grade irritation jolted me from my page, and I was up and around my desk, moving at speed. I opened my door to see Steve gesturing to Claire with the universally approved cop wave of "keep it going."

Rolling her eyes at him, Claire nevertheless launched into an animated argument with someone who apparently thought she was the antichrist and wanted to share with her all the ways she was going to suffer for her sins. After two or three rounds of this, Steve finally gave her the thumbs up. With a decisive click of a key, she cut the man off mid-rant and turned on Steve.

"Did I seriously need to sit there and listen to that asshole for that long? Or were you just enjoying yourself?"

"Well, both those things can be true," he said, reasonably enough. "But I got a lock on the phone number and a geolocation for it, all coded by my team, thank you very much. I think I'm going to call this app SpoofProof, you know? It's really gonna be—"

"Steve," I broke in, and he swiveled to me, not missing a beat.

"All the calls are coming from the same house," he said. "Which is good and bad news. Good news in that we don't really have a public nuisance problem, bad news in that whoever has decided to target us, which almost definitely is Dark Streets, they're organized. So, even if they are just seeding the hysteria mill now until it can build up on its own, it's a problem."

"It's definitely a problem," I agreed. "But maybe we can get out ahead of it and—"

The sound of the office door buzzing made us all jump, especially as I could hear the buzz distantly echoing in rooms down the hallway.

"For heaven's sake," Claire protested. "Have they tracked us all the way here? Where's Sergei?"

Still, ever the dutiful office manager, she spun and connected the intercom. "Thompson & Associates?" she began brightly.

"Oh, my God, hi! This is Sandy, Sandy Shaw? I'm new here. It's my first day, and my keys are in the office, and I was so hoping that you could let me in just so that I could start unpacking. I'm so excited to be here, I just totally forgot what the code was. Would you mind letting me in?"

This had to be the same woman I'd seen in the parking lot. I gave Claire the thumbs up, then stepped forward as she held the speaker button down.

"I'll be right down," I said, as Claire's phone rang again. "Just hang on a second."

"Oh, my God, thank you!" Sandy Shaw said, and I pointed Claire to her phone.

"Continue answering whatever comes in and track it all. If this keeps up to the point where we've got a serious case for harassment, we could maybe call Officer Hernandez. Even if she can't help us, she might know more than we do about what we're dealing with."

"On it!" Steve said as Claire picked up the phone. "We should have plenty of data to work with by the end of the day."

I stepped out of the office and into the quiet of the hallway, considering Sandy Shaw's new arrival with a grim smile. If she rented out the space in this building hoping for solitude, she might be disappointed.

Sandy stood just a few feet away from the door, her smile broadening as she caught sight of me. Her corkscrew brown hair seemed to move of its own volition, separate from her body, which was sturdy, rounded, and brimming with energy. Up close, her caftan revealed itself as a masterwork of multicolored scraps of cloth, woven together with indiscriminate needlework.

"Hi!" she announced as I opened the door. "It's so great that somebody is actually here. When I stopped by a few weeks ago to tour the place, it was pretty much dead. I'm glad there are actually living, breathing people here!"

"Same," I said smiling. "I'm Delia—Delia Thompson—and I'm happy to meet you, Sandy. Here, let me take that."

She laughed again as she handed over the box of bouncing balls. "Thank you! This totally super-built guy just hanging out in the parking lot helped me collect them all when they went flying everywhere. I packed in such a hurry this morning, way too eager for sanity, and I guess I didn't gauge the weight right. He did some foldy thing with the bottom of the box and said it would hold for a bit, but we'd better hurry unless we want another Easter egg hunt. I'll just run back and get a few things!"

It turned out that Sandy Shaw's office was about five doors down from the yoga studio on the first floor, around the corner and occupying a cheerful open space with windows on two sides. It didn't have a back office, but she stepped into the room like a girl entering a castle.

"Isn't this the *best*?" she said, turning around with palpable joy. "I do holistic therapy, a lot of tactile work, connecting people with their inner child. You'd be surprised how many of us need playtime in today's world—well, you probably wouldn't be surprised since you work here. What do you do?"

"A few different things," I hedged, not quite ready to dump exorcism on the woman yet. "You work with clients of all ages, men and women?"

"I work with anyone who needs me!" she agreed with another quick smile. "But yes, all ages. My background is psychology, and I did a few years at a trauma center in Minneapolis, where I saw some things."

"Things," I echoed, and she nodded, her mood moderating a bit.

"Things, for sure. Enough to make me decide that private practice was probably a better fit. But it gave me some great experience, and I'm super grateful for the opportunity that brought me here. I think I just have one more load!"

"I'll go with you," I said. "I can let you back in, and I need some fresh air, so this works out."

"Fresh air is the *best*, and what a gorgeous day it is," she agreed. "Chicago in June can sometimes be absolute murder, but it's been just a glorious summer so far, hasn't it?"

She flowed down the hallway beside me, chirping enthusiastically. I suddenly realized I was smiling too. The expression felt odd on my face, and I found myself glad that Sandy Shaw had chosen this building. Hopefully, she wouldn't come to regret that decision.

We stepped outside, and I waited as she trotted down to her car, my smile only deepening as she pulled out the last thing in the back seat, a large throw pillow shaped like the sun.

"Hello, beautiful," she cooed, and swung around toward me —then her attention diverted, her eyes pinning to the side of the lot. "Oh! Well, hello there! Aren't you a sweet thing?"

I turned as well, then froze.

Standing at attention in the middle of the parking lot was the red-leash dog, the brown, black, and white beagle mix I'd seen so unconcernedly walking with the hallucination I now knew as Thomas Keegan. Only this time, there was no hallucination and no red leash, since I still had it in the office. And the dog itself looked like it'd been through some things. His fur was dull and stained with something dark on one side, his tail low and dispirited, barely twitching. Even his ears seemed to droop.

The dog looked straight at me and, with an odd, melancholy purse to its jaws, yodeled. Beside me, Sandy mewed again in distress. "Oh, my goodness, is that blood on your side? What happened to you?"

After leveling me with another accusing stare, the dog turned, gave a violent shake, and took off running.

I raced after him.

FOURTEEN

"Hey!" Moving fast in my ready-to-run clothing, I followed the dog at a dead run, catapulting down the small hill that served as the drive to our back parking lot, and bursting out onto the sidewalk.

Were there more cars on the street than usual? It seemed more congested, but I mainly noticed the cluster of vehicles because the dog was running in between and underneath the ones parked along the street. It slipped out of sight between two SUVs before bursting out again, a brown and white bullet, racing away from my office in the opposite direction of the coffee shop. I hadn't done much exploring in the neighborhood that hadn't involved a caffeine run, but I wasn't surprised when I saw the pocket park up ahead—I'd vaguely known it was there, and clearly, the dog had too. Which meant the animal must know the area. Which further meant it was real and not a hallucination—also indicated by the fact that Sandy had seen it.

Speaking of Sandy, my new neighbor had slowed down only long enough to fling her sunshine pillow back into her convertible, then she'd come clomping after me in her well-worn

Birkenstocks. The fact that no one should *ever* try to run in Birkenstocks didn't seem to be slowing her down.

"Hey, buddy! It's okay!" she called out encouragingly, which seemed to spur the dog to move even faster.

I leaned into my run and picked up the pace as well. As fast as it was moving, there was something definitely not quite right about the dog. It burst forward, then seemed to catch itself, turning back to me every few yards with a fresh wobble, its gait strangely lopsided. Then it would right itself and dash forward again, as if chased by the hounds of hell.

Sandy had been right about the blood on its fur, though. If that was real, what had happened to this poor guy? Forget his potentially demonic owner, what sort of monster would hurt a *dog*?

When we reached the park, the beagle dashed through the entrance, awkwardly catching a kid in the shins as he was exiting through the turnstiles.

"Hey!" The kid shouted, looking from the beagle to me. Behind him, another young teen stopped and turned, a basketball forgotten in his hands as he stared. "Is that your dog?"

"Please—" I shouted, waving frantically for good measure. "He slipped his leash again. Could you help me catch him?"

"Sure!" Kid number one took off, and the second boy dropped the basketball he was carrying, then dashed off after the beagle. "Hey, buddy!"

"He's hurt!" I heard the first boy gasp over his shoulder. "Kind of bad, I think!"

"Oh no!" I shouted back, not knowing what else to say and trying furiously to come up with a plausible-sounding dog name in case they asked. Apparently the dog was a he—I hadn't given the animal that close of an inspection, but I was willing to go with the kid's assessment. No more conversation was needed as the boys herded the dog against the chain link fence that surrounded the half-court basketball platform. The beagle didn't try to run away, just crouched against the fence. He started to shiver uncontrollably as they approached.

"It's okay, buddy, we've got you. You're good," the first boy said. He crouched down and crab-walked forward, giving me a clear look at the beagle's head as he swung his snout from kid to kid. His tail was up again and wagging furiously, and he shivered even harder as the first boy got closer, then finally swung his gaze to me.

Oh shit.

"Wait!" I began, but the first boy already had the dog in his arms, the second boy crowding in. Then the beagle started wriggling and writhing with fresh energy as it glared back at me, a long, terrifying yodel escaping from its jaws.

"I've got him too!" the second boy shouted, clamping his hands on the dog's flanks as it tried to get purchase on the first kid. I yanked off my cardigan, rushing up behind them.

"Wrap him up in this," I shouted, with enough command that the kids took my sweater and wrapped it around the flailing limbs without asking any questions. "Be careful—he may jump!"

Sure enough, the dog half scrabbled up his primary captor's chest, lunging over his shoulder as if to launch himself away. The boys shouted and clamped down, while I grabbed the beagle's head and shoved my face toward him, ignoring his bared teeth as he wriggled vigorously in the kids' arms, his howl turning into a long, protracted wail.

"Oh, no you fucking don't," I snarled, locking my gaze on the dog's eyes. Because I'd already seen what I needed to see about this poor creature. Of course, I had.

There was something inside it, slimy and foul, skulking around the skull of the unsuspecting animal who'd done nothing but be in the wrong place at the wrong time, a runaway who smelled like old dirt and fresh death, but who hadn't escaped his red leash before picking up a very unwelcome passenger.

A passenger I'd been able to name the moment the dog and I had locked eyes.

"Hello, *Gahmel*," I growled in a voice low enough that both boys froze—and so did the dog. "You picked the wrong day to fuck with a dog, you know that? Surely, you heard what I did to Alaria."

The dog's eyes jittered, a new, broken howl that sounded suspiciously like a plea starting low in his throat before cutting off abruptly. I leaned forward. "This dog has done nothing to you, Gahmel. Why do you trouble this small creature? You have no right to trespass here, you know that. And since when does a Sloth demon choose a beagle? That was poorly done."

"Who is she talking to?" I heard, or I thought I heard, as the sunny presence of Sandy Shaw drew in close behind me, her breath coming fitfully through her teeth. Distantly, some wandering synapses of my brain linked up and recognized that this was probably going to be a very short-lived friendship, but there was nothing I could do about that now. Right now, I could only focus on the second-level entity of filth and rot that had wedged itself inside this unsuspecting beagle's brain.

I picked up more too, in that searching glance, the scent of fear and frenzy coiling up with car exhaust and sunshine. The gash along the dog's side had come from a terrified attempt to escape the heavy red leash that had kept it locked to a fence not unlike this, vulnerable to capture by the man—and it had to be a man at least to start, some human whose mind could be bent to do a demon's bidding, then discarded when his need was over. A human...or a shedim, maybe? Human-like enough to pass?

The more I thought about that, the angrier I got. "You're not smart enough to be in there on your own, Gahmel," I snarled. "Who put you in here, and how fast can you get out?"

Inside the dog, Gahmel shivered, and the dog shivered with it, emitting more terrified half-yodel sounds as its jaws dripped muck. Whoever had kept him hadn't been feeding him well, and I latched on to the mind of the creature cowering behind the demon, the wide-open, boundless brain of a beagle that couldn't be vanquished even by the quivering glob of evil that had been thrust upon it.

"Hold him tighter," I commanded, and there was a shuffling around me, then a shift in pressure as the dog was transferred to Sandy. She gathered the creature against her body, its legs still wrapped in my destroyed sweater. Whether it was the sheer volume of fabric and warm body surrounding it or if Gahmel was beginning to understand what was coming, the dog's yodel turned into a low, ululating howl that seemed to be coming from its back paws.

"Who asked this of you?" I pushed Gahmel. "Because I know you didn't come up with this idea yourself. And if you've been paying attention at all, you know I'm the exorcist. You know what I did to Alaria. You want me to do the same thing to you?" At this, the dog's lips peeled back from his teeth, and his head craned away from me to utter a long, mournful denial. Distantly, I heard more youthful curses uttered in surprise, sensed the flash of light on glass. But after the protracted howl, the dog's face lulled forward again, his beleaguered yap sounding almost like a word. Almost.

"Try again," I demanded. "I didn't get that."

"Fuck," one of the boys muttered, and the beagle yowled again, then croaked out a noise that no dog should ever make. A noise that sounded remarkably like "Zagan."

"Excellent." I wasn't going to speak the demon's name out loud, not here, but it felt right to me, it felt true. Ignoring the fact that my hands were slippery with dog slobber, I took a firmer hold on the beagle's jaw and leaned in close, staring deep into its soft, terrified brown eyes. "Now you, Gahmel, will leave this blessed creature, formed of the Creator, and you will never return to trouble it or me or anyone near me. And if you breathe one word of this day, I will find you, Gahmel, and you will pay. So, go. Now."

The beagle howled again, his body shuddering violently, and I refocused barely in time for me to pull the dog away from Sandy, holding it under its front legs. I whirled in a wide arc toward the nearest stand of trees—away from her, away from the boys, away—

A burst of pitch-black shit detonated out of the back end of the dog in an explosion of stink and rot.

"*Fuck!*" the boys howled, louder than the beagle even, and I swept the dog over to the nearest patch of unviolated grass, easing him to the ground. I retrieved my shredded sweater and sluiced the worst of the muck off the creature's shaking hind quarters, my own hands trembling at its absolute surrender and relief. The dog absolutely reeked, but as I worked, he licked me unrestrainedly, which was not my favorite experience of the day, and yet I didn't have the heart to make him stop. Backing away from him, I murmured my best post-exorcism invocation for dogs, and he staggered upright.

He stumbled a bit, dazed and confused at what had just happened to him. I knew how he felt.

Looking up from my crouch, I realized why the kids had both stayed and had remained fairly quiet. They both had their phones in their hands, trained on me. "Guys," I groaned, more tired than I expected to be. "It's been a really bad day so far. Could you maybe wait before destroying me online?"

"No way!" the first burst out as the second chimed in, "Are you kidding? That was so cool!" They were laughing and shouting, and the dog bounced around, oblivious to his destruction of the park.

"And it smells so *bad*!" The boys burst into cackles, then ran off, zigzagging across the open bank of grass to collect their basketball. I looked up at Sandy Shaw, whose beautiful, bright caftan was now stained with more fluids than I could count.

"So, hey there," I groaned, as I used my forearm to brush my hair out of my eyes. "I'm Delia Thompson, and I'm an exorcist."

"And *this* is the best day ever," she countered with a grin. She reached out a hand and pulled me to my feet. "But I kind of figured out you color outside the lines. That's fine by me—the kind of work I do, a lot of my lines turn into squiggles. That said, I'm super glad you're on the side of angels, Delia Thompson."

I snorted at that but didn't respond. I wasn't so sure anymore.

We headed back to the office, and to my surprise, Sandy didn't try to force me into conversation. She glanced behind us a few times, though, and when she did speak, her voice was low and easy. "So, you know the dog is following us, right?"

"Yeah." I'd sensed its presence as well, and when I looked back, I wasn't surprised to see the beagle was only a few yards away. He stopped when I did, tail wagging experimentally as he tilted his head to the right. Funk surrounded him like a storm of regret.

"We can't just, like, leave him, right? Poor thing looks like he's been out on the street for a minute. But I can't take care of a dog, and he's probably going to need help."

I smiled wearily. "I don't suppose you do dog therapy?"

"I mean..." She tilted her head much like the beagle, her corkscrew hair floating in the breeze. "That'd be pretty awesome, wouldn't it?" she said with a bright smile that reminded me of Claire. "It could be a whole new modality!"

"That's...undoubtedly true." We continued to trudge on, and I kept my gaze down, trying to make sure my feet didn't slip out from under me. My white skin looked almost ghostly in the sunshine, the bruises standing out now in starker relief. I should probably do something about those, I thought distantly.

If Sandy noticed, though, she didn't comment. Her steps didn't falter until we turned the last corner back toward the office.

"Wow," she announced. "Our place got busy."

I looked up to see that there were more cars bunched up around the entrance to our Oak Park wellness center. Sergei stood at the top of the drive, a glowering traffic cop who was keeping away anyone he deemed not to be an actual customer, which, considering the cars lined up and down the street, was almost everyone. A gaggle of onlookers spilled out over the sidewalk in front of the building, and they seemed to multiply as we approached.

"This isn't good," Sandy said, her tone still light.

"I bet I can fix it." I turned back. "Hey, buddy," I cooed, holding my arms out. "You wanna do me a solid? It's not like I'm not already disgusting."

In response, the beagle trotted forward, his tail whipping around in a full circle, like he might take off and fly away helicopter-style. When I crouched down, he came willingly into my arms. Though my eyes watered at the stench, I gritted my teeth and hauled him up, then turned back to the office with grim determination.

"This is going to be good," Sandy murmured, as we marched forward, our pungent odor rolling out ahead of us. "Coming through!" she shouted. "Please, sick dog—make way!"

"Oh, my God!" somebody said, a sentiment that was shared all around as we parted the phone-toting crowd like the Red Sea. When they recognized me, however, the questions came fast and furious. "Are you Delia Thompson, the exorcist?" demanded the closest spectator, the question layered with a heavy amount of sarcasm.

The next question was more urgent. "What did you do to that *dog*? Or what did the dog do to you?"

"Do your neighbors know what you're doing in here?" came a third challenge. "Just how legitimate are you?"

"How did I not know we had a demon dog lady in Chicago?" someone else demanded.

"Clear a path, clear a path, everyone. Therapist at work!" Sandy announced abruptly, not breaking stride. "I can't tell you how grateful I am to Delia and her efforts in relieving the agony that was visited upon this abused dog. I'm Sandy Shaw, and I'll be beginning my own treatment of dog therapy tomorrow. You can read all about it on my Instagram, @ShawYourColorsTherapy! Check it out for other therapeutic tools!"

By the time she finished this recitation, we'd made it almost all the way through the crowd and were safely within Sergei's hula hoop of protection. If he noticed the stench of the dog as we hustled by him, his glowering face didn't betray it, and we were by him and almost to the back door of the office building just as Steve came out, keys in hand.

"Hey, Delia!" he began, then staggered back. "Whoa, little man! What went and died on you?"

The beagle turned in my arms and nearly wriggled itself into another dimension before leaping out toward Steve, who deftly caught him under his front legs and held him out from his body, the dog's little beagle legs churning.

"I don't suppose we have a bathroom or somewhere you could clean this guy up?" I asked. "He kind of ran into a demon problem."

"That's what demon ass smells like?" Steve demanded, his voice betraying equal parts awe and revulsion as the beagle continued his air dance. "Sir, that's some serious Son of Sam funk. You need to be de-fumigated. I got a blanket in the car that I can wrap you up in and then burn after we're done. Then we'll get you checked by a vet who specializes in demon douches, how about that?"

Still laughing, he swung away, dog in tow. I shook my head and looked down at myself, still far worse for wear despite the source of my funk being removed.

Sandy punched me in the arm. "Come on down to my new office, I've got a spare caftan or six you can choose from," she said brightly. "I'm sure I've got just the thing for the Demon Dog Lady."

CHAPTER
FIFTEEN

The next morning, I stood in the middle of Sandy's now fully decorated therapy studio and finally understood what it would be like to be mugged by a kaleidoscope. While the rest of the building deliberately and explicitly boasted office after office of soothing, understated neutrals, Oak Park's newest wellness practitioner had gone rogue.

In Sandy's defense, she hadn't used paint, but fabric—piles and piles of fabric, reds and purples and yellows and blues. They flowed from sturdy hooks that now marched along the top of the wall and framed the windows that remained open to the sunlight. The floor was covered in a mosaic of carpet squares, each large enough that you could have your own color-coded island, and the space's pre-existing comfortable chairs and couches were draped in thick, fluffy throw blankets in rich jewel tones. Add to that fully two dozen throw pillows that looked like they'd been designed by a very cheerful acid trip—and enough crystals to stock a New Age shop—and the place made you feel like you'd died and gone to heaven in a Crayola crayon box.

It should have been overwhelming, a hyper-stimulation nightmare of chaos and color. Instead, it felt oddly…safe.

"You like it?" Sandy emerged from behind a screen draped with yet more fabrics, her hair in a messy topknot and her smile wide. Today she wore a flowing pantsuit, its creamy mix of neutrals markedly less chaotic than her colorful surroundings. She beamed at me as I struggled to find the words. "You like it. I can tell. How's Angel?"

I blinked, now completely disoriented. "Who?"

"The dog! I ran into Steve last night when I finished setting this place up, and he was taking him around the building with that gorgeous pile of a security guy." She tilted her head. "Do I pay for him, partly? Does he come with the building? Because that's an amenity they need to put in the brochure."

"I…" I shook my head, following her as she floated across her new domain. "Steve named the dog Angel?"

A knock at the door had us turning, and I smiled to see Claire step inside with wide, disbelieving eyes, Grace right behind her. After I'd told Claire about my introduction to Sandy Shaw, she'd immediately booked Grace an appointment. That was why I'd decided to visit Sandy at this particular time, but I hadn't at all been sure the young woman would show.

Now Grace looked around with obvious surprise and more than a little edge. "You're kidding me, right?" she asked, and I mentally noted that we weren't dealing with what I'd started to refer to as Ordinary Grace, but this wasn't Frozen Grace either —and though Steve insisted that Mystical Grace showed up most often for him, I hadn't seen her at all.

"Grace, welcome." Sandy turned to her and smiled. "I'm Sandy Shaw. I'm so glad to see you."

"Oh, I bet." Claire and I exchanged a glance as Grace's shoulders straightened, her chin lifted. "I think I'll try my luck with the yogi wannabe down the hall after all. This place sucks."

"That would be the new instructor, Hannah, I think she said her name was," Claire said evenly. I noticed Grace remained glued to her side as she moved deeper into the room. The angry act didn't give her agency, just edge. "She cornered Grace after I buzzed her in. I found them in the studio. I mean, hooray for more yoga options, I guess, but she did kind of seem fixated on Grace."

"Right," Grace scoffed, folding her arms. "She was fixated on getting a new member for her yoga class. But at least she wasn't colorblind."

"Is the room overwhelming? We can move," Sandy said, settling into professional mode with impressive ease. Despite her studio looking like a unicorn had decorated it, her demeanor was completely grounded. "But if you'd like to stay, where would you like to sit? You get to choose."

Grace surveyed the room with a critical eye before selecting a chair positioned nearest to the door. Smart. Sandy watched her, clearly taking mental notes, but her smile gentled further as she moved to a chair opposite Grace's. "Delia, would you like to stay with us? Claire?"

"I really need to get back upstairs, if that's okay, Grace? Delia can stay for as long as you'd like this first time, like you asked."

"Whatever." Grace shrugged, her hands twitching at the purple throw that had found its way to her lap. Her posture shifted, shoulders rounding as her voice rose to an almost child-like pitch—Frozen Grace taking a bow. "You'll come down here to take me home?" she asked. "I don't have to take an Uber back? I hate Ubers."

"I'll absolutely take you home," Claire assured her without hesitation. "That's no problem at all." I wasn't sure what I was paying Claire, now that I thought about it, but clearly, she deserved a raise.

I waited for Grace's glance to sweep over me as Claire stepped out of the room. When it did, I peered at her, waiting for the connection with whatever was curled inside of her—if anything was curled inside of her.

But there was nothing. No cold wash of certainty, no snap recognition of something hiding in the dark.

Whatever was going on with Grace, there wasn't a demon riding shotgun today. Which meant this was purely human psychology territory—exactly what Sandy was trained for.

"So," Sandy began, her voice warm but professional as I took a chair several feet away from both of them. "Claire mentioned you've been having some difficult experiences lately, Grace. Something you might want to share with someone new. Would you like to tell me about those in your own words?"

Grace's laugh was sharp, dismissive. Back to Angry Grace. "Difficult experiences. Right. As if anyone would believe me if I told them what's really going on."

The sound of footsteps in the hallway made me tense, but I relaxed when Lucian appeared in the doorway, somehow managing to make a basic white button-down and black trousers look perfectly natural. To my surprise, though, Sandy bristled—a reaction that drew Grace's attention immediately.

"Excuse me," she said, her voice polite but firm. "We're in session here."

"My apologies," Lucian said, but his gaze locked on me with an intensity that made my pulse spike. "But Delia? A moment, if you will."

I made a face, glancing back at my client. Grace looked bored. Sandy...a little too interested. I realized she hadn't met Lucian yet, but now wasn't the time for introductions. "Sandy, would you mind if—"

"Of course," she said, then slanted a glance toward Grace. "We can wait?"

"Not necessary on my account," Grace informed her coolly. "We keep going. I don't want to waste my time."

"Excellent," Sandy said, and internally, I breathed a sigh of relief. I'd take a demon any day over this chick, I decided. Lucian had just given me a greater gift than he realized.

I stepped into the hallway with Lucian, clocking his agitation with some concern. Whatever had brought him here, he was radiating tension like heat off summer asphalt—and his jaw looked tight enough to crack walnuts.

"What happened? Are you okay?"

That made him blink, and he lifted one impossibly elegant brow. "You do remember I'm the demon in this equation?"

I rolled my eyes, but he continued before I could respond to that. "There's chatter among the horde that you need to be aware of. Someone's been asking questions about you. And about your newest client."

That stopped me. "Grace? Why?"

"It's become a focal point for the betting community of shedim. No one seems to know who's damaged her, and that— invites curiosity. Curiosity is never good for the horde."

"They don't know?" I frowned. "What if that just means she's not possessed?" Even as I said the words, I discounted them. Something was wrong with Grace beyond her instability. I just couldn't figure out what.

Before I could process that fully, the distant sound of the door buzzing around the corner of the building corresponded with a ping to my phone. I pulled out my phone—and froze.

"Holy shit." I turned the phone to Lucian. "Claire says...the police are here?"

"Stall them," he said tightly, and with a sudden shift in air pressure, he was gone. Just—gone. Not running, not leaping, simply disappeared. I took off at a run myself, skidding around the corner as the first cop cleared the far entrance. To absolutely no one's surprise, I recognized her. Officer Hernandez.

I didn't think this was the time for me to trot out her first name.

"Officer Hernandez!" I began brightly, jogging up to her. "Claire texted you were here—my goodness, what's all this?"

"This is a warrant, Delia." Officer Hernandez held out her hand to one of her compatriots, a stocky man in his late thirties who obligingly handed over a piece of paper. "You can have your lawyer explain it to you."

"I don't have a lawyer." I opened the paper, but the words ran together on the page, my mind churning for excuses to slow them down. "I'm not trying to stop you from doing whatever you need to do, but can you explain to me what's going on? A warrant for what?"

Realization struck, and I jerked my gaze back up with a jolt. "Are you arresting me?"

"Not yet," she said tersely. "We walk and talk."

Not waiting for my agreement, she kept moving up the stairs, three other uniformed cops behind her. For once, I was glad the building was virtually abandoned at this hour of the day.

"But what is it—"

"Rabbi Mordechai Schneider's notebooks and journals, and any other printed material previously in his possession that we deem of interest," Hernandez said, not remotely winded despite moving up the stairs at a trot. "The whole lot."

"But those are mine!" I protested, genuinely confused. "I didn't steal them. He sent those to me!"

By now, we were up on the second floor, but I couldn't slow down Hernandez any more than I could fly. I matched her stride and entered the office first—

To see Claire sitting at her office, perfectly composed. Too composed. Steve was nowhere to be seen.

"Delia!" Claire chirped as Hernandez and her goons piled into the room. "What's going on?"

"Are these all of them?" Hernandez pointed to the shelf behind Claire, heavy with books.

I looked at the men and their boxes and smiled at her tightly. "Not exactly," I said. I marched across to my internal office, praying that Lucian wasn't still in there stuffing books into a pillowcase, and opened the door.

My heart sank. No Lucian, but no evidence he'd been there, either. My desk was neater, admittedly, but I'd put everything back, and the shelves looked as heavy as ever. I turned back to Hernandez. "You're going to need a few more boxes," I told her grimly, then waved the paper at her as one of the men pushed past me, the others currently behind Claire's desk.

Hernandez unbent. "We received an anonymous tip that provided evidence suggesting you may have materials relevant to Mr. Schneider's death. They were kind enough to send an example of said evidence, a journal."

She pulled out her phone and swiped at it, then turned it to me. On the screen was a picture of a thick, bound book with a battered cover. A six-pointed star surrounded by dots was stamped on the cover of the book, and I peered at the looping script in the center of the star. I couldn't make it out, but I'd seen enough of these books before that I was genuinely curious.

"They sent you that? I mean—it's Mordechai's, right? It looks like his."

"I don't know. I think so, but the handwriting—we'll need to see more of his handwriting to be sure. You've got other journals? That's primarily what we need."

"I mean, yes..." I panicked for a moment, thinking maybe Lucian had somehow spirited them away—and sincerely wishing he had—but no, there they were, lined up on the shelves. "Right there. Those *are* my property, Officer Hernandez. I want them back unharmed." Property. More like my world.

She gestured to her men. "Every item will be cataloged and returned to you once we review it."

"But...what is it you're looking for? I just don't—I mean, what was in the book you got?"

Her smile turned grim. "The journal we received detailed his exorcism methods. Methods that, according to our source, may provide motive for his murder."

The word 'murder' hung in the air like a toxic cloud, and I watched, numbly, as they boxed up book after book. They knew exactly what they were looking for—not the general occult library the old man had accumulated over the years, but specifically Mordechai's handwritten journals and files.

"Do you have a current address you could give us, Delia?" Hernandez asked as her officers began boxing my entire professional foundation.

"I'm staying at the Palidor Hotel," I said, my voice hollow. This wasn't exactly true, since I'd checked out earlier this morning—for good this time—but fuck them. They didn't need to know about the Victorian on Ash Street.

"The journal we received was quite detailed," Hernandez continued conversationally as her officers gutted my workspace. "Descriptions of experimental procedures. A young girl subjected to dangerous supernatural exposure. Very compelling reading."

"Seriously?" I peered at her. "That seems...super specific. I haven't found anything like that in his other books. You could just look at them here, you know."

"I think we'll make headway faster on our own."

"The timing is interesting, don't you think?"

"Isn't it?" Hernandez nodded as her men started carrying the boxes through my door. "We've got more boxes in the car."

They left with a dozen crates of materials and my sense of security in tatters. I stood in my gutted office, waiting for Lucian to return, when Sandy appeared in the doorway, her bright eyes staring around wildly, all her good cheer gone.

"Delia," she demanded. "Have you seen her? Did she come up here?"

The words didn't compute at first. "Seen her?"

"Yes. We were having an absolutely productive conversation—I have my own thoughts on her diagnosis, but it's early yet, more work to be done. But she stopped being angry and turned almost, well, ethereal, very light, very New Agey. Then she sort of froze up—like a little girl—and demanded to go to the bathroom. I told her where it was and offered to take her because she didn't seem to understand what I was saying. The minute I did that, we were back to her being angry."

"Really. So, you think it's DID?" I waved her off before she could tell me that she couldn't discuss anything specific about the diagnosis. "Sorry—forget that. But Grace didn't come back after she went to the bathroom? She just walked out?"

"I don't know *where* she went, or why." She flapped a hand in dismay. "I've seen trauma responses that don't fit standard categories, and this may be that—or something else. It really fits more with OSDD-1b, which has far too many initials to explain, but it's really too early to tell—and, of course, is a confidential conversation for Grace and me. But when she didn't come back, I was surprised. She talked some more about that new yoga instructor, so that's where I went to check on her, only..." Sandy's professional composure cracked a bit. "The yoga studio is empty. The woman's things are gone. It's like she was never—hey!"

I was out the door before Sandy even finished speaking, hitting the stairs at top speed.

I reached the first floor to see Lucian heading into the studio ahead of me. By the time I entered, he was striding across an empty space that still smelled faintly of incense and duplicity, his fingers fanned wide as if he was picking up the room's vibes.

"This was planned," he announced as he turned back to me, his voice carrying undertones that made the hair on my arms stand up. "The warrant, the yoga instructor, Grace's vulnerability—all of it carefully coordinated to hit at the same time."

"Why?" I demanded, unnerved by the expression on his face. It was anger, but not only anger. Something deeper and messier. Something that looked almost like guilt.

"Planning this for how long?" I tried again. "Grace only became my client a few days ago. No one could have guessed that would happen, and according to Steve's and our best guesses, she's been screwed up since she was *twelve*. I haven't even known Steve for that long. This doesn't make any sense!"

"Nevertheless." Lucian fanned his fingers through the air again as Sandy breached the doorway, waves of her concern flowing across the room. "Whoever is behind this has had ample time to watch, to wait, to catalog all the unfortunate innocents in the city and their weaknesses, keeping their fractures fresh, their wounds on the brink of re-opening. It may have been just a matter of waiting for the opportunity to present itself. Then, they push the pieces into place and set the game in motion."

"A game..." I echoed, staring at him. As much as I hated to admit it, his explanation made sense. I looked over to see that Claire and Steve had joined Sandy by the door. "Did Grace ever talk about hurting people before a few weeks ago, Steve?"

He screwed up his face, dark eyes staring into the distance. "Not that I can think of. Kind of the opposite, actually. She was always going on about her manifestation practice, all the good she could do in the world, how powerful it made her feel. Nothing like making her roommate eat slimy leftovers."

"A few weeks ago." I winced, so numb deep in my gut I didn't think I'd ever warm up again. "After I...did what I did. After Mordechai died."

"Who?" I heard Sandy ask, but no one answered her.

I stared at Lucian. "This is my fault," I said, the words hanging in the charged air between us. "Grace was targeted because of me—because she was a friend of Steve's. I did this."

Lucian's smile curled into something hard, dark, and feral. His words, when they came, curved around me like talons. "And now we shall both undo it," he said.

SIXTEEN

The exorcised beagle was sitting next to a ranting Steve outside our building when Sergei drove me up the short drive the next morning, like some kind of supernatural doorman. Steve gesticulated wildly as he argued with someone on his phone, but the dog—now named Angel, if Sandy Shaw was to be believed—didn't seem to mind. Two days since I'd expelled whatever had been playing tagalong inside his brain, and Angel had apparently decided we were a pack now.

He looked better too—the matted blood gone, his coat cleaner, eyes bright and alert instead of that hollow, haunted look possessed creatures got after they'd harbored a demon too long. Definitely an improvement.

But there was still something off about the dog, I thought. The way he turned to look at Sergei's SUV with a knowing look in his brown eyes, the way his ears pricked as he glanced down the long building, as if seeing something that wasn't there. Was he still suffering the effects of a demonic afterglow? I really didn't want a repeat of the Sloth demon stinkfest from the park if I could avoid it.

"Yo, Delia," Steve turned to me as I got out of the SUV, stuffing his phone in his pocket. "Angel here wanted to show off his new de-stinkified self, and he's a good hang, I gotta say. I also got an expense report to file that is probably going to get us audited, just wanted to warn you."

I snorted. "There's going to be a lot of those, I think." I glanced back at Steve. "Anything new on Grace?"

"A few things, yeah," he said, keying the passcode to the backdoor and ushering me inside, Angel at our heels. "It's sort of a tough situation though. I mean, she's a grown-ass woman, so there's not a lot we can do. And I don't want to call the police if she's just pissed off, you know?"

We'd spent most of yesterday reeling from the coordinated attack—my office gutted, Grace vanished, and Lucian's suspicion that there was a demon out there with a seriously high delayed gratification threshold. But the day hadn't been a total loss. Lucian had managed to spirit away half of Mordechai's journals before Hernandez had hit the office, and he'd given those to me for safekeeping at the house on Ash Street in case the cops came back to ransack us a second time. He'd made some vague comment about doing his own research and sent me home with Sergei as a watchdog. I hadn't seen him since.

I'd convinced the burly Romanian to protect me from inside the mansion instead of his SUV, which at least ensured I wouldn't be attacked by anything human. Sergei hadn't been fazed by the creepy old house, but I'd spent the night reading Mordechai's journals until my eyes crossed, opting for a blanket on the couch in the front room rather than deal with a house I didn't know in the dark, while Sergei bunked down on a couch across the room. I got maybe three hours of sleep, and those had been filled with shadows, dark hallways, and someone calling my name from far away.

Super restful.

"Any word from her parents?" I asked Steve as we headed upstairs to survey the wreckage of my professional life.

"Actually, yeah." Steve headed over to his desk, his workstation remarkably unscathed since Hernandez's warrant only covered Mordechai's records. The man barely knew how to operate a computer, let alone use one for filing his cases, so the computers had been strictly off limits. "I called them this morning. Interesting conversation."

"'Good' interesting, or 'we're all going to jail' interesting?"

"Depends on your perspective." His fingers flew across the keyboard. "They were surprisingly calm about Grace going missing. Turns out this isn't the first time—though she always has come back, obviously."

"Seriously?" I frowned. "Shouldn't we have known that earlier?"

"Known what?" Sandy asked from the doorway, juggling a takeout tray of questionable-looking green smoothies that clashed violently with her orange and yellow caftan. Claire was right behind her, carrying a similar tray but with what I prayed was coffee.

"Grace has a history of going poof," I offered as Steve accepted a cup from Sandy, then set it on his desk like it might bite him.

"Hmm," Sandy said, depositing a second cup on the coffee table near me. I took a careful step back. "I definitely should have known about that," she said.

"Here's the thing," Steve continued. "Her folks never reported them as missing person incidents because she always came back within twenty-four to forty-eight hours. Always safe, always claiming she had no memory of where she'd been, but, you know, she was a teenager. They just figured she was acting out."

The pieces clicked together in my head like a prison deadbolt. "Dissociative episodes?" I asked Sandy. "When one of her alters takes over, the others don't retain memories of what happened?"

"If that's her diagnosis, then it's possible," Sandy said carefully. "But I don't want to make too many assumptions here. It's very early days. I still haven't talked with her primary therapist."

"Yeah, though, you know—mental condition or demon possession, kind of a toss-up on what's worse, yeah? And here's the kicker," Steve said. "After the third incident, her folks had a microchip implanted. One of those GPS tracking devices designed for people with dementia or memory loss who might wander off."

I stared at him. "Grace has a microchip?"

"Grace has a microchip," he confirmed, grinning, picking up the cup beside him and toasting us with it while I diligently stuffed down my renewed thoughts of chipping Lucian. "And her parents just gave me the access codes."

He took a deep swig of the drink—then choked, gasping as he stared down at the cup. "What is this, grass?"

"Wheatgrass!" Sandy announced. "It's good for you."

As he invited the dog to come over and try some wheatgrass, I felt a spark of hope. "Can you track her?"

"Already am." Despite Sandy's protestations, Steve poured the smoothie into a travel bowl for Angel, then swung back to his computer. After a few keystrokes, the screen lit up with what looked like a street map covered in colored dots.

"Anndddd...bingo. Looks like she's been moving through the city in a very specific pattern. Not random wandering. Girl is on a mission."

Claire moved to his side. "What's the timeline?" she asked.

Steve clicked through a series of screens showing Grace's movements over the past twenty-four hours. "She left here around 11 a.m. yesterday, during all the police chaos. Moved northeast toward Lincoln Park, then south toward the Loop, then back north again. Almost like…"

"Like someone was giving her a tour of the city," I finished. "Or taking her to specific locations."

Angel finished slurping up the smoothie, then bounced off to explore the office some more, sniffing at the shelves where the police had removed my confiscated books. His behavior was getting more agitated by the minute, and I was starting to wonder if the smoothie was maybe not Steve's best idea.

"What I don't love is how fast she's moving," Steve said. "Look at this. She stops for a few hours, then moves a far distance. Stop…move. Stop. I didn't ask for the results of her previous walkabouts, but I'm thinking this isn't her pattern. She didn't have a car, you know? You really think she's Ubering all these places?"

"Not a chance," Claire said. She looked fresh and perfectly pressed in her lemon-yellow sweater and fawn-colored slacks. I looked down at my own tank top and jeans, and grimaced. I'd only gotten three hours of sleep. This was the best I could do. "She prefers to drive with people she knows. She told me that like half a dozen times."

My phone buzzed with a text from an unknown number. The message was short and obnoxious: *Check the pod. You have two hours.*

"Oh, for fuck's sake," I muttered, but I knew what was coming. I'd been bracing for it ever since we'd scattered the onlookers with Angel's funk the day before. "Steve, I think we've got another post to deal with from Dark Streets. Can you call up their channel?"

"Yeah, I've already been up to my neck in those assholes today." Steve grimaced, switching his monitor to a new browser. He angled the screen toward us. "When you got here, I was getting the download from Rook and the rest of my gamer buds. That Willows chick has been working this story hard. Like, way too hard for someone who just likes posting spooky shit for horror nerds, you know? I don't know what her deal is."

I didn't say anything as he queued up the Dark Streets podcast and hit play, but the opening image of the video made my teeth clench. Sue Willows stood in front of what looked like an abandoned warehouse, her perfectly styled flame-red hair whipping in the wind as she spoke directly into the camera.

"...anonymous tip led us to this location in North Lawndale, where sources suggest a young woman with known mental health issues has been taken against her will," she said. "Chicago PD is reportedly preparing a raid on the building behind me, but questions remain about why this particular case has attracted so much official attention—and what led to this poor woman being abducted."

"What the fuck?" Steve protested as Claire leaned forward.

"I call bullshit," she snapped. "Check her location, like, right now. There's no way someone would have tipped off a rinky-dink podcaster. They would have called actual media outlets. Or, you know, the police."

"Location, Steve?" I asked as Sandy clenched her hands in front of her.

Steve's gaze zipped over his second screen. "Grace's signal puts her about three blocks from that warehouse—so not there, but too damned close for comfort. And even worse..."

He broke off as he leaned forward, and Sandy turned on him. "Worse?" she demanded. "How can it be worse?"

"Well, it looks like the feed just updated after glitching for God knows how long. According to this data, she's been stationary for three whole hours—that's a new record. Either she's taking a nap in a fucked-up warehouse in North Lawndale, or—someone's got her."

"And they want us to find her by ratcheting up the panic," I said darkly. "It's not enough to bring us, they want to bring us in at a frantic scramble."

"So, you bring in another antagonist," Sandy said, nodding. "A big-mouthed podcaster, with a shadow threat of the police. Nicely done."

"Too nicely," I finished, thinking about Lucian's suspicion that someone was carefully orchestrating this whole set piece. I had to admit, I was beginning to think he was right. "It has to be a trap."

"I gotta think you're right," Steve agreed, swiveling back to the pod. Back on the first screen, the broadcast looped and started up again, and Steve muttered a low curse. "Guys? Grace's signal just glitched again. Either she's down in some bunker or—shit, I don't know. But something's goofy with it. I kind of don't want to ask the parents if that's happened before, either."

Claire held up her phone. "Sergei's got us covered, though he's definitely not happy about our trajectory. Where's North Lawndale? I completely don't know it."

"You wouldn't," Steve and I both said at once, and our gazes met in a moment of shared connection. This was a guy who'd seen me at my worst—and I'd returned the favor. But the exorcism that'd taken me into North Lawndale had been one of Mordechai's messiest, and it'd happened right after Steve had moved into the duplex with me, about six months after my mom had died. I'd been more than messy myself back then—and I hadn't even known I was carting around a demon at the time.

I thought about that as we exited the office and piled into Sergei's SUV—including Angel—only half-listening as Claire brought Sergei up to speed, answering his gruff questions as she urged him to move faster. How much of Mordechai's exorcisms had I all but sleepwalked through, faking normal as best as I could while my brain tried to cope with some grimdark entity wrapped around my guts? And, once again, why hadn't Mordechai done something about it all those years? He'd waited until I was twenty-five and getting snotty about taking on more responsibility? That had triggered him into trying to help me?

But why?

Another thought ripped through me, unwanted and unbidden. Did Hernandez's mystery journal contain the information I'd been looking for to answer that exact question? And was the answer bad enough that she thought I had something to do with Mordechai's death?

What had Mordechai written in that journal that he'd then, what...lost? Hidden? Thought he'd destroyed? And why was it suddenly surfacing now, fifteen years later, just in time to make me look guilty as hell? Had someone been sitting on it all this time, waiting for the perfect moment to twist the knife?

And did Lucian know more about who that someone might be than he was letting on?

My stomach started to cramp from all the acid I was generating.

Twenty minutes later, we found ourselves in an industrial neighborhood I didn't recognize, but Sergei clearly did. Angel started yodeling under his breath, and Sergei responded with a burst of rough-sounding Romanian, so harsh I flinched.

Angel just helicoptered his tail.

"This seems to be it," Steve said, peering down at his laptop. "And the signal's strong here too, which I don't love."

"It's not safe," Sergei said. "For anyone, but especially not you."

I stared out the window, knowing he was right. The warehouse in front of us squatted in the industrial wasteland like a predator waiting to pounce—three stories of crumbling brick and shattered glass, surrounded by a chain-link fence that had been cut in so many places it was little more than a tetanus shot waiting to happen. Weeds pushed through cracks in the concrete, and a loading dock at the far end of the building looked like it'd been reinforced against the zombie apocalypse.

My phone buzzed again. Another text from the unknown number: *CPD heading your way. Should make for some good video.*

"Asshole," I breathed, turning my phone to Claire. "It's maybe a trap, maybe a police raid, and definitely something we're going to regret."

"You shouldn't go in there," Sergei said again. "It's a trap."

Angel turned and fixed me with his soulful brown eyes, and I grimaced. "I know it's a trap," I said. "That's the whole point of this. But if we don't go in there and try to get Grace out— she'll cease being useful to them. That's no good either."

In the silence, Angel yodeled a low, panicked wail.

"Preach, brother," I told him. Then I got out of the car, Sergei right behind me.

CHAPTER

SEVENTEEN

"Hey, wait a minute," Claire began urgently. "We're coming too."

She pushed out of the SUV and dropped to the concrete, Sandy right behind her. The dog also leaped out and danced a few feet forward.

"I'm her therapist," Sandy reminded everyone in earshot, though she focused on the bulky Romanian bodyguard who merely scowled at her, unimpressed. "If she's in the middle of some traumatic event, I can help her."

"You can help her, yes. But not if she's dead," Sergei said, his tone flat and unhurried. "You will stay in the SUV, and you will keep the doors locked. Anything disturbs you, anyone tries to open the doors, additional security will arrive. You will need to get down below the windows. You will also need to protect the dog."

He stared at Angel, who now stood at attention, his tail whipping enthusiastically in a helicopter whirl. "You will also stay here," he informed the beagle. "I cannot worry about a dog."

Despite myself, I stifled a smile. I suddenly had no doubt that Sergei would absolutely worry about the dog, probably more than his human charges. Strangely, I didn't mind that.

To her credit, Claire read Sergei's expression and mine and didn't try to push the issue. She got back in the SUV, calling Angel in with the promise of treats. She clearly already had the beagle's number, because he abandoned his effort at protecting us without a backward glance.

Sandy hesitated a moment longer, her gaze swiveling from Sergei to the abandoned warehouse. But no matter how much of a badass she was in the mental health realm, she wasn't hiding a ninja warrior beneath that caftan, and she knew it.

"I'll just get in the way," she finally decided, bitterness lacing her words. With a sigh of regret, she got back in the SUV, leaning out the door at the last second. She pointed an orange-polished nail at Sergei. "But if there's a clear path, and I can help Grace, even just to keep her calm, I'm literally right *here*. And I can help."

"You will help by staying put," Sergei said, glowering at her until she closed the door. Once the locks were audibly engaged, Steve and I turned, following Sergei's lead as he strode toward the loading dock at the end of the building.

Sergei grunted, gesturing forward. "This will be the closest access to open space," he said, though I hadn't asked. I hadn't needed to. With every step we took, my sense of awareness increased, my nerves prickling with anticipation and dread. Something was waiting for us inside the warehouse, I was pretty sure. Something besides Grace.

The large garage-style doors were padlocked shut, and the human-sized door beside them was reinforced with heavy locks and covered with spray-painted slurs and graffiti. But when Sergei tried it, the door opened easily, courtesy of the hole that had been shot through the handle.

"Whoa," Steve managed, eyeing the door as it drifted shut again.

"They are not trying to keep us out, and they are not trying to hide," Sergei said. "They want us here."

"So, it's an ambush?" Steve pressed, but before Sergei could speak, I shook my head.

"Not exactly," I said. "They're making a point. Grace is only part of that point."

"I agree." Sergei turned to me. "So, you should understand. Their goal is not to kill Grace. Not to harm her either, I suspect. She's not the purpose of this demonstration."

He pointed at me. "You are. For Grace, that is good news and bad news. Good news in that she will not be their immediate target, bad news in that they will make her a target in an instant if it suits their needs. Just be aware."

I winced, looking at him. His assignment from Volkov probably didn't extend to taking care of my client list, which meant Grace really would be left hanging if something bad went down.

Steve had figured that out as well.

"She's a friend," he said quietly, peering down the corridor. Sergei sighed but said nothing further as we pushed into the warehouse.

The moment we stepped inside, I could feel a brush of awareness, the faintest touch. Not only from deeper inside the building, but distantly. *Lucian*, I decided, more grateful than I wanted to admit. Was he reaching out to me? Or was this sensation just another artifact of our fading connection?

A low, haunting tune started up from deep inside the warehouse, scattering my thoughts. A chillingly familiar song.

"What the heck is that?" Steve muttered, going stock still for a second before moving again.

The tune had no backing music, and someone was actually

singing it, I thought, with four distinct notes repeated over and over again, up and down the scale. This wasn't a recording. Each note was held for a different length, and the pattern was inconsistent, loud enough to set my teeth on edge.

It was the same melody that I heard the hallucination I now referred to as Thomas Keegan humming when I first saw him walking the dog. The same song I'd been hearing in my dreams or catching myself humming whenever I thought of the guy.

Something about the memory of Keegan walking his dog poked at me, but the song drowned out all other thoughts. His signature tune wasn't an actual song from the radio, I thought. I'd recognize it if it was, wouldn't I? And if it had been something that Keegan had hummed all the way back a decade ago, during Mordechai's exorcism of Keegan's demon, I definitely should remember it. But it wasn't striking me that way. It simply wasn't *that* alarming.

But should it be? The way it was being projected through the warehouse felt deliberate, goading, as if to say "Remember me? This was part of your nightmares," in the time-honored way of TV villains. Only, I'd been up to my neck in a real villain during that time, so maybe it hadn't fazed me that much? I didn't know. There was too much I didn't know.

"Is he gonna keep that up?" muttered Steve as we made our way along the empty corridor. The space was remarkably undisturbed by trash or feces, no doubt due to the lack of windows on the first floor and the heavy padlocks that had held until this morning. "What's the point of it?"

"No idea," was the best response I could offer as we took a hard right turn and I peered down another long corridor with more unfamiliar doors. I tried to cast myself back to the girl I had been at fifteen, seeing if it would jog loose a memory. Most self-respecting teenagers wouldn't have caught themselves dead wandering around with a shawl-covered rabbi who smelled of tomato soup, I knew that much. They'd have been hanging out with their friends, yelling at their parents, living on their phones. But I hadn't had any friends, my mother was someone I was better off avoiding, and my phone was only good when Mordechai called me for a job.

How quickly had that become my life after I'd met him that first day, walking some old lady's dogs? It probably didn't speak too well of my mother that she had gratefully and eagerly allowed Mordechai to become my surrogate babysitter. But she hadn't asked too many questions once she'd figured out that he was a "sort of priest, right?" and after they'd spoken a few times on our front porch. She'd been happy to relinquish any pretense of giving a shit. And I'd been happy to let her.

Idly, I wondered if Sandy might have a therapy opening for me sometime soon, after all this was over.

My ruminations were cut off when Sergei lifted a hand. We stopped.

Keegan's song got louder as the bodyguard gestured toward the doorway at the end of the corridor. Unlike the others, it stood open and gave the impression of space and concrete beyond. A steady wash of bright light shone through the door, not the flickering swaying light of a loose bulb, but industrial-strength fluorescent panels.

I smelled fear, but also curiosity, skateboards, and jumping fences, and I slanted a glance at Steve beside me. He met my gaze as if he had been expecting it, gave me a half smile.

"It just occurred to me, I guess we're going to find out if that Hallow stuff was some bullshit," he murmured quietly, and I jolted.

I'd forgotten all about Steve's secondary protected status among the horde. When I'd found him in Descent last month, right after Mordechai had died, he'd been trapped in a party room with demons, but hadn't been possessed. I'd managed to get him out of danger before they could get a foothold on his soul. Apparently, that near miss made him special, or at least more special than he already was.

"That's right." I smiled back at him. "You could have your own podcast."

A sharp command in Romanian shut us both up, and we followed Sergei forward into the room.

We saw Grace immediately.

Grace was not doing well.

Looking smaller and more frail than I remembered her, Grace was seated upright in the center of the room, her waist zip-tied to the chair. Her arms were free, flailing around, while her legs were tied at the ankles to the chair's legs. A neck collar kept her head upright and her body from pitching forward too violently, also attached to the back of the chair with yet more looping zip ties. But it was clear at a glance why such restraints had been deemed necessary, because Grace was putting on a show.

First, she froze, shoulders up, fists at her side, eyes wide, mouth trembling. Tears and snot ran down her face, and she shivered uncontrollably.

"Please!" she wailed when she caught sight of us. "Please! I'll be quiet. I'll leave you alone. I'll do anything you say!"

My heart squeezed tight at the high-pitched childlike voice, then stuttered a bit as angry Grace took hold.

"You fucking bastards," she snarled, jerking her gaze around as if she could pierce the shadows. "Do you even know who I am? Do you know what I can do? You think the moment I get a handle on the cocksucker you unleashed inside me, who's made me stronger, tougher, you think I won't come after you?"

Another shift, and Manager Grace was back in play. She stared around the room, blinking owlishly. "What is this place? Why have you brought me here? I don't have any money and I don't know anybody, I promise. I'm seriously not that interesting. Just talk to me, and I'm sure we...*Steve!*"

When she caught sight of Steve, she craned her body around to follow her face, but she couldn't do much given that her chair was bolted to the floor. Steve started forward, only to be restrained by Sergei's heavy hand. Instead, I moved forward, feeling the bodyguard's gaze heavy on my back, his anger practically a living thing, smelling of broken bones and bullets and blood, so much blood.

I was really glad Sergei was on our side.

"Grace," I said loudly. "How badly are you hurt?"

Back we went to Frozen Grace. Her whole body seized, drawing in, appearing almost a third smaller though she didn't shift size at all. "I'm so scared!" she bleated, or tried to bleat, her little-girl breathiness rendering her nearly mute. "Please help me. I'm sorry, I'm sorry, I'm so sorry!"

Unbidden, I thought about the photos in Grace's morning room. The happy family pictures marching along until they weren't so happy anymore, until they were staged. I didn't know what had happened to Grace, but it hadn't been a demon possession. Not at first. Something had happened that had nothing to do with demons and everything to do with the people who were supposed to take care of her, people who'd betrayed her, who'd let her down.

Not all demons lived in the dark.

"Hush now, all of you. We just need to believe, don't we?"

The voice changed so abruptly that I stopped, startled, hyperaware of wrongness as Grace shook her head back, as if she could fling the smudges off her face, reset her hair with the casual toss of her head. I hadn't heard this voice before, this tonality. "The mind is probably the greatest tool we have second to the heart," she cooed. "The heart leads, and the mind puts its intentions to work, recognizing the synchronicities that are brought into your field."

A second chill chased the first down my spine.

"Grace?" Steve's strangled call made her smile go broader, and she twisted again to see him, but again couldn't quite turn her head that far.

"Steve, I'm so glad you're here. You really did the right thing, bringing me to your friend. You didn't know, and I didn't know how to tell you, but I leveled up a few months ago. I got strong—really strong. And shouldn't I be strong? I think I should. I'm the only one who's fucking going to therapy. The side of me that's just a pitiful little girl won't say a word. I try my best to not let my pissed-off side get out and then my goodness, there's the one who's pulling all the strings, the one who's always in control, but she kind of wanted me to be in control too, you know?" Grace's voice dropped, going conspiratorial. "I've got a secret, Steve. These last few months, they've *all* wanted me to be in control. You want to know why? Because I'm not myself."

The strain began to show around her smile, and I looked at her sharply, rapidly redefining my assessment of this young woman. "You know the power of manifestation."

"I sure do!" she said cheerfully, her eyes shifting away from my face despite giving every indication that she wanted to meet my gaze. As if somehow, she knew that she shouldn't do that.

Holy shit. I'd been looking for the demon buried inside this woman, but I hadn't been looking in the right place. "Why would anything dark latch on to the essential lightness and goodness of a heart-led practice?" I asked carefully, moving closer to her, and Grace blinked several times.

"Get the fuck away from me!"

She hurled herself against her bounds, damn near choking herself before her brain caught up with her body. Still, angry

Grace was back in play. "We're finally getting some work done here, bitch. We're finally making people pay. And the moment, the absolute fucking *moment* that we get a chance, we're going to make more people pay, the people who actually deserve to pay. Not my stupid fucking roommate and her stupid fucking need to borrow every goddamn thing that I own, or even my professor, who was a total dick to me, the fucking asshole trying to tank my GPA. He should have known better, but he didn't, because people are stupid. But *I'm* not stupid, and you are not going to screw up this opportunity for us. We've worked too damn hard for too damn long to miss this chance."

"Delia," Sergei grunted the warning, and I stopped before I could get within arm's reach of Grace.

Behind me, I could hear Steve's hissed intake of breath, could almost feel him drawing closer to Sergei. As he did, Grace changed her voice again. I expected Manager Grace this time, but no, we were back to Woo.

"I had no way of understanding why I'd suddenly gotten so much better at the things I wanted to manifest, you have to know that," she said calmly. "At first it was great. My specialty has always been parking spaces, getting them to spring up out of nowhere, but that skill got better first. Then my parents announced that they were spending more money on me, paying for this meditation retreat that I seriously want to attend. My grades came more easily than ever before, my mind was sharper. But it wasn't all good."

She sighed, her head dipping, while her voice dropped to a mere murmur. "My heart was heavier, you know? I didn't understand why. And then of course the bad things started happening."

Her face twisted into a snarl but just that quickly she smoothed it out, the agony of expressions warring on her face suddenly weighing on my bones.

I still wasn't close enough to see the demon behind her eyes, though. I didn't know its name, I didn't know its court or its purpose. I needed to get closer. I needed to see.

"It's okay, Grace," I said. "It's not your fault. You were doing everything you possibly could to hold it together. You're doing great."

"Yes, I am doing great, unfortunately." She sighed again, then glanced up toward me, her eyes hooded by her lashes. "I did this to you. I didn't mean to, but you're here because of me. Because they wanted to meet you."

She stretched her neck from one side to the next, as if she were preparing for a long restful yoga session. "Some people hear voices come on whispers in the dark, telling them to do terrible things. But that wasn't my experience. I heard entire conversations, conversations I didn't understand until just a few days ago when I met you, and then I met someone else I recognized, deep down inside. Well, maybe *I* didn't recognize him, but the creature within me did. He knows so much more than I can possibly understand, Delia, but—I'm learning, I think."

I grimaced. "Those aren't lessons you really want to know."

"Maybe..." She looked at me clearly for the first time, her eyes wide and fixed, but also excited. "I'm sorry, Delia. They so wanted to meet you and, in the end, well, I couldn't say no."

The lights went out, and new lights replaced them, flares of flame flickering to life around us in a stumpy circle of fire.

"What the hell!" I yelped, but it was too late, of course. It'd been too late that first day in Grace's drawing room, when I didn't realize what was going on with her, didn't see the trap drawing close.

Keegan's mournful tune cut off, and when Grace opened her mouth again, it twisted into an ugly snarl of a voice I hadn't heard before.

"Palemerious's little pet," it croaked out, the words slithering and snide. "Now we get to see why he's hiding you from us."

The wall of fire roared up around us, heat nearly knocking me flat.

"Lucian!" I screamed.

CHAPTER

EIGHTEEN

LUCIAN

L ucian gasped into a raging dust storm, reaching out with fingers that were no longer fully formed, but morphing between the slender, elegant fingers his shedim form allowed and the thick, broken-knuckled claws that ended in viciously sharp talons. And then, even that was denied him. The Ravening winds of the blighted realm swept over him with sand and fire, stripping away every last vestige of his form, whittling him down to dust.

He tried to fill his wasting lungs, but there was no air here, no oxygen—no sweetly fragranced mist hung with the taste of ocean and sunshine. There was nothing at all but wind and death.

The tribunal had started its summons. In truth, the only demons who should be affected by the call were those titillated by the possibility of a judgment of their own one day, but that was enough to draw plenty to the city. Worse, it was within Asmodaea's rights to provide him a taste of his punishment, should he be found guilty, which he almost certainly would be, he was coming to understand. The generals were restless, the horde was bored, and bored, restless demons were a certain prelude to chaos. The example of the Nephilim had taught everyone that lesson millennia ago. And so Lucian would have to pay for stepping out of line.

Daggers struck from all directions, ripping out what was left of his flesh. He knew this place, this horizonless wasteland on the edge of oblivion. He had glimpsed it only days ago when he'd sent Mirr tumbling toward it, screaming with the kind of terror that no demon believed he could feel. Lucian had shoved him willingly, with intention and focus, because Mirr had dared to test him. And now Mirr was dead. Would he be next?

He could no longer feel Delia, no longer sense the bond between them. It had been fading already, but with Mirr's banishment, it had fallen away like rocks off a cliff. Worse, he was losing control of his shedim form, flashing more and more often into shadows and fury. Even there, fully in his glory as a seventh-level commander, he felt lost, unsettled. And then, of course, the memories returned.

Lucian gasped again, struggling to draw breath with lungs squeezed tight with pain.

It was strange, really, how time bent and twisted. It had been barely seventeen years since he had slipped away from Belial's court into the unsuspecting human child, not to torture or taunt the whimpering creature into hideous acts, but simply to slip away in her shadow, to venture into the wild world separate from the Ravening Court and Belial's hold. It had been a good plan. He had been careful. It would have worked.

But the child had fallen ill, and one of the wretched doctors that had been brought in to help her had realized that something more was troubling this child of Abraham than a disease of the flesh. Palemerious had been prepared for that. He knew the ways of exorcists, knew he would be driven from the girl.

But if he moved quickly enough, he could still escape, still flee into the night. It had been a good plan.

It had not ended the way he had envisioned.

He twisted now as the winds kicked up, knives cutting, stripping the last gobbets of his hard-won flesh away. He wasn't only being shown the future but also the future's future. As if there might be a way station between where he stood now and his ultimate destruction, a chance to make a different choice. And when his mind caught on that idea, on the idea of this choice, this decision, the sensations assaulting him changed. They swelled and danced through him, and all that was dark and beautiful of his existence was returned to him in a rush. He spun through the shadows once more, power rekindling deep in his core, his energy radiating out, bursting from his newly restored shadow form, lust rising like a needful tide. He gloried in the fullness of his seventh-level power, no longer constrained by any residual fourth-level shedim weakness. Once more, he was Death and he was dire song, and he knew his own power.

How long had he walked the earth as Palemerious? His lips curled into a satisfied smirk. Since the Fall, of course, but...since well before the Fall as well. He had been one of the chosen, an elite even then, tasked with making the world and burying its treasures into running lava or the folds of bedrock, glittering stones that would excite the eye of humans centuries, millennia hence. He knew where all these treasures were buried, because he had placed them there. He had been sunshine and water, fire and joy, and he had not been willing to give it up when the Creator had crooked His finger, summoning his angels home.

He had not wanted to go.

And so, he hadn't.

He'd remained when the chosen of God had risen. He had fallen, and he had reveled in the Fall. The stinking muck that humans so often ascribed to the demonic realm was not untrue, but he and his brethren *lived*. They lived! They were real and visceral, and the pain and fury of the realm that served as their base simply reminded them of what it was to be alive. What it was to *feel*.

That sensation dimmed in the human realm, where he could only experience through a host's fear and desire, their need and their want. But it was still a glorious existence, and humans over the centuries were always in flight, moving toward the light or away from it, while he watched their shifting passages from the shadows. He would trade nothing, not a single decision. He was Palemerious, and he was power.

But had he been something else for a moment? Had he chosen a different path?

A foreign, abstract thought dug into the center of him, wan and forlorn and strangely terrifying. The touch of a hand on his body, the curve of a smile caused not by his own manipulation but by the human seeking to connect. Connect! And maybe more than that. The fragile tendril of an emotion that he had given up all claim to except for in its most perverted, corrupted form. It reached out to him now as if from very far away, beckoning pleading, begging him to remember.

Remember what?

A deep crimson tide rose up in the distance, flickering with flame, calling him home. But even as he moved toward it, a wisp of soft blue smoke and shimmering mist spun up to the other side, a world where there was pain and doubt, hope and vulnerability. What was this? What were these emotions, these sensations cascading through him? Who was this? Who was he?

Lucian. That was it, but now the name felt thin, wrong, meaningless. Why had he chosen that human word? He was Palemerious, the seventh-level commander of the Ravening Court. He was power and desire, and he could send a human sprawling with the lightest touch, or bring them crawling back with the twitch of his finger.

That was what he had learned in all these centuries of service to the darkness. He had learned that humans were weak and demons were strong because demons had been formed first. They were the servants and helpmates of a higher being, and they had dared to turn on the All That Is, turned and danced and fled from His command. This was who he was. This was his birthright, this was his choice, not...

"Lucian!"

The urgent call arrowed through him, gutting and harsh, opening a wellspring of haggard loss. Heeding this call would make him weak, he knew. If he embraced that lower calling, that broken form, he would be killed. He should be killed. Stamped into nothingness and abandoned like the fool he was. No human should have such power over him. No human should be able to warp and twist him to their service. That was not to be borne.

He was meant to rule, not be ruled, to drink until he was sated and devour all that was spread before him, bite by delicious bite.

The next time the word came, however, it was different, high-pitched and frantic, calling for him and only him. *"Lucian!"*

He turned back from the flowing crimson, the belching fire, the rolling smoke that spread before him like an invitation. He turned back toward the mist and the sorrow, the pain and loss, the hope and shattered dreams and ruined lives—and the trying, the trying, the trying and the failing, the loss and the pain. The blight of humanity didn't beckon to him like the crimson tide of darkness; it threw up barriers of fear, doubt, and shrinking, shriveling wretchedness.

And in the center of it, she stood. He could see her now. She was surrounded by fire, which didn't make any sense. Surrounded by fire, fear, and taunting laughing voices that he knew deep within his bones. Voices that sang to him even as they pushed and mauled her into making choices she should never have to make. She was trapped. They were hunting her. She was their plaything, as all humans were.

The bond between them crackled to life once more, shaking off the hoarfrost that he hadn't realized had settled upon it. It pulsed and writhed, a human thing, a living thing, but also burrowed deep within him, scraping all his bones.

His bones.

His shedim form solidified again, and Lucian dragged himself upright, staring blindly out at the sparkling surface of a distant lake, the sun shimmering high above the water, its rays dancing through the clouds.

He was Lucian and she had called him. He had touched her, taken her, gloried in her, and now he heard the sound of his name again, faint and terrified on her lips.

"*Lucian.*"

He turned toward the door, shedding his shedim form as quickly as he had reclaimed it.

He burst out into the street, seeing humanity as it had ever presented to demons, as shadow forms and cattle, with the occasional burst of fire, the whisper of greed, the violence of anger, the bright white purity of light and hope. Not all humans were shadows, though many were, more and more every year. It made their pleasure easier, but it also made seeking out those still with energy to burn a delicious effort. But his focus was not on these drifting souls, not now. His focus was on Delia. He'd damaged the flame that burned within her, he'd turned it from something good and pure to something twisted and dark, something stronger, something worth fighting for...

Or at least with.

. . .

By the time he reached the door of the warehouse, the wailing of the creatures within had intensified. Dimly, he acknowledged the presence of Sergei's SUV, the humans and the small animal that crouched within. Spreading his field of vision wider, he noted the dark paneled van that cruised toward the warehouse, the quavering interest of the people within it. The van bore no taint of demon, which struck him as important, but he had no time to spend on it. He reformed into his shedim husk as he pushed through the door of the warehouse, racing down the corridor faster than any human. He didn't need to breathe, his feet never sounded upon the floor, but he did not fool himself into thinking he wasn't noticed. He was part of the point.

"Palemerious's little pet," the taunt croaked out, a voice he recognized. "Now we get to see why he's hiding you from us."

The fourth-level ankle biter puffed up on his own power, Lucian thought. *Zagan.* He wasn't attacking now. He was watching with rapt attention, mesmerized by the bound red-headed woman in the center of the room who sat in front of Delia. The bound human who was inches away from breaking into so many pieces she might not ever find her way back to whole again.

Delia could wait out this demon until it made a mistake, Lucian thought. He certainly could. But the woman held in the demon's thrall on the chair...she could wait no longer.

He fled back toward the parking lot, little more than smoke.

NINETEEN

"What in the hell?"

I staggered back, trying not to choke on the stink of burning sulfur as I took in the shooting gouts of fire that surrounded us—then I noticed Sergei and Steve looking at me strangely. They were also inside the circle of flames that had erupted around us, but they seemed not to give a single shit.

"This version of Grace is the problem, Delia," Steve said helpfully. "Maybe it's time to ix-nay the emon-day?"

"I..." I broke off, staring at them hard. "You don't see any of this, do you?" I asked, gesturing at the fire around us. Sergei peered back at me.

"I have received a blessing," he rumbled. "As long as I protect you, I'm protected, at least to a degree. He's a Hallow."

"Seriously?" I squinted harder, my eyes tearing up from the smoke. "Is this how it works in Descent? You just don't see... anything?"

Sergei shrugged. "Sometimes. Sometimes, only one person is affected in the whole club. They usually don't last too long."

The voice croaked out of Grace's mouth again, now curiously flat. "This demonstration isn't for the blessed, Delia. It's for you. Unless you'd rather they see what you see? Feel what you feel? We could arrange that."

A heartbeat later, Steve screamed and nearly leaped into Sergei's arms, while the burly bodyguard bristled to almost a third again his size. Did the man have purebred bear in his ancestry?

Another moment passed, and they both relaxed, and Sergei stared at me. "There is no fire. But if this woman sees that—"

"Hey!" I turned in horror to see a small, bounding Beagle, hurtling like a shot out of the shadows, followed swiftly by pant-suited Claire lugging her signature exorcist-supply tote. Sandy rushed in last, her flowing caftan a fire hazard waiting to happen.

"Watch out!" I shouted, but they also didn't seem to notice the leaping fire. They didn't even break stride, except for Angel as he passed over the perimeter of the flames. He stopped, whirled, then barked as Claire and Sandy reached me. As they approached, I felt the pressure of their nearness in a way that I normally didn't. And not only theirs. Everyone in this small circle leaned into me, adding their weight to my shoulders. The laughter started again, and on the heels of it, Thomas Keegan's tuneless song echoed through the room, notes running up the scale and down again in no discernible pattern.

"How is she?" Sandy asked, her eyes on Grace.

I struggled to focus on her and not the fire surrounding us. "Shifting between alters," I said, and blew out a breath. "I'm glad you're here. I can get the demon out, but she's not stable, I don't think. I'm not sure how it's going to affect her."

Something shifted in the shadows beyond the wall of flames, something that sounded heavy, like a crate dragged against the concrete.

I glanced over at it, then back to Steve. "Did you hear that?"

"What?" he said, and Sergei shifted closer to me, the dog at his side. At least Angel was staring in the same direction I was, his nose flaring as his lips peeled back from his teeth.

Sergei folded his arms. "You do what you need to do," he said tightly. "Anything that comes at you will have to come through me."

I stared at him considering. "You know, that's pretty good," I acknowledged, "that could almost work."

The moment the words were out of my mouth, crates the size of coffins ripped across the open space behind Sergei, hurtling toward him, toward me. Despite his assertion, I screamed, dropping my shoulder and shoving into him, knocking him aside. He spun away, still well within the circle of flames, and of course the crates disappeared.

"Sorry," I muttered as Sergei cursed. I turned, then, coming face to face with a grinning Grace, the possessed manifester version.

"Now you begin to understand," she said cheerfully, though her voice sounded strained. "We draw to us that which we most fear. I certainly did, and though it gave me strength I didn't expect, there was a price to pay. A heck of a price."

"Grace?" Sandy asked gently. "I'd like to tell you that you're safe here, but I don't think you are. You can move toward safety, though. We all can move toward safety." With that, Grace turned on her, her face turning surly above her straining collar.

"The last thing I want is safety, thanks," she informed Sandy, who took the response without a flinch. "I've spent my entire fucking life trying to be safe, held back, held down. I don't fucking want to be safe. I've got abilities now. I can do what I want."

"But not you, right?" It was Claire who spoke up, earning her a tight-lipped scowl of disapproval from Sandy, not that she seemed to care. She took another step toward Grace, gripping her tote more tightly. "This version of you, the snotty one, that's not who's really in control. If it were, don't you think that's who would have the power here? Because I do. I totally do. You're just along for the ride, aren't you? Piping up in the background loud enough that Grace throws you a bone every once in a while, but you're not the one in power."

"We're all in this together," Grace said, with the measured tones of the young woman I'd first met. Manager Grace, I thought. "I don't know what we're doing here, but this doesn't seem good. Steve?" She gave him a wide, desperate smile. "Can we go?"

"Not yet," I said grimly. I refocused on Grace and spoke out loud as if to her, but she wasn't my real audience. Where the hell was Lucian? I knew that he had work to do for his tribunal, or whatever, but I needed him—we all needed him.

What was the point of having a seventh-level demon commander on hand to help you defend against evil, if he was permanently MIA?

"So, this was your plan all along," I said to Grace, and she blinked at me with startled eyes. The team around me stiffened, and Angel let out a small querulous yodel.

"You waited until..." I stopped, a whisper of understanding pushing through me, words forming in my mind. Words that sounded like Lucian. *Third-level tops, controlled by Grace's illness, circumscribed by it. No way it's any higher than third. Not the leader.*

I gritted my teeth as Keegan's song spiraled through another round of discordant notes. So it wasn't Keegan influencing this woman directly, I thought, or whatever demon was wearing Keegan's face. Grace had been pretty consistently altered for months now. Something was inside her, somehow, even if I couldn't pin it down.

So, what, was she possessed by one of Keegan's demon's

minions? He was strong enough to have minions? That marked him as at least fourth-level, maybe fifth, and that tracked too, didn't it? Fourth-level meant shedim. Maybe he'd been a low fourth-level when he'd possessed Thomas Keegan, just getting his power on? And now, ten years later, he was just impersonating the guy?

A shedim wouldn't need a human form—they had one of their own. And although Lucian had moved backward to claim his shedim form, that wasn't the usual trajectory of these assholes. Plus, Keegan's demon would have to have enough juice to command Gahmel too, the demon who'd possessed the dog—*and* to command whoever was inside Grace, now. So, no lightweight, no matter what level he was.

I processed all that in a few seconds as I leaned toward Grace. The howling beyond the circle of fire got louder, more excited, but I felt strangely settled. Lucian was here—I could feel it. He hadn't shown himself yet, maybe couldn't show himself if that meant the risk of capture or attack, but he was here, which meant I could focus on drawing out this motherfucker.

"Sandy," I said, drawing the therapist's startled glance. "What do we know about Grace?"

"Delia, I—"

"Please fucking answer the question," I said tightly. "It's important."

Sandy drew in a sharp breath. "Grace is a remarkable young woman," she said brightly. "She has managed to endure significant trauma yet create a life for herself that is rich and full."

"I thought so too." I nodded. "How in the world was she able to do that? Was she just that smart?"

Sandy smiled. "Well, she tried very hard to make everything okay for everyone, and eventually she got more tools that helped her do that. Remember, Grace, you told me that first book of your sister's that you read? Even though she wasn't very happy with you."

Sandy faltered as Grace shifted in her chair, her eyes going wide, her shoulders drawing in. "I'm sorry!" she said, the words heartbreakingly young and vulnerable.

Then Mean Grace reappeared. "Will you shut the fuck up? That bitch had no idea what she was reading."

"It was wrong to take something that wasn't mine, but I did find the book very valuable," Managing Grace said. All of these answers came out in a rush, but they weren't the one I was looking for. Then, unwittingly, Managing Grace did me a solid.

"It's really not that big of a deal," she said, waving a hand. "They're just self-help books. I enjoy them, nothing more than that."

"I do *more* than enjoy them," Manifesting Grace countered, her chin coming up, her hands flattening on her knees. "I learned something new from every single one. I studied them more than I studied anything in school. And I'm a very good student. Very good." The intensity of her words was not lost on me. As much as I was trying to draw the demon forward, Manifesting Grace was trying to assert her own independence, her own voice. The voice that had helped her cope for all these long, lonely years from age twelve on.

The rustling in my own mind kicked up. "You're boring us, Delia. We want to know what you're thinking too. Let us into your mind, or we take theirs instead."

The flames blazed around me in a circle, throwing Sandy, Steve, and Claire into bright relief. Manifesting Grace lost control as Frozen Grace took over again, her voice carrying over Keegan's song. "I'm sorry! I'm sorry! I didn't mean to take it!"

"If you would just stop your sniveling," Mean Grace growled.

"We're fine, I'm fine. Can we leave now, Steve? I'd like to go," Managing Grace said again. "Why are we here?"

"Faster…" breathed the rush and tumble of voices, carrying over Keegan's song, Grace's words spinning up in my mind, clawing at my foundations, shaking loose my every thought. "Faster—"

"No!" I screamed.

I pressed my hands to my ears and dropped to my knees in front of Grace, washed over with a tidal wave of my own memories and fears, every experience from my childhood on, well before that day with the dogs and the little girl and Mordechai. I was assaulted with vision after vision of my mother's screaming fits, her tears and slaps, pushes and angry words. The endless rounds of cleaning, the broken bottles, the brave and angry face I put on for my schoolmates, the bright smile and cheerful demeanor I managed for my teachers.

The weight of it pressed me down into the concrete, nails spiking through my feet, my hands, my back. *She would leave me alone*, I thought. My mother would leave me alone in the house, with the doors locked and only the upstairs windows open. It was hot, *so* hot, because she didn't want to pay for fans when she wasn't there. And air conditioning didn't happen at all, not back then. Not before I had the voice or ability to complain. It was so *hot*. I was so *alone*. I would always be alone if I wasn't good.

My head whipped up, and I knew what to do.

"Thank you," I whispered to no one and nobody but my own feverish, broken mind, but I knew what to do now. I dragged myself forward, still on my knees in front of Grace.

"I need you to teach me how to manifest, Grace," I said. "I need help, your help. Right now."

She was cycling through all of her alters so quickly, it was tough to track.

Angry snarl, frightened eyes, exasperated confusion—and then I had it. Manifesting Grace smiled at me.

"Of course!" she said joyfully, eagerly as her eyes widened, then widened further.

And then I saw him. Because of course I did. "Raza," I breathed out, relishing the way that Grace sat up straight, as if she'd suddenly been struck with a cattle prod. I wasn't proud of that, but I was still happy. I didn't have my props, I barely remembered any words, but I didn't need to know all that. Not here. Not with the fucking horde surrounding me like a bunch of screaming teenagers.

"Hello, Raza," I spoke in a clear, low voice. "Looks like you're not even smart enough to know when to duck. Whoever took charge and ordered you inside this daughter of the Creator was doing you no favors. I will, though. But you don't want to make me mad, or I'll not only pull you out of this human, I'll cast you into the wind, far away from the court that has treated you so poorly. Oh, how they mock you."

"What?" Grace asked in her lilting Manifester Grace mode. Then it slipped into a flat croak. "No one treats me poorly."

And I realized that this was the hook, this was the lever. Demons might be the spawn of evil, powerful enough to make a human's bones turn to water, but they had their hang-ups too. They had their triggers and hot buttons, and humiliation seemed to be one of them.

I leaned in. "I can set you free of this trap some other demon has laid for you. Set you free and set you in the wind long enough for you to find some other place. You will get stronger, you will survive, but not if you stay here. Here, there is nothing for you but shame as others laugh..."

I cycled through all the miserable things I could think of, but this was a demon I was talking to, a third-level mischief maker who delighted in making things suffer. For this demon, maybe for all demons, there was only one threat that carried any water.

"Here, there is nothing for you but death."

That was too much, and Grace shifted again, her eyes shuttering and closing off the demon behind another wall.

"You lie!" The voice that came out of Grace was high and clear, but no longer frightened. This was an impossibly young child version of Grace, before the trauma, before the breaking apart. "You can't kill me. You lie!"

"*I* don't lie."

I felt the cold wash of energy sweep up next to me, then a moment later, Lucian stood at my side, holding his hand out toward Grace. She shrieked in absolute horror, and I turned to see the creature that he allowed her to see, the demon that had attacked me in his apartment, horns and teeth, scales and fury.

He spoke, and I could understand the words. I wasn't the only one.

"I will hunt you down and send you into oblivion," he said, my human ears recording the language as snarls and garbled howls, but my soul tracking their meaning. "I've done it more than once, Raza. I have a taste for it. Do you think for a moment I don't long to do it again?"

He wrenched out a taloned hand and raked it across Grace's forearm. Making her scream.

"Now," he commanded. "Out."

Black blood geysered out of the wound on Grace's arm, making Steve shout and Sandy rush forward, her body held back barely in time by Sergei. The demon spewed forth in the blood, shooting straight up as I wrapped it in the words that Mordechai had taught me all those years ago, the words of release and forgiveness, the words to speed it on its way to anywhere that was far away from here.

The fire guttered out and everything went still—no

screaming demons, no Lucian, no Raza. There was only sobbing Grace, her zip-tied waist, ankles, and collar being cut off by Sergei, Claire and Steve huddled together, and Sandy on her knees in front of Grace, holding her hands, lending her strength.

And somewhere far across the room, I heard an excited, "Got it!"

I slumped to the floor.

CHAPTER

TWENTY

"Delia!" Claire rushed to my side, but not before my head cracked off the concrete, which did a better job of reviving me than any of her panicked ministrations.

"Oh my God, Delia, are you all right? Are you dizzy? You don't look damaged. And no vomit. You're getting better at this."

"I've got her," Lucian said, and he knelt beside me, reaching for me as if he intended to pick me up. But I hadn't imagined what I'd heard in the shadows.

"Fuck that!" I said, and I rolled to my feet, staggering. "Who else is in here?"

"There you go, dear." Sandy's voice nearly drowned me out, probably deliberately so, and I whirled around to glare at her, catching her stern gaze as she angled Grace over the line of chalk that had been circumscribed in a wide arc around the central chair. I neared it, smelling the faint odor of rotten eggs, and wondered what the barrier's purpose had been. Were the demons watching this show trying to keep me enclosed? Or were they trying to keep other demons out?

Something about that bothered me, but my thoughts were derailed again as Sergei emerged from the shadows, dragging a man into the pool of fluorescent light. The man clutched a camera to his chest, and he stared at us with wide steady eyes, his shoulders hunched, his blunt-cut hair looking almost white in the harsh lighting. He was a giant of a man, probably six foot four and broad-shouldered, bulky-armed and legged, but he wasn't strong like Sergei or even fat. He was just big...and easily pushing 60.

"Are you with Dark Streets?" I demanded. It was the only explanation that made any sense.

He grimaced. "Well, that's a long story, but the short answer is, I was, but I'm not anymore. Dark Streets started as a pet project of mine about fifteen years ago. I thought I was too tired for this business when things blew up about three years back. Sue Willows had the fire and energy I just couldn't seem to summon anymore, and away we went."

"Wait a minute," Steve said, peering at him. "Are you Roy Granger?"

The older man actually blushed—which was a terrifying sight in the weird light.

"Now, how would you know my name?" he asked with a soft quirk to his mouth.

"Masters of the Universe Magic Tournament, 2010. Ring a bell?" Steve demanded gleefully, but I lifted a hand to cut off this impromptu reunion.

"What are you doing here?" I asked slowly. "And who else is with you? Who else knows that Grace was held here—and is Dark Streets getting your video?"

Sergei bristled beside Roy, and the videographer raised both hands in surrender. "Not fucking likely," he said, then immediately blushed again. "Sorry. Barb was always after me about my language."

He seemed to shake that off and started over again. "Dark Streets is *not* getting this feed, no. They're videoing a distraction, if you will, in a warehouse about three blocks away. They've also tipped off the cops, you should know, so all things being equal, we should get our asses out of here. But I, I…" He rubbed his face. "Okay, I need to start over. It's kind of a lot to explain."

"Then you should explain in the vehicle," Sergei said. "If there is a possibility that we will have police here, we need to leave."

"I'm not sure Grace can…oh!" Sandy's startled words broke off as Sergei turned smartly on his heel, marched over to Grace. Leaning down, he picked her up easily—Grace, who looked like she'd never been picked up in her life. She placed one hand on Sergei's bulky chest, her eyes going wide and glassy, and managed an echoing "oh!"

"There's no possession here. And any entities that were in the mix are gone." Lucian's words floated across the open space, a moment before the man appeared. He was once again in perfect Lucian form, dark eyes fixed on me, before shifting to Roy Granger. His lips twisted. "I see you continue to pick up strays."

"I'm just passing through," Roy said, but Lucian had already turned to head out the corridor ahead of Sergei and Grace. Sandy followed close behind, and the rest of us, suddenly without much to do, followed as well. The dog was nowhere in sight.

We stepped out into the bright sunshine of full day to see Sergei now walking with Grace beside him, no longer carrying her. Lucian had disappeared, and Angel jumped excitedly around the front of the SUV, just a dog fresh back from a walk, nothing interesting to see here.

With as few words as possible, we piled into the SUV, Claire,

Grace, and Sandy in the third row, Steve and Roy in the center, while I got in the front next to Sergei, Angel at my feet. The dog immediately torpedoed over the console so that he could join the guys in the center. "I have a car a few blocks away," Roy began, but Sergei cut him off.

"I will bring you back to it. It's hidden well?"

Roy shrugged. "Well enough. Sue isn't really the type to pay attention to those kinds of details. If it wasn't on the shot sheet, she didn't much care. And the people around her are in the business of making her look good. I was just the content review guy and researcher toward the end. Suited me fine enough, but…"

"Did you see where Lucian went?" I asked Sergei quietly as Steve started peppering Roy with questions. In the far back, Claire and Sandy sandwiched a now completely passed-out Grace between them.

"It will be our last stop," Sergei said, which made no sense at all.

As if she could hear him, Sandy piped up from the back. "We're going to need to take Grace back to her house, reconnect with her parents, and understand what kind of care they can get her. She's not in a place to make decisions for herself, but she needs to be checked out by a medical professional, not just a mental one. This cut on her arm doesn't look bad, a heck of a lot better than I expected it to, based on what I saw inside that warehouse, but it doesn't mean that she's not a potential for infection. I kind of doubt that she's had her tetanus shots updated recently."

"Should we take her straight to the hospital?" Steve asked worriedly, but Sandy shut that idea down.

"If we can talk to her parents first, that would be better. We need to understand what their insurance situation is and their medical decisions. If Grace has been undergoing treatment that we don't know about, it's better to do it by the book. And she doesn't seem to be in distress."

In response, Grace opened her mouth and issued a long, satisfied snore.

Steve chuckled. "I'd say she agrees with you."

He swiveled back to Roy. "So, you went from low-level podcaster to mid-level podcaster, and then Sue Willows, what, took notice? Came up to you at a video shoot?"

"I met her at a con," Roy said. "She was bright, funny, easy on the eyes. Great voice, the whole package. People seemed to draw closer every time she spoke. And I've been doing this a lot of years. My wife passed a few years back, and, you know, you don't lose your interest in the hunt, but you can lose your taste for everything else. Anyway, we started talking, she came on as a guest on the pod, and listeners liked her, then she asked to start doing a few solo episodes. Her stuff was popular, and it generated more comments. Plus, she knew how to promote. It wasn't a hard decision to give it all up."

"But you didn't give it up," I said. "You're here. That means you clearly know what's going on."

He blew out a long breath. "I still work for Dark Streets, yeah. Like I said, I mostly do research and production work now, which works out great. But I was in the studio when the delivery came a few days ago, addressed to Sue but in a small enough package that I knew it had to be some sort of book or journal."

I froze. From the back seat, Claire's voice was careful and exact.

"A journal?" she asked.

Roy shifted in his seat, reaching into the pocket of his light-weight but voluminous jacket. He pulled out a book wrapped in plastic. It had the same heavy cover as Mordechai's other journals, bound in what looked like leather and branded at the bottom with a kabbalistic tree of life.

I fought the groan. "How many journals did this guy have?"

To my surprise, Roy chuckled.

"Funny you should mention that. I got the feeling that this wasn't the first time he'd written the words in this journal down, if that makes any sense. There were no scratch-outs, no hesitation. The writing was swift and even. It reminded me of being in grade school and having to write the same sentences over five hundred times as punishment."

"Dude, are you serious?" Steve asked him, clearly aghast. "Your teacher made you do that?"

Roy smiled. "My parents. Good Catholic boys, Jim and me. By the time we finally flew the coop, we knew all about how to make a good penance. And we had plenty of reason to apologize."

He glanced up at me. "Jim's my brother. About ten years younger than I am, but we still managed to get into a mess of trouble. He used to be in the same business you are."

I blinked. "Exorcisms?"

Roy chuckled. "Yeah. He moved away some years back, all the way to New York. Anyway," he said, shaking himself. "I didn't intend to steal the journal, but these last few weeks, Sue hasn't really been herself. Not possessed or anything—" he waved off my question. "More *ob*-sessed. And frankly, running with stories I didn't have time to validate. You get a lot of crazy stuff doing the work we do, and about half of it is bullshit. The other half will turn your hair white."

He grinned at his own joke, then we broke off as Sergei announced that we were getting close.

Sergei looked into the rearview mirror. "Your vehicles are still at the office. I can have them sent wherever you need, if you give me the keys. Or I can return to collect you when you're finished."

"We can Uber back to the office," Claire began, then broke off as Sergei glared at her. "We're going to have to have a conversation about this sometime," she said sweetly, but she remained quiet as Sergei parked the vehicle and got out to assist them and their still-woozy cargo into the house.

I craned my neck around, but it didn't look like anyone was in residence. "Where did you say her parents were?" I asked Steve.

"Belgium, I think the mom said. She's in international commerce, and the dad is in investments. They travel a lot. They always have, really, for as long as I've known Grace."

He held up a phone. "I should probably go in there too, you know? She knows me, and we gotta get the information together about her medical care. You're going to be okay?"

"Oh, yeah. I'm good." I gestured to Roy. "I think we'll go somewhere where we can check out this journal in private. If it's the same thing that the police got, that would help a lot. You be careful, Steve, okay?"

Angel yapped in solidarity beside him, and I pointed at the dog. "You go with Steve and try not to get possessed again," I told him. "It's been a long day."

Sergei had another surprise for us when he got back in the vehicle. "We're not going back to the office, not yet," he said. "Sue Willows landed there twenty minutes ago, waiting for your return. We go to the house."

He looked at Roy Granger in the rearview mirror, and I turned to see the older man reviewing footage on his camera.

"Can you put together some kind of counterprogramming?" I asked. "Just to occupy her?"

Roy looked up, his eyes kindling with a new light. "Like a rogue pod?" he asked, scratching his chin. "I could do that. I've got enough dummy accounts that she'd never figure out who it was, and the voice masking they have now is off the chain. If I had an avatar running some lines and just let the video do the talking..." He paused. "For how long?"

"Three or four days to start? After that..." Sergei shrugged. "It may not matter so much."

I looked at him sharply. Three or four days was about the timeline for the tribunal, but it wasn't like our problems we're going to instantly go away after that, were they? Was that even a thing?

I refocused on Roy. "I know you've recorded at a studio or whatever, but what do you need as far as set up?" I asked.

"That part's easy," he said. "All I need is a really quiet location. Maybe soundproof walls if you've got them? All my equipment's in the car, mobile setup. So, we'll just need to swing back and get my car and then maybe—"

"Of course, I will get your car," Sergei said. "You can record in the house." He slanted a glance at me, and I made a face.

"It's kind of a creepy house," I warned him, and Roy laughed.

"Creepy is what I do. I learned a long time ago that the scariest things aren't waiting in the dark, they're inside us."

His comment hung in the air as I leaned back in my seat, watching the streets of Chicago flow by. Where had Lucian gone off to, again? He'd been right there when I needed him, finally, and now—once more gone. Was this how things were going to be between us? Me never knowing if he'd show up, if I could depend on him, or if one day I'd wake up and he'd suddenly be gone? Transpo'd back to Hell without so much as a goodbye?

I didn't know, I couldn't know. All I could do was move forward.

I pressed my lips together and watched the lights start winking on in the city, forcing myself not to scream.

CHAPTER

TWENTY-ONE

Sergei drove us back to the warehouse district and parked the SUV several blocks shy of where Roy had left his car. He glared at me until I promised I wouldn't move a muscle, then the two of them got out. Roy had told him there was no way that Sue Willows and her entourage were still creeping around the warehouse district—not when they had their own video to refine and post—but Sergei wasn't hearing it. The two set off at a swift trot and were out of sight in moments.

I sank back against the car seat...and didn't stir until Sergei touched my arm seconds later. I blinked at him in confusion. Why was he turning off the car again? Why were we no longer on a run-down street of chain-link fences and dark-windowed buildings?

"What?" I asked, struggling upright.

"We're at the house." He scowled, looking up at the gothic Victorian mansion, its shaggy flowering bushes dancing in the light breeze. "Your temporary house, anyway. You need to get inside."

"I slept all the way through—all of that?"

But, of course, he didn't need to reply to that, and my attention was immediately distracted by Roy Granger's jaw-dropped expression of awe as he looked up at the building.

"Dear God, I must have driven by these houses a thousand times, imagining what they look like behind the walls and gates. This street is notorious. You know that, right? The houses up and down the lane were considered to be the headquarters for some of the most active spiritualists in the late 1800s. I don't remember all the lore off the top of my head, but there's a lot of it."

He turned his startled gaze to me. "You live here? This is your house?"

"Not permanently," I corrected as we exited the SUV. "I've just been loaned it for a while."

"Well, it's pretty epic. You could probably do a three-part series just on...ah."

The abrupt change in Roy's tone had me looking over, and I followed his gaze up to the man standing on the porch of my temporary home.

Lucian Gray had never looked more elegant. It seemed like the greater the danger we faced, the more impossibly sophisticated-looking he became...at least when he wasn't a snarling demon. Now he strolled down the steps of the Victorian mansion as if he really did own the place, moving toward Roy, who stood rooted in place.

Lucian held out a hand. "Lucian Gray," he said. "We haven't formally met. Sergei tells me you need a quiet room."

"I do. I do," Roy finally managed, then he reached out his own hand and grasped Lucian's.

He blinked. "I wouldn't have expected that," he said. "You feel human."

A ghost of a smile crossed over Lucian's face, but I didn't share the reaction. It was *that* obvious to Roy that Lucian was a demon? Surely, he wasn't the only psychically sensitive hunter in the city. How vulnerable was Lucian to being identified?

Lucian slanted a glance at me. While our demonic bond might be weakening by the moment, it was clear he could still read my thoughts.

"The Granger family has been known to our kind for generations," he said. "Roy pursued his work in the public eye, while his brother chose to practice on an even quieter level than Rabbi Mordechai."

I blinked at both of them. "You're aware of everything going on in the city?" I asked Roy, but he raised his hands in denial.

"Oh, no, I wouldn't say that. I know enough to be dangerous, and for the sake of my business, I've had the opportunity to investigate a lot of haunted houses in this city. It tracks that if there are a lot of haunted houses, there are a lot of demons, but I'm not an expert on specific ones. That would have been far more my brother's line of work. I just find them where they're squatting and record the tale."

He squinted up at the house. "But yeah. If you've got a room here that I can set up in, I can put together something. A new pod, maybe Darker Truths, yeah? That has a nice ring to it."

"We can see what works for you." Lucian turned and led us into the house, and I unabashedly trailed a few feet behind Roy, who huffed out in surprise and wonder with every new room and corridor. I could relate. I hadn't taken the time to investigate the house beyond the first floor—drawing room, powder room, kitchen in the back. I knew I'd need to figure out how to shower, eventually, so I was relieved when we climbed the narrow staircase next to the entrance to the kitchen to see it served as sort of a servant's entrance to the second floor, where room after room of opulent chambers stood, a central bathroom tucked into the rear of the building.

"This has stayed the same all these years?" Roy finally sputtered. "No updates?"

Lucian didn't respond to that, leading us past heavy oil paintings and delicate marble statuary—angels with knowing smiles, gargoyles with too-human eyes, figures that belonged in museums rather than private homes.

"Jesus," Roy muttered, peering into a library lined floor-to-ceiling with leather-bound books, then glancing down a hallway where crystal chandeliers cast flickering light across Persian runners. He nearly squeaked with excitement as Lucian finally led him up a narrow spiral staircase to the turret.

"I suspect this room will be best for your needs," Lucian said. "It is...unusually soundproof, we've discovered. The windows are also equipped with interior shutters, should you want to avoid natural light."

"No, this is..." Roy's voice faltered as he looked around with surprise. "Wait. There's no echo."

"What?" I asked, as he clapped his hands loudly, his eyes going wide. He dropped his case to the floor, unzipping it, his movements speeding up as he unloaded.

"This is great. This is perfect," he said, speaking faster too. "I'll need two hours—maybe more, but not much. I can't...I mean, I can't believe the sound in here! How is this possible?"

He swung his gaze toward the window, grinning. "And the *light*. I don't need the light—I sure as hell am not going to be on camera, but I can *see*. And for an old man, let me tell you, that's something. How is it so soundproofed with all these windows?"

He practically bounced with excitement, then his gaze met Lucian's. "What—oh. Sorry."

He dove for his jacket and pulled out the book. "Forgot all about that thing. Good luck with whatever you find in there. It's kind of cryptic to me, but I..." he blew out a long breath. "I knew I didn't want Sue to get her claws into it. I don't know why."

"You did the right thing," Lucian said simply. He took the book and we stepped outside, leaving Roy giggling like a ten-year-old with a new bike.

"We'll go downstairs to read this," Lucian murmured, moving down the curving stairs and along the hallway, past the staircase we came up. He opened a door that revealed another steep staircase—this one also flush against the wall and too narrow for comfort.

"Why do I have a feeling that none of this is up to code?" I murmured.

He chuckled. "We'll be sure to bring it up to the real estate broker when we sell."

We passed the first-floor landing but kept going down another flight to a door that opened up on a room with another entrance at the far end—much larger than the one we entered. But the room itself was a wonder. It wasn't the same library we'd seen before, but books lined floor-to-ceiling shelves on two sides, a long bar stood on the third next to a fireplace, and in the center was an imposing table of inlaid wood, cushioned chairs drawn up all around. Around the perimeter of the room, more chairs stood next to lamps and side tables.

Every single lamp was lit. A huge grandfather clock stood in the corner, pendulum swinging, and I absently noted the time—nearly 2 p.m. We'd need to go find Roy by four, I thought, and make sure the turret room hadn't swallowed him whole. The idea made me smile as I scanned the rest of the room—the books, the chairs, the fireplace crackling in the hearth.

"A fireplace in the basement?" I asked, blinking in surprise.

"A not uncommon feature of the times," Lucian said, waiting as my eyes adjusted to the lights. And then, of course, I saw them.

"Mordechai's journals!" I gasped, moving toward the wall in surprise.

"I wasn't able to spirit away most of them—just a few of the more recent years. When the police return the rest, we'll store them here for safety."

"If they do," I grumbled.

"Oh...that won't be an issue." He directed us to the table. "We should sit."

I blew out a long breath and took my seat, not objecting when Lucian pulled up the one right next to me. These weren't typical library chairs, but plush and deep, inviting the reader to sit back and savor a book—at least when they weren't tilting forward on the edge of their seat nervous about what they were going to read. I *definitely* was feeling pretty nervous right now.

He slid Mordechai's journal over to me as the clock chimed with two echoing bells. Before the sound fully died, I'd opened the journal to the first page.

"There are no dates," I said. "Just these hash marks. That's different. Was he trying to hide something?"

Lucian didn't answer, and I bit my lip, trying to stem my nervous commentary. It didn't take too long before I found an entry I hadn't read before.

She came to me on Thursday. I meant to see the family Wednesday but was delayed. Delayed. Would everything have changed if I had not been delayed?

The account continued, and Roy was correct. There was no hesitation in the writing, no skips or scratch-outs. It was like it had been copied over carefully, studiously, an acolyte performing a penance or recording a perfect copy for his master. And as I read, I thought of another journal, perhaps exactly like this, sitting in the police station downtown. Violation wormed through me along with horror. And before I realized it, I was speaking out loud. Pulling the book back close to me to read it more clearly under the lights, subtly withdrawing from Lucian, but needing him beside me more than ever.

She was a rough child from the beginning, unruly and unkempt, with a strange sort of ferocity that you could see in her eyes and the way she held her jaw, locking it against the strength it took to keep the yapping dogs in line. Three dogs. One little girl. They barked uproariously, dragging her into the house where I'd been summoned, shocking Mrs. Edelbrock, who apparently knew the dogs.

She pulled the animals away from the child, apologizing for the ruckus and explaining that these dogs loved her daughter, her daughter who looked so different from this new, strange little girl in our midst, this little girl who now was staring at sweet Adele, whose skin had turned papery thin with shadows roaming beneath it. Sweet, weak Adele, her body breaking down with the strength of the creature that squatted inside her, not moving, not breathing. Not exhorting her to demonstrations of evil or darkness or filth or vice. A demon who was doing something that demons should not, did not do. It was hiding.

"What's wrong with her?" the little girl asked. "Why is she so sick?"

I should have sent her out after Mrs. Edelbrock. But she didn't give me the chance. She walked right up to Adele, nudged her, and when the girl opened her eyes and looked at her, she said it. Just as simple and certain as that. "His name is Palemerious," she said. "And he doesn't want to go."

Lucian's sharp intake of breath drew my head up with a snap.

"Do you remember this?" I demanded as he pushed away from the table and stood, stalking around the room.

"I do not," he said tersely. "I don't remember anything about you other than you were there both before the exorcism and after."

I turned back to the book, unable to keep from reading the truth any longer. The words now tumbled out swiftly, jangling around the room as Lucian stopped at the far end of the table, his hands gripping another chair.

I did not hesitate, for the Lord had delivered the name I could not draw out myself in the face of the child's weakness, her sickness, but I knew it to be true. It was right and convicting. And so I leaned down next to Adele, one child at my arm, the other on the bed, both of them watching me with eyes too young to know the truths they had seen. The demon watched me too, furious then cold, already calculating what would happen next.

I felt his sneering laughter, his certainty, his pride, and his strength. And then I felt her strength as well. This little girl, bruises on her arms, too thin, too pale, too strong for a ten-year-old child. I did not think she would be in danger. No one is ever in danger who walks in the Lord's shadow, but I did not walk with the Lord that morning. When I drew Palemerious out and he unfurled his shadow wings to fly, I knew he would not listen, he would not leave. He would soar up into the heavens and out over the wasteland, and return in a rush of darkness and sin to strike again, to befoul and plunder, to leach away the goodness of God's beloved children. They were all at risk, they all would be struck. Or...perhaps just one would be, until I could do more. And into that one I commanded him.

"What?" I shoved my way back, the book skittering across the table, caught by Lucian who moved in the blink of an eye to keep it from falling to the floor.

"He *put* you inside me? You didn't choose it? You weren't trying to possess me?" I looked up at him, and he stared back at me, his face blank except for the hollow, haunted look of uncertainty.

"I don't remember it." He shook his head. "I don't know the words he used, these commands he speaks of. There was only the first child and then the second—what happened in between was lost."

His mouth tightened, but he said no more.

"But how is that possible? And if he put you in me, why didn't he take you out?"

In response, Lucian gave the slightest flick of his fingers, and the book came sailing back toward me, landing in front of me, the cover flapping open, the pages flipping until they stopped several pages past where I had first started reading. I stared at him, not at the book, even as my hands snaked out and drew it closer.

"Do you know what's in here?"

He nodded. "After you opened it, yes. You had to touch it first but now..." He shrugged. "Yes."

I forced my gaze down again.

She makes me stronger.

I blinked, the words blurring but not going away, though I wanted them to go away. Those and the words that came after.

From that day forward, with her at my side, no demon dares to ignore me. I cleansed the afflicted faster, more completely. I knew why. Because this vessel I chose as a temporary trap for a seventh-level demon has become its prison. And she is imprisoned as well, but it's for the greater good. The greater good. I could never do so much as I am now able to. I can help so many more people.

"He used me," I whispered. It wasn't a question, and Lucian didn't give me an answer. He didn't need to. "That's all I was to him?"

Only it wasn't, of course. Because Mordechai also watched me like a researcher hovering over rats in a cage.

It was all there. Every mention I had made of a nightmare, every muttered aside, every rambling confession that had leaked out of me after the exorcisms that we went on together. A detailed accounting of the state of my mother's house and the state of my mother. The quiet donations he had made to ensure that I would have clothes to wear to school, books to read, tuition paid at a private Catholic grade school, then a high school, then a solitary university class a semester. All of that, along with the unflinching admission that he could have taken Palemerious out of me at any time...he simply didn't. Even when he started to become ill, wondering idly if this new affliction was brought to him as penance for the violation he was rendering upon me, even then, he didn't stop, wouldn't stop. He listed the number of exorcisms, notations in the margins, comments made, and after each one, he wrote the same word, underscoring it heavily even in this sanitized copy. Pride.

Pride.

Pride.

"He trapped you inside me, and he wouldn't let you go, and he wouldn't let me go because... Because he couldn't do as well without me? Without you—"

"That isn't all of it, Delia," Lucian said softly.

I looked up to see him staring back at me.

"What?" I demanded. "What could be worse than this? He was my mentor, my *caretaker*. He was the only fucking person in my life who gave a shit about me, and he did all that because of what I could do for him? Because I gave him what, notoriety? People whispering as he walked by, sending him admiring glances? He was a rabbi! He wasn't trying to get laid or anything. At least *that* I could understand. But no, he was just getting off on people thinking he was helping them. Except the only way he was helping them was by hurting me—and hurting you too."

"No."

The roughness of Lucian's voice cleared my mind, and then I finally noticed his fists clenched at his side, his jaw tight, his eyes flaring more red than black.

"He wasn't hurting me, Delia. I never suffered for the time that I spent attached to you. You were not a cage to me. For all that he may have wanted to believe otherwise, at least in the early going, I could have left. It would have been difficult. I would have needed to avoid his efforts to redirect me once again, but I could have left. And I didn't. Even as I damaged you, year after year, exorcism after exorcism, even as I wore down all that was right, good, and true in your soul, I could have left. I didn't."

I opened my mouth to form the question "why?", but I couldn't get it out.

Lucian continued anyway. "There's a reason why Grace was chosen for this particular demonstration, Delia. There's a reason why the creature that crawled into her did so through the window that opened onto the soul of her burgeoning manifestation capabilities, the truest form of human achievement granted to all, but only honed by a few."

He drew in a deep breath, shifting his gaze to the bookshelves, telling his story to them. "I have long enjoyed the taste of spiritual souls. The closer to the edge of proper societal constraints, the better. I relish their ability to see the world with different eyes, and I revel in the act of seeing through them. The horde knew this about me, so they chose Grace for their demonstration as...as a joke. To remind me of all they knew."

I started to speak, but he turned to me, staring at me across the broad expanse of the table. "And that day fifteen years ago when I found myself in you, witnessing your ability, and when I saw how the great and powerful Rabbi Mordechai was using it to devastate more demons, well...I wanted to be a part of that power. It was new, interesting, and for a demon, *interesting* is a potent drug. Over time, I grew to crave the exorcisms like an addiction, yearning for them. Prodding you to return to Mordechai for the next, and the next, and the next. And, you should know...I would do it again."

I set my jaw, but I nodded. "You would."

Fury and betrayal surged within, but something else did too, something more dangerous.

Understanding.

Lucian, this elegant apparition in front of me, this mask of gorgeous male over a dark, infernal beast, was telling the truth. And demons were never more dangerous than when they told the truth. "You want inside me again?" I asked him. "You want to possess me?"

He met my eyes and didn't look away. "Those are two different questions, Delia. And right now, there's only one I'm interested in."

TWENTY-TWO

All the air in the room seemed to go still, the fire still crackling in the hearth but making no sound. My heart beat faster, my blood starting to thrum.

Lucian stood opposite me across the room, the heavy table between us. I knew I was seeing the form he wanted me to see, this well-constructed shedim façade that even now seemed to shimmer a bit at the edges, as if the effort to keep it whole was taxing him more than he wanted to admit, but I didn't care. Lucian wasn't just the skin he wore or the eyes he glared out of, glinting red at the edges. He was allowed to want me for whatever sick and twisted reasons he could conjure up—my spiritual gifts, whatever the fuck those were, the way I felt when he was inside me, the way he felt too.

I'd take that. I wanted that.

Because I wanted him too. I wanted his mouth and teeth on me, tasting me, marking me. I wanted his grip hard upon my wrists and his knees shoving my legs wide. I wanted his breath hot on my body, smelling of cinnamon and smoke, knowing that he had used me, tortured me, damned near ruined me, but

I had come out on the other side stronger. Smarter. And definitely more certain of what I wanted.

And I didn't just want the gorgeous form he was presenting me, the heat and need and want that burned behind his devastated eyes.

I wanted the darkness underneath.

"Delia," he rasped, and he gripped the back of the chair he stood behind, my name sounding ripped from his throat. His body shimmered and twisted a bit more in the brightly lit room, shadows seeming to converge upon it, and I felt the smile curve my lips.

"Lucian," I answered him, and I stood, pushing my own chair to the side. "Tell me what you want."

If anything, his form loosened further, the edges of his suit seeming to roughen and expand, as if the body beneath it was bulking up. His breath hissed out in a long, sinuous slide, and his words, when they came, were lower, more dangerous.

"Delia, the tribunal is less than a day away," he said. "You…" he blew out a shuddering breath. "You don't want to do this right now."

"Oh, I'm pretty sure I do," I said. I reached down and pulled my shirt up in one movement, baring the simple bra I'd thrown on without thinking about it this morning. I pulled it off next, not missing how Lucian leaned forward, his eyes now fever-bright. "In fact, last time I checked, you were a demon of the Ravening Court. A lust demon."

This last I said as I drew my hands along my own body—not lush by any description, but still raw and true and mine. My breasts felt heavy, full, and my waist dipped in then flared over hips still trapped by this morning's half-asleep choice of dark jeans. A good choice for an exorcism, as it turned out. Which reminded me.

"You performed your own exorcism today, commanding Raza out of Grace. You did that, not me," I murmured, sliding my hand around to loosen the top snap of my jeans, tugging down the zipper. "That had to feel good, didn't it?"

"Did," he growled, and there was no denying it. Lucian was definitely losing control of his shedim form. A small, distant part of my brain clocked that, holding it for safekeeping, as a cold, furious fire awakened deep in my belly. I drew in my own breath on a hiss, the unexpected outrage rushing up within me, steeling my spine, twisting my hands into fists as I met his glare with one of my own. If any one of those cock-sucking generals took my demon from me...

A snarling roar was my only warning.

The sound that tore from Lucian's throat was nothing human, nothing that should have been able to emerge from the elegant form he'd been maintaining. It was pure predator, pure need, and the careful construction of his shedim appearance shattered completely.

What lunged across the table toward me wasn't the beautiful, controlled man who'd been gripping that chair. This was something larger, rawer, with shadows that clung to his skin like living things, and eyes that had gone completely crimson.

"*Delia*," he growled, but it was my name wrapped in smoke and flame, and when his hands found my shoulders, they were shaking with the effort not to simply tear through me to get to whatever it was he needed, buried deep within. "I can't—I don't know how to—"

"I *know*," I practically screamed back, and I did. I could see it in the way his form kept shifting, the way his fingers dug into my skin not to hurt but to anchor, like he was drowning, and I was the only solid thing in his universe. "I've got you."

The sound he made then was broken, desperate, and when

he kissed me, it was with the kind of hunger that felt like starvation. His mouth was hot and demanding against mine, and I met him kiss for kiss, bite for bite, because if he was falling apart, if he was exploding into a downward spiral of smoke, pain, and oblivion, then I was going down with him.

"The *tribunal*," he managed against my lips, even as his hands moved restlessly over my bare skin, mapping every curve and hollow like he was memorizing me. "Tomorrow night, they could—"

"Fuck the tribunal," I said fiercely. My hands found the edges of whatever his shirt had become—fabric, shadow, or something in between—and I pulled, needing to feel skin, needing to confirm he was still real under all the supernatural chaos. "Right now, there's just this."

His form shuddered under my touch, and I could feel the moment his control finally snapped completely. The careful boundaries he'd been maintaining, the measured responses, the way he'd been holding himself back—all of it crumbled like a dam bursting.

"I need—" The words came out cracked, raw. "Delia, I can't control—can't stop what I want—"

"Then don't," I told him, and I meant that too. My jeans hit the floor somewhere between one heartbeat and the next, and then there was nothing between us but skin and want and the desperate need to prove that whatever we were, whatever this connection was, it was real.

He lifted me like I weighed nothing, carrying me the few steps to the thick rug by the fire, but when he laid me down, it was with a reverence that contradicted the barely leashed violence in his eyes. His hands shook as they traced the line of my collarbone, the curve of my ribs, like he was afraid I might disappear.

"I've wanted this," he said, and his voice had gone rough,

almost unrecognizable. "From the moment I understood what wanting was. But not like this, not when I'm—" He gestured helplessly at himself, at the way his form kept shifting between human and something far more dangerous.

"But I do," I whispered. "I want this—*this*! Here. Now. This. Exactly like this."

"Yes…" The kiss that followed was different—slower, deeper, like he was trying to pour everything he couldn't say into the press of his lips against mine. And maybe he was. Maybe we both were.

His mouth moved down my throat, finding the pulse point there and lingering, and I felt his teeth scrape gently against my skin. The sensation sent fire racing through my veins, and when I arched beneath him, pressing closer, the sound he made was pure masculine satisfaction.

"*Delia*," he murmured once more against my skin, and there was something almost worshipful in the way he said my name now. His hands found the curve of my waist, the flare of my hips, touching me like I was something precious and dangerous all at once.

I could feel his form stabilizing above me, the chaotic shifting settling into something more solid, more present. Like my acceptance of what he really was had given him permission to stop pretending to be something else.

"Show me," I whispered against his ear, letting my teeth catch his earlobe. "Show me who you are. All of you."

His response was immediate and devastating. He pulled back to look at me, his eyes now a steady, burning crimson, and what I saw there wasn't just hunger—it was recognition. Understanding. The same desperate need that was clawing through my own chest.

"I am this," he hissed, and then his mouth was on mine

again, and there was no more room for words, no more space for doubt or fear or the weight of tomorrow's tribunal.

There was only this moment between us—heat, want, and the absolute certainty that whatever happened next, whatever the courts decided, whatever price we'd both have to pay, it would be worth it for this moment of perfect, honest need.

Lucian reached out his hand, spreading his fingers wide. For just a second, the hand elongated into sharp, cruel claws. Then that glamour broke as well, and a different hand appeared. Golden, long-fingered, shimmering at the edges like it was filled with lightning trying to escape.

I met it with my own hand, our fingers tangling, and the golden energy moved from his hand to mine. It shot up my forearm, the heat painful and prickling beneath my skin. Reflexively, I pulled back, and his hand clamped down, claws reappearing to cage my fingers. Then he was back in his shedim form and yanking me toward him, his other arm going around me and hauling me close as he toppled me on top of him in front of the roaring fire.

The rug here was thick, ample, more to ward off embers thrown from the hearth, I was pretty sure, than impromptu lovemaking, but I didn't care. The energy in this room was nothing like the drawing room where he'd first taken me in this place. It was warmer, inviting. Human.

And in this room, I'd pinned a demon beneath me, my hands shackling his wrists, my knees spilling over his waist. Even though I was technically in the position of power here, I felt vulnerable, like I'd caught a tornado by mistake and all I could do was hold on.

"Kiss me," Lucian murmured, and I leaned down over him, releasing his wrists to stabilize my hands beside his head. His arms snaked around me, and I dropped my lips to his, tasting salt and heat, and the heady mix of exotic spices...and something else beneath all that, something that had me pressing closer, my tongue dipping into his mouth, trying to catch quicksilver magic with my lips.

"You taste like sunshine," I murmured, my words lost as he deepened the kiss, his body curling beneath mine, his arms lifting me, then smoothly rolling me over so that our positions were once more shifted. He laid my head back on blankets I hadn't noticed, and he stared down at me, but his eyes were strange, now, almost alien. Not only black and red, but shot through with blinding white-gold light. I stared up, transfixed, and he dropped his mouth to my ear.

"Shhh," he murmured. "Say nothing."

I shivered as he moved down my body, his lips soft and searching, not the ripping binding heat that I knew we could share but something different, something almost reverent. He suckled my breast, teeth grazing my nipple, the sweet slide of pain and pleasure making me arch beneath him and moan incoherent words of encouragement.

He chuckled then, the sound once again sounding heavier than it should, as if coming from a different place deep within him. It rumbled through my body, settling in my bones, but when he dropped his mouth to my rib cage, then to the curve of my belly, I lost all memory of it. Instead, I groaned, arching up to meet him. My hands gripped his shoulders as he took me with his mouth, breathing damp heat between my legs, licking and tasting, murmuring words I didn't understand, couldn't follow as his tongue found the quivering, sensitive nub of my clit, then teased and tortured it, washing me in waves of heat and cold, a crashing, conflicting tide.

I built and built toward climax, but just as I was about to peak, he shifted, allowing his mouth to roam over my thigh, my hip bone, trailing hot kisses along my sensitized skin before circling back to send me soaring again. By the third time, I was shaking. By the fourth, when he finally levered himself up and over me, I could barely breathe.

"Mine," he said, sliding into me, stretching me wide. I blinked, and I saw it again, that electric shimmer chasing over his body, his skin seeming to go almost golden, then blue-white, energy arching up and away from him almost like, almost like—

Something in my face registered with him, angering him, clearly, because he sharpened his gaze on me, his mouth curling into a harsh sneer. The glittering light winked out, and now, hovering over me, driving into me, was a demon. Not the ugly beast that I had witnessed scaring the daylights out of Grace, but the large, raw-boned, dark-haired, bronze and broken creature I had painted on my walls, his hair long and lank, his face haggard and wet with tears and blood, while charred angry stumps stretched up from his shoulders as if once glorious wings had been ripped away, burned off him alive. Lucian fell on me as if cast out of heaven itself, and I wrapped my arms around him, my body overwhelmed with emotion. In a blink, my own climax spiked, and I shattered with him inside me, spasming around him, unable to stop.

"Delia," he whispered, that single word slicing into me like a dagger, deep and low.

"*Mine*," I cried out, my voice muffled against his shoulder, my teeth rending his flesh, as I held on with all my might. For in that moment, he was being taken from me, I somehow knew. He was being ripped away. He was being pulled out of my feeble grasp and tossed into oblivion.

"You can't *leave* me," I ordered, and I anchored my hands on his back, my legs around his hips, pulling him into me, driving him deep as I arched my body up to meet him thrust for thrust. "You can't, won't. We are *bound*. That matters!"

He stared down at me with eyes as black as pitch, red fire

dancing around the edges. There was no more gold, now, no more blue-white light. There was only heat and darkness.

"*Bound*," he gasped, then he shuddered over me, and heat spilled through me like molten fire, so hot, too hot, but I wouldn't let go. I couldn't let go. I would never let go.

The clock struck 4 p.m.

TWENTY-THREE

Lucian and I walked along the Victorian's secretive, murmuring corridors without touching, without speaking. The energy that vibrated off us was already too much. It seemed to shimmer off the walls, ceiling, and floor, clamoring and twisting like a living thing.

When the clock had struck four bare minutes ago, we'd rolled away from each other like we'd been caught out by the house itself. In some ways, I suppose we had. Still, in that moment, I hadn't felt awkward or embarrassed. It probably would've been more normal if I had. Instead, I'd felt strangely comfortable. Accepted, as if the house had witnessed Lucian and my frantic, desperate lovemaking, and approved.

I didn't think notching the approval of the haunted house was my best move, but here we were.

Beside me, stalking along the velvet-wallpapered corridor, Lucian remained silent, as if he, too, was afraid to break the fragile bond of solidarity between us. Did he feel the energy of the house as well? The approval? Did he have a better handle on whatever was happening between us?

He chuckled softly, and lifted his hand as we walked along, then let it fall gently down. Though he wasn't touching me, I felt a trailing pressure along my arm, drifting down to my wrist.

I jerked away, turning on him as I stopped short in the middle of the hallway. "Stop that. You did that before," I accused. "After I left your apartment, after you *attacked* me, I felt your hands on me as I rode the elevator down to the first floor—the whole way down! What is that? How can you do that all of a sudden? Because you couldn't do it before. Or you *didn't*, at least. I thought our connection was, I don't know..." I flapped a hand at him. "Fading."

"It's supposed to be fading, yes," he said, his eyes dark and stormy, as if he *could* sense the same shimmering intensity between us, the same disquieting touch. "And this isn't the same as the bond of possession. With that, I knew what you felt. I understood it intellectually, but I couldn't feel it, myself. If anything, I tamped down your senses—sight and smell, taste and touch and hearing. I was a weight that dragged."

I frowned, though of course, I knew what he meant. I hadn't thought about it at the time, because I hadn't known anything different. But he definitely had been a weight on me, dragging me down without me realizing it. "And now?"

He shrugged, but started walking again, and I fell into step beside him, the energy sparking again between us. "Now, in the moments after we entangle ourselves together, whether in rage or passion, I can retain that connection. I can still *feel* you— touch you. It doesn't last, but it's there." He frowned. "It's as if, for a few moments, I'm human."

I snorted. "Let me assure you, humans don't connect like that. Not by a long shot."

Something flared in his dark eyes as he glanced at me, the red flame brightening around the iris, and then we were climbing the final set of stairs to the turret room and no more conversation was possible.

I had no problem with that. I didn't want to think about how wrong this developing connection with Lucian was...I just didn't want it to go away.

Roy glanced up with tight, focused energy when we entered the slightly ajar door of the turret room. Any concern I had that he'd notice the impact of the last two hours on Lucian and me was immediately dispelled as he launched in.

"Figured you'd know what to do when I propped open the door, but we're good," he said excitedly. "We're more than good. It's been a minute since I've done one of these, but some things you just don't forget. I put it up under Darker Truths, did a voice masking with some AI rolled in, and off we go to the races. For good measure, I used a spoofed email account to alert some of the diehard fans in the city, and they're already starting to sniff around."

"A spoofed account?" I questioned. "Won't that make people nervous?"

"Should, but we're not talking ordinary people here. We're talking people who want something spooky to come out of the dark. I was just today's spooky. And I didn't include a link, just directions on how to find the link. That kind of secured instruction plays pretty well. Throw a couple crumbs down, and they'll follow along for a bit if the smell is good enough."

I smiled at that. Granger's scent had caught me when I first walked in the room: granola, lemon pudding, and steadiness. I found myself hoping irrationally that his podcast took off, for no other reason than I liked to see him smile.

"Any movement from Dark Streets yet?" I asked.

"Oh, yeah. First thing I did was set up analytics on the pass-through page, and I'm the one who designed their system, so you could say I am uniquely qualified to know who's checking us out and from where. But they haven't tapped over yet. Need-less to say, they weren't on my email list." He grinned. "How-ever, they *have* put up a preview of the next show which is going to be dropping probably within the next hour if I know their cadence for promo. We're going to want to keep an eye on that."

Lucian hummed under his breath. "What will they feature?"

"Unknown. I don't think they're going to have anything remotely as good as us, but what they have could be interesting —nothing to do with the warehouse incident, I'm thinking, but something. Sue has been hella jacked the last few days, and not secretive about it, either. She's not one to read the room. Prob-ably why she didn't make it as an actress, though she's got a hell of a voice."

My phone buzzed, and I pulled it out. "Claire's ready," I told Lucian. "She wants to know if Sergei can pick her up or if she can, and I quote, Uber like a normal person."

Lucian's lips twitched. "I'd say she's effectively given up her claim on normal for the foreseeable future."

"I'd say you're right," Roy said, standing as well. "But I'm done here, so I can head out too. It'll just take me a minute to pack up."

I exchanged a glance with Lucian, but we were instantly aligned on this topic.

"If you don't mind, I'd like you to come with us and leave your stuff here," I said. "It'll be perfectly safe, but there's a lot of loose energy running around, and it would probably be better if we kept tabs on the pod."

He chuckled. "As well as on me, I get it."

His eyes swiveled to Lucian again. "You're a shedim, aren't you? Heard of you guys but never met one in the flesh. To be honest, didn't know if that was Jewish mumbo jumbo, but I'd be the first to tell you that a lot of what we think is mumbo jumbo turns out to be stone-cold truth. Wouldn't mind having a conversation with you sometime."

As he spoke, he hastily gathered up several things for his bag, including a laptop, two different phones, and a boom mic.

"You'd like to interview me for your show?" Lucian asked with amusement.

"Well, it wouldn't be a bad idea—whoa!"

He took a step back, and I shot a startled glance at Lucian, but he looked the same to me. Maybe shimmery around the edges, but otherwise the same.

"What is it?" I asked.

"We should get going," Lucian said tersely. He turned on his heel and exited, leaving a clearly unnerved Roy staring in his wake.

"Holy shit," Roy muttered, but he didn't look at me, didn't look at anything but the floor in front of him and then the stairs as he clattered down after Lucian, leaving me to follow in his wake. "Holy shit," he muttered again.

Sergei already had the SUV running when we exited the house, clearly notified by Lucian. Roy got in the back with me, Lucian riding shotgun, and I eyed the older man with curiosity as he opened his laptop.

"Everything okay?" I asked, but whatever Lucian had allowed him to see in the turret room had dimmed in importance to what he was seeing on screen now. He gave a low, intrigued whistle.

"More than okay. Damn, if I had had these kinds of tools back in the day? Not only able to put up content, but track it like this? Game changer. And Houston, we have liftoff."

He turned the screen toward me, but if he expected me to be impressed with the colorful graph that danced across it, he was destined to be disappointed. He didn't seem to mind.

"What that's showing is that we're already getting likes,

comments, and views," he said. "Goddamn network in Chicago, always hungry for the real shit, and they can sniff it out a mile away."

"Are they saying anything about your video?" I asked, but he shook his head. "Not yet, no, though we've got some action from one of Dark Street's top commenters. Basically, dude's acting like an ad for Sue and the gang, saying we ain't got shit, that theirs is going to blow my post away. Ordinarily, I'd have a mod take that down, but not in this case. In this case, the denial just gives me credibility. And nobody's saying jack about the quality of my video, which is good because it's some of my best work. So much faster now." He shook his head. "It's like night and day."

The synapses in my brain finally started firing with that comment. I frowned at him. "Speaking of, we should probably know what you put up."

He grinned at me. "Wondered when you'd get around to that. But I don't think you'll have a problem with it."

He turned the laptop toward me as Sergei announced we were three minutes out from Grace's house. Lucian said something in response, but I could track nothing but the video unspooling before me. "Sixty seconds?" I asked, looking at the timestamp. "That's all you got?"

"That's all I'm showing," he corrected. "Cold audiences have the attention span of goldfish. They can sign up for exclusive access if they want the full enchilada. Which, as it happens, I'm still rendering. But I think this is good enough to start."

It was more than good enough.

The camera panned up over the charred chalk circle to show the backs of Sergei, Claire, and Steve. Through their figures you could see a woman sitting bound in a chair, but only portions of her torso, her gripped hands on her knees. Beside her, kneeling, was another figure which I knew to be me, but I was smudged and indistinct. Some sort of editing powers on Granger's part? Or was that how the video captured me?

I thought back to Lucian, the way his body shimmered and wavered at the edges. Was that happening to me too? Wasn't I supposed to be getting better the further away I got from exorcising him out of me, not worse?

I stiffened as Grace threw her head back and screamed, the sound playing out on the video as a second person's voice—mine—exhorted her with garbled words. And then something else appeared. A figure larger than any of us swooped down with a distinct form of talons and meaty legs, wings, and horns, so fast I was convinced I missed it. It hovered and spoke words as garbled as mine, then shot back up, all in the space of a few seconds. Then blood burst from Grace's arm, smoke billowed, and the camera went sideways.

I looked up to see Roy grinning at me, practically bouncing in his seat.

"Your camera didn't go sideways," I said.

"That's all you have to say? That is largely *unedited* video! I mean, yes, I added the effect of dropping the camera, but before that, everything on there was *actual* footage. I didn't do jack shit to it. There was no augmentation or amplification. It was straight up real, and I *caught it on camera*."

Lucian's voice flowed back to us. "And did you consider why that was allowed?" he asked, the soul of reason.

"Ahhh...no?" Roy made a face as I peered at Lucian.

"Uh-oh. Is this a problem?" I asked, which earned me a low chuckle.

"Not a problem in the eyes of the Creator, I can assure you. But whenever a demon offers you a gift, you would be wise to question it."

"We're here," Sergei announced, and I looked up to see that, in fact, we were in front of Grace's home. Claire stood in the front walk, on her phone. She hustled toward us, sliding into the back seat once she realized the middle seat was taken up with passengers and electronics.

"Grace's parents are on their way back from Belgium as we speak," she said. "Steve and Sandy are staying with Grace until some aunt or another arrives from Cleveland to stay with her. They apparently have an entire treatment plan worked out with Grace's main therapist for her dissociative disorder, but they never pursued it because Grace got much better at managing her episodes." She made a face. "You ask me, her parents wanted to believe that her condition was a problem that simply went away. They'll make sure she has someone watching her 24/7 until she's in a more intensive program, though, to make sure that she stays stable. Honestly, it'll be super interesting to see how quickly she improves. I mean, yes, she had her disorder long before she got infested with a demon, but now that it's gone...maybe her disorder will improve as well, you know?"

I opened my mouth, but she cut me off with a wave. "Before you ask, no. She's exhibiting no signs of Post Traumatic Possession Disorder that I can see. Manifesting Grace, when she comes to the fore, spends a lot of time crying and wanting to wrap her arms around Steve. Sandy thinks that's a good sign, and the parents have already signed Sandy on for ongoing care once Grace gets cleared by a more advanced therapy team. Steve, however, is officially freaked out."

I snorted, but still, I had to agree. "That's a very good sign, I would think. She's got a long road ahead of her, though."

Claire sighed and sat back. "She's got an interesting road, for sure," she agreed. "What do you guys have going on?" She peered at me as if suddenly catching something. "Is everything okay? You seem different."

Before I could answer, Roy shifted beside me.

"Check it, they dropped the pod. It's short. It's sort of like mine, actually, a teaser. And I don't think that's what they intended. Their audience isn't cold. But they maybe rushed the production of the thing, and, of course, I'm not there to serve as backup." He scratched his jaw. "I hadn't quite thought that through, but oh well, a problem for another day. You gotta check this out."

He turned the laptop toward us, and Claire leaned forward in her seat. The video showed Sue Willows talking with a man in a half mask and dark clothing. The guy was sitting back in a chair, one shoulder drooped, one hand splayed over his knee.

"...very special guest here today, someone who has looked evil in the face and lived to tell the tale, but not without suffering grave bodily harm," Sue said, in her best serious voice. "We've masked his identity for his own safety, and the voice that you'll hear has been modified as well. But it doesn't make his story any less frightening. There'll be more soon, but we couldn't wait to share this piece with you."

She turned to him. "Tell us what happened and where, while you were there," she said, her voice turning cold. The man's mouth below his mask turned into a petulant pout, and Claire sat up straight.

"Oh, my God," she said as a voice came out over the speaker that was in no way human.

"I've only been in the city a little while," the man said. "Just long enough to get my feet underneath me, you know. I'm a drifter. Have been for a while now. I like it that way. But I couldn't *not* share this story."

Sue broke for a promotional plug insertion, while the energy inside our SUV exploded.

"He's lying," Lucian put in, but Claire flapped her hands.

"That's Jay," she squeaked. "I'd recognize that thing he does with his mouth anywhere. He may be lying, but he's mostly pissed off that he's not getting his way about something. I saw that more times than I could count when I was in high school. I don't know what deal he made with Sue, but he's very much reconsidering it, and he's a snake. He can pivot on a dime if he needs to."

"He'd better," Sergei put in. "Volkov determined he was the source of the leak about the activity at Descent. He was allowed to remain in the back rooms too long when we had another incursion of mischief demons. He knows what will happen if he is indiscreet again."

"What?" Claire bleated, while on the screen, Jay continued. "I'm telling you the truth. I was attacked by dark forms, larger than anything I'd ever seen. Claws, horns, teeth."

"Interesting that this happened in one of Chicago's most popular night spots," Sue Willows put in. "You'd think the owners of Descent would be more careful."

Whatever she said struck a nerve with Jay, and his eyes narrowed.

"Uh-oh," Claire murmured beside me, and I nodded.

"Not Descent," he said, and for the first time, his lips tweaked into a smile.

"What?" Sue said, appearing genuinely surprised. "You're telling me you're changing your story?"

"That's exactly what I'm telling you." He leaned forward urgently. "I couldn't tell the truth when we first talked. There were too many people listening. But if you want to see where these creatures are, you need to go to Storm Court, not Descent. That's where the action is."

Roy whistled under his breath. "I've heard that name before," he said. "Not here, though. It's a club in New York. Didn't know they had an outpost here."

Jay kept talking. "There's been a whole lot of movement in and out of that place, and only some of it's human. I'm not joking." He spoke with such certainty that Claire muttered sheesh under her breath, and I turned to see her staring wide-eyed, her skin pale.

She met my gaze. "He scared me," she said. "When he got like that. He could convince you to do anything and make you believe it was your idea. Still…" She cast her gaze forward to Sergei, who seemed to be spending a lot of time eyeballing her in the rearview mirror. "He's been hurt?"

"Not bad," Sergei said, but coming from the burly Romanian, that wasn't much comfort to Claire.

Sergei kept talking. "Where is the Dark Streets studio? Where are they recording? We should find out what else he says before it is broadcast for all to hear."

Roy rattled off the address, and Sergei changed direction, speeding across Chicago as the show continued. They were pitching it as a teaser with a full interview to follow, and Sue Willows closed with a meaningful stare at the camera. "For the latest and most complete information and the most authentic podcast in Chicago, stay tuned to Dark Streets."

"Sounds defensive, don't you think?" Roy said with a grin.

"Definitely defensive," Claire agreed.

"He's been located and detained," Sergei said, earning him startled looks from everyone but Lucian. He abruptly changed course again, not speaking more until we turned into a crowded parking lot and drew up next to another vehicle, this one a paneled van. Claire yelped as her door suddenly popped open and a mid-sized male was shoved in next to her, his head in a bag.

"Jay!" Claire said automatically as the door slammed shut, and she reached out and ripped the hood from the man's face.

"Um…Claire?" Jay stared at her, an angry bruise blooming along one cheek and his pallor much more pronounced than it had seemed in the video. His hand was bandaged as well, which made me wonder if he had fought back in the back rooms of

Descent. His skittering eyes bounced around the vehicle. "What's happening?"

"We saw you just now. On the podcast. I recognized you," Claire said, her voice strong and sure, though I was pretty sure she hadn't expected to come face to face with her high school tormentor this evening.

"But how would you know to look for that?" he sputtered. "They literally just started airing it." Clearly confused, he swung his head around, and then he saw Sergei in the front of the vehicle. He went still.

"She's a friend," Sergei said, leaning into his Romanian accent. Jay clearly had seen him before, and he swung his eyes back to Claire.

"It's like high school all over again, isn't it?" he said bitterly. "You're always one step ahead."

"What do you mean?" Claire asked, genuinely taken aback. "You were the one who harassed me."

"Yeah, yeah, I did," Jay said. "And then you got out. I don't know how, I don't know what happened in that fucking lab, but by the time Lily and I got out of the hospital, everything was jacked up. She blamed me, made my life a living nightmare until I left, and nothing was ever right again. I just wanted to be a part of her world, I guess, thought I *was* in her world. But I wasn't. You got out ahead of it, and I got kicked out. And it seems like all I do is get kicked out, no matter what I do."

Guilt had clawed its way across Claire's expression, freezing her mouth in a rictus of distress, and once again, Sergei came to the rescue.

"You hurt her?" he rumbled.

"Yeah, I guess I did," Jay said, glancing toward him. "I was a kid, and I got caught up with the wrong girl. But I never laid a hand on her. Just a lot of talk and stupidity."

"He's right," Claire said, though it clearly pained her. "Lily wasn't an idiot; she kept her threats to blackmail. Jay never hurt me though."

"And you got out ahead of it," he said again. I didn't know what he meant exactly, but Claire seemed to.

Sergei grunted, his eyes still watching her in the rearview mirror in between checking traffic. "You changed their attention to focus on Storm Court," he said.

Jay shifted in his seat. "Yeah, I did. Sue and I talked once—just once!—and I told her about Descent. I love her podcast, and, well, it's kind of a scary place. I thought she'd be into it, and she was. But once she started talking about bringing in cameras and planting spies and all that, I realized what I'd done. I mean, I feel bad about what's about to descend on Storm Court, but..."

"They can worry about their own," Sergei said. "They are prideful and a problem. It was a good redirection."

The expression of surprise and hope on Jay's face poked at me, and Claire bit her lip. "You need anything for the pain?" she asked.

He smiled a little lopsidedly. "A stiff drink maybe," he said. "And I won't talk to Sue Willows again. Not unless it helps."

"Good," Sergei said. He drove on and a renewed silence settled over the car, punctuated only by Roy tapping on his computer.

"Where are we going anyway?" Jay asked, and Lucian turned back toward him, something in his expression making Jay back all the way up against his seat.

"Do you really want to know?" Lucian asked, before he dissolved completely into mist—just...disappeared.

"*Shit*! No," Jay said quickly, his eyes going wide. "Maybe you could just take me home?"

TWENTY-FOUR

LUCIAN

Lucian regained his shedim form a block from Descent, and he wasn't surprised to find a man similar in size and stature to Sergei waiting for him at the private entrance. It was barely four o'clock, and the club itself wouldn't be jumping for hours, but the horde didn't keep a schedule like humans did. They were always up for a party.

He fought to maintain his form as the guard led him down a corridor with polished parquet flooring and heavy oak doors. He was meeting Volkov in his private offices today, not simply the viewing rooms of one of the club's dance floors.

At least Volkov was taking this seriously. He should. The summons that had ripped Lucian bodily from his vehicle had been impossible to ignore. The temporary attempt he'd lodged against it had cost him, gutting him with pain that rivaled what he'd felt in his building a few days earlier.

It was an effective leash. For the first time in all his millennia of life on this earth, he'd felt the possibility of a banishment he might not return from, a banishment beyond the reach of Hell itself. Of course, there was always the possibility that the Creator would be waiting for him on the other side of that banishment, but Lucian didn't like his odds for that meeting. He needed a different strategy.

The bodyguard stopped at a door that was indistinguishable from the others, and he knocked but didn't wait for permission to enter. He simply pushed in and stood to the side, gesturing Lucian ahead of him. Lucian didn't know this human. Then again, up until a very short time ago, he hadn't paid much attention to humans of any stripe.

Nikolai looked up as he entered. The self-appointed mafia kingpin of the demon-human crossroads in Chicago wasn't sitting at his imposing desk in the corner. Instead, he reclined at the large central table set up with dark wine and darker spirits that glinted in glittering tumblers.

"You really know how to rush a party," he said as Lucian stepped into the room. The bodyguard quietly closed the door behind him.

"If I'd realized I was so popular, I might have come back sooner."

"I guess that's the sticking point, isn't it?" Nikolai gestured for him to sit. "Everyone wants to be wanted, even apparently the generals of the horde. You hurt their feelings, Lucian, trying to flee Belial's court. You made them feel unloved."

"Yes, well, I'm not sure they'll be pleased to find that I haven't learned my lesson. But it's you that I need to have a conversation with, not them."

"And not me either, for that matter," Nikolai said. He took a glass and handed it to Lucian, one of the small cut-crystal tumblers with dark liquid swirling in its depths.

"She is my responsibility should the need arise," he continued. He toasted Lucian and waited for him to tip the drink back before lifting his own glass to his lips and drinking the spirits down. Without Delia present, Lucian expected the liquor to taste like a slurry of ash, like most drinks tasted to him. To his surprise, it didn't. The taste wasn't as rich and rolling as he'd come to expect when Delia was near, but there was no question that he had an unusual connection to Nikolai Volkov as well. Interesting.

Nikolai made it more interesting.

The other man set his glass on the table and met Lucian's eyes with his own hard gaze. "After you return, which I expect you will, we don't have to face this impasse again. Together, we can make her stronger."

The tension stretched between the two men, quivering in the air.

"Safer," Lucian corrected. "It is more important that she is safe."

Nikolai shrugged, still watching him with his one fully working eye. The other was now protected beneath a black silk patch. "The strong are always safe," he pointed out.

Lucian settled back in his chair, but the human wasn't wrong. Still. "If I don't return, her safety is on you. And no matter how far away I am cast, I won't forget that."

Nikolai had no sooner nodded, his smile curving his lips, than the door behind Lucian burst open. A horde of fifth-level Rage demons exploded into the room, sweeping around him in an instant, wrapping him in chains. Lucian and Nikolai locked gazes, both of them knowing that this would be the last human he would see until it was all over, and Lucian didn't miss the fact that Nikolai clamped his own hands on the arms of his chair, forcibly restraining himself from leaping up to intervene. That would solve nothing, and the human had his own job to do here. At least the drink had tasted halfway decent.

The screaming of the horde filled Lucian's ears as they crashed through the floor of Volkov's office and raced down,

down, the chains wrapping tighter around him instead of loosening as they fell, acknowledging his seventh-level status. A status that had taken some demons millennia to attain, but not him. He'd started out at the top. He was going to remain there.

As he fell, the pressure of Delia's body beneath his played back over his mind. These last precious moments, before his thoughts would be opened and violated by the scourge of fools that dared to stop him, he'd think about what he wanted to. After that, he would lock it down.

They imagined that he gave a shit about what they thought he should do, who they thought he should be. But he had miscalculated, for all his dismissal of them. He hadn't protected himself against this. And now the very idea that they might keep him from this life he had only now begun to form, to give flesh and life and breath to, filled him with such rage that he had to force himself to remember that he was the accused, not the accuser. He was the one being dragged forward and held accountable, not the one passing deadly judgment.

They were lucky.

As if the assembled courts could sense his fury, the chains tightened around Lucian as he dropped into the center of a large chamber, his knees buckling as he slammed to the floor, but not breaking. Never that. Instead, he straightened, fury driving through him as he glared at the assemblage of his peers —and it was only peers too, or close to it, demons from the fifth-level up. No shedim here, excluded in part for their lack of strength but also, he suspected, because the higher-level horde didn't want to think too much about those among them who could walk with humans, talk with them—touch and take them. They had worked hard to reach their station and had no interest in looking back...and they certainly didn't realize that dipping backward the way he had, still maintaining their hard-won higher status but making adjustments to accommodate the lower form, brought more carnal delight than they could possibly imagine.

He wasn't about to enlighten them.

"Palemerious." The sinuous slide of his name on Asmodaea's lips made him stiffen, but only internally. He wouldn't give the highest-ranking commander of Samael the pleasure of believing she could best him. As his primary accuser, these proceedings were hers to direct, but that was all she would get from this.

He met her gaze across the room, taking in her affect with a curl of his lip. She was beautiful and sleek in this form, her Wrath connection displayed in the wild tumble of her dark hair, the daggers at her hips. She wore leather, as most Wrath demons did when they chose human glamour in the demon realm, and the dark sheath hugged her hard-angled figure, looking as angry as she perpetually was.

So of course, he piled on.

"Asmodaea." He inclined his head, and when he brought it up again, meeting her gaze, he brightened his internal anger the barest notch. It was enough to turn his dead-gray iron chains to purest gold, and then to dissolve that gold into dust, pouring off him until he stood in the center of a sea of glistening sand. As predicted, the demons of the tribunal keened with joy—all that was pretty in the human world never failed to fascinate them, even when he was supposed to be the entertainment.

"Enough!" Asmodaea howled, and with a slashing command in the ancient tongue of the damned, she ordered his bindings to be reset. Lucian allowed it, his chin up, his eyes narrowing as he surveyed the horde around him. The Ravening Court was poorly represented here, which was actually to his favor. Belial, of course, reclined in the far corner, watching him moodily, with something approaching desire beneath his hooded eyes. Belial desired everything; it was why he had chosen this court overall to command. But what he lusted after was not total subjugation like some of the other generals, simply effectiveness. And the signal that he showed by not having his other lieutenants in attendance was a revelation to Palemerius. If he could survive this, Belial had already determined a use for him. For just a moment, Lucian allowed himself to wonder what that use would be.

First, of course, he had to survive whatever Asmodaea and the other generals planned to throw at him. Each of the courts was represented—Belial, of course, of the Ravening Court, and Asmodaea for Wrath, but also functionaries from Pride, Indulgence and Envy, Greed, and finally, Sloth...in fact, there were more representatives of the Indolent Court than he would have expected, up to and including their corpulent general, Leviathan. That struck him as wrong, somehow, problematic, but he didn't have time to consider it too closely as Asmodaea took up her case.

"Generals, commanders, and agents of darkness all, I speak today not only for myself, but for all of you," she said, strolling onto the chamber floor where Lucian stood, once more wrapped in restraints, this time of heavy iron. He watched her with amusement, but as she neared, he could sense the power she wielded.

It was stronger than he remembered. He'd been gone a scant fifteen years, but Asmodaea had used the time to her advantage.

"The crimes that Palemerious has committed have not been solely against me," she continued, "but against the very nature of who we are. The pulsing, needful urgency that props up this abysmal plane and ensures that it remains livable for all of us, lest we devolve into a squabbling horde that the righteous are so eager to describe us as. But we are not the horde, not at this level. Our strength is in our unity and our structure. We have honed the art of our existence over long millennia since we chose to remain on this earth, and our few rules are sacrosanct, even sacred. And yet, here we have Palemerious, who would want to break those rules for his own fickle will. Palemerious, who, if you will recall, disappeared without a trace seventeen years ago, apparently burying himself as the possessor of some insipid child. Not your usual taste at all, Palemerious. We well know you have cultivated a slightly more rarefied palette, feasting on humans who aspire to see beyond their pitiful station. But no, not this time. You slunk into a child and almost made it out if the accounts are to be believed, and there always are accounts, Palemerious. You above all should know that."

Lucian watched her with disdain, burying the first tremor of doubt that slid through him at her constant repetition of his name. It was, in its way, its own binding ritual, rooting him to the floor of this chamber as effectively as his iron bonds.

He couldn't show weakness, of course. He certainly couldn't show fear or any emotion that a demon of Wrath would feed upon. But, in truth, he felt weakness, doubt, fear, and some surprise. How did she know so much about him? How had she guessed? Mordechai's accounts didn't have a record of his reasoning for entering the first child, only why he had chosen to transplant him into Delia Thompson. How in the world had Asmodaea discovered his plan?

No one could have talked, because he had told no one. No one could have known, because no one had shared his thoughts. No one...except Delia herself, unknowing, unwitting. Delia, talking in her sleep, writing on her walls.

Asmodaea continued. "But his plan was foiled by an agitator we knew all too well, the rabbi exorcist who wielded his puny powers day and night to save his flock. And it was this *rabbi*," she said the honorific as if it were a slur, "who managed to catch the trailing edge of Palemerious and imprison him in a new human host, a human host who *did* possess the kind of characteristics that we all know have delighted Palemerious over the centuries. A young girl who grew up to become the exorcist's assistant, as he increased his power and reach with each new challenge to our strength."

She smiled, turning to address the gallery, who regarded her now with rapt fascination. "Do you think for even one moment that Mordechai's remarkable ascent of power through our ranks, his ability to achieve his success, was solely due to the efforts of a *child*? I don't believe it for a second. If I'd been looking for it, it would have been evident to me long before now. Alas and alack, I, like all of you, was duped by Palemerious's strategy. But...Palemerious was caught off guard too, I think. For when he was buried in that pile of human offal, that simpering child, he *did* develop another taste. One for harming his own kind."

She circled back, and Palemerious had to hand it to her, she was making a convincing argument. He hadn't thought about his enjoyment of Mordechai's activities as anything more than the passing pleasantry of a human well chosen, especially given that he thought that he had done the choosing. But Asmodaea wasn't wrong. He *had* enjoyed punishing demons, routing them from their insidious nests, and sending them on their way, perhaps with a bit more pain than Mordechai ever realized. He'd relished the opportunity to defy them and deny them their pleasure of possession, even as he enjoyed his own more deeply with every passing year.

"And as if all of that wasn't bad enough," Asmodaea said, clearly relishing the attention lavished on her by the slavering onlookers. "When he was finally exorcised by his very own human, he still chose to hide. He didn't return to Belial and pay the attention due his own general. No, he slid into the lesser form of a shedim so that he could continue his liaison with the human, never mind the shattering boredom of that form. He had to do it for some reason, after all, he is a demon of lust."

She turned, her purred words floating out over the gallery. "And what would that reason be, do you think?"

Lucian stiffened. He hadn't thought this through, at all. If they realized, if they understood the passion, the *power* that he had experienced with Delia, if they had one iota of it, she wouldn't be safe. Neither would other humans, but he gave not one shit about that—only Delia. He had put Delia in danger.

Drawing in a careful breath, he gathered his strength, building it, condensing it, supercharging it. He would die, he thought. He would absolutely die and go to the ends of the universe to face the void eternal, before he would let a demon—

Then Asmodaea shocked him.

"Because he wanted to kill again," she announced.

She whirled as if this were the greatest crime, and of course, to a demon it was, but Lucian met her gaze evenly, grimly hoping she couldn't see the relief in his eyes.

"And he did," she seethed. "The first chance he got, he sent Mirr not simply back to his origin within the pits of Hell, but he obliterated him from this earthly plane entirely. What say you to these crimes, Palemerious?" she challenged, practically gloating. "How do you plead?"

Lucian smiled with perhaps more pleasure than he should. "Guilty, of course."

The court erupted in fury, and Asmodaea turned and delivered a second surprising blow, cutting to the end game of the tribunal without entertaining any more challenges—or defense.

"Generals, stand forth!" she called. "For to you it falls to judge the twice fallen—and remove him from our sight."

CHAPTER

TWENTY-FIVE

LUCIAN

"No."

Lucian held himself very still as Belial roused himself from his lazy sprawl in the gallery and stepped forward, but he noted that none of the other generals stood. Leviathan probably couldn't, rooted in place through his own spreading bulk, and Caim of the court of Envy was simply watching with amusement. Astaroth of the Gilded Court looked appropriately bored, his aristocratic glamour pale, blond, and untroubled, and Lucian spared a thought for whether or not he knew about the raid forthcoming on his own human outpost, Storm Court.

A problem for another day; he needed to keep his focus on Belial.

The general of the Ravening Court didn't often trouble himself with the dramas of the court he ran. His was the purview of lust, but it wasn't the lust for power, simply plea-sure. Lucian had always appreciated that about him. But that didn't mean that Belial wasn't capable of great strength or the

253

ability to deliver exquisite pain. Pain was one of the few things the demons could experience, after all. In the vernacular of these times, fear and pain were a demon's love languages, even among themselves. And pain could be as addictive as any other vice.

Belial strolled down to the chamber floor. "You summoned us here at your own expense, Asmodaea," he said. "But you cannot command us—even me, who ordinarily would have a say in these proceedings, which you conveniently seem to have forgotten. I would suggest caution, if you understood the subtleties of that state."

Asmodaea stiffened. Lucian fought the smirk. In her own court, she was revered as even more powerful than Samael, rumored to be his assigned successor should there ever be a need. But she wasn't holding forth in the Court of Ruin, now. She was in Belial's presence, acting as a proxy general without any of their power, and her own protector wasn't present. By the time Belial reached the chamber floor, the room had gone fully silent.

She didn't stay quiet for long.

"The question isn't about my role here, but that of Palemerious," she drawled his name to bind him anew, disdain oozing from every word. Though she spoke in a low, almost mesmerizing cadence, her voice filled the space, commanding attention.

She turned with a dramatic flourish. "When, exactly, did Palemerious begin betraying his pledge of service to those of us who walk this path by his side? When did he stop honoring our sacred past and cleave to...well, not the human realm, certainly, but neither is he honoring what we have fought to preserve so strenuously over time. When did he choose the path of betrayal? I suspect that with careful review, we could answer this question. Don't you, Belial?" She turned back to him. "Don't you crave the answer?"

Another hush swept over the room, and Lucian, perhaps for the first time in longer than he could remember, felt the first brush of real fear. Because Belial was no longer mocking Asmodaea, he was regarding her with keen interest. Her attack, the way she twisted the knife into Lucian's carefully constructed persona, this was something that interested him, something he could enjoy.

The genuine exploitation of a seventh-level commander was by any account a delicious consideration, all the more so because Lucian didn't speak. Yet he couldn't speak, he knew. He couldn't plead his case, not now. Not after taunting Asmodaea and the entire gallery with the admission of his guilt. He was no fool. He saw what was coming, and all he could do was endure.

Belial didn't give him too much time to think about it.

"You may show us his full history," he purred, leaning against the low wall that ringed the gallery, and gesturing indolently toward Lucian. "We're all in need of a good show."

The floor opened up beneath Lucian and...

He fell.

First, because Asmodaea was a vicious bitch and understood the power that she held over him, over all of them, she allowed him to embody the being he was before. The glorious angel who was feted and adored above even many of his own peers. The radiant child of the Creator, his wings arcing out in crystalline waves of light and buoyant energy, giving him the speed to race over the mountains and valleys the Creator had made, filling him with pride, joy, and life.

Then of course, it was ripped from him.

The pain came first, the staggering punch to the chest where all breath was stolen away and replaced by fire and choking smoke. Then came the ripping knives, rending his flesh from his bones, slicing through his veins. As if the punishment he deserved was his complete unmaking. But only then, hurtling through the planes of night and day to night again, did the cruelest violation come. His wings. His glorious wings ripped from his back and thrust away from him, spinning, tumbling, shattering into darkness, bursting into flame. It made no sense —it hadn't then, it still didn't—that he somehow could feel their destruction more strongly than any other violation.

He fell for a very long time, and when he finally crashed into the stinking rot of hell, he was grateful. Because this...this was something real. This was feeling and sensation. There was pain, yes, but it was glorious pain. The pain that reminded him of what he had done and why he had done it. Defying the Creator himself that he might remain among the living.

It hadn't quite worked out like that, of course. Once again, to truly experience the human condition, he had to walk among them, had to taste, touch, and breathe their very essence from the realm of shadow. But that hadn't been a hardship. He'd never wanted to be human; he'd simply wanted to live. And though his craven nature demanded sacrifice from the humans from time to time, to feed his own lustful needs, he had made it worth their while.

Lucian watched the parade of terrified souls he'd driven to madness, despair, and worse—so much worse—and he had reveled in it. It was his divine right, after all. The mere fact that he, that any of them, could do this work, could exist, was proof of that. The Creator may not appreciate or approve of the acts his creatures wrought, but he didn't kill them, either. Not yet. That didn't mean that they couldn't be killed, of course. Mirr hadn't been the first.

"We already know that he has no loyalty, no love. We, none of us, would trust each other, but Palemerious has always taken that to an extreme," Asmodaea cooed as his first murder was played out in vicious glory.

At least in this, Belial could take some comfort, Lucian thought, though he didn't give himself the luxury of looking over at his general. He had taken down another seventh-level in the first millennium after the Fall. A commander of extraordinary power, who had whispered of the horde regaining their strength, rebuilding their path to the Creator. Heady stuff, dangerous stuff. He'd had to go, everyone knew it —and Belial had sanctioned it.

Lucian hadn't hesitated. The gallery shifted and muttered as the commander exploded, bursting into so many pieces that they would never find their way back across the universe. And still time marched on, the years turning to centuries, the centuries to millennia until his alliance with Asmodaea was formed on the back of another betrayal, another murder, once more at Belial's request.

But this one…was different. This murder, five hundred years past, had been a demon of the Court of Wrath, one of Samael's pets. He'd fallen for a human, defied the horde, and Lucian had trapped him, playing upon his desire, his need until the demon had been weak and defenseless, crazed with the human he couldn't have. And then Lucian had taken him down without a second's thought—brutally, viciously.

Lucian watched the battle from hooded eyes, his throat tight. He'd forgotten most of this, he mused. Buried it. But had a seed been planted in himself, all those long years ago?

"Asmodaea, I'm finding myself less impressed than I want to be," Belial announced, and Lucian looked up then, surprised to realize that he was on his knees. When had he collapsed like this?

He should be feeling better, he thought. He didn't. Because with a rush, time tilted and sped forward, bringing the gallery up to the events of the last few weeks. To his first steps as a shedim. To the moment he walked into the bright office of Delia Thompson and saw her through eyes that were not her own. It was all displayed for the restless courts, the gallery of his peers leaning in to see what had driven him to unsanctioned murder, what had caused him to break their highest code.

Here it comes. He steeled himself.

In vivid color, for all the howling demons to see, far clearer honestly than they typically viewed humans, Delia looked up at him, her temper flaring, her blood rushing under her skin. Anger leaped and sizzled between them, and the demon horde hooted in approval. They tracked her reaction to him, her fear and outrage...but there was nothing more.

Lucian stared right along with them, forcing his expression to remain flat. He had lived those moments with Delia, had watched her react to him, gloried in it. But not just because she reviled him, and not only because some deep and shameful part of her was attracted to the darkness that he brought to her. Humans had always had that weakness, drawn to that which they most feared.

But there had been more in Delia's eyes than lust, though he never would have called it true affection. It was something less than love but more than simple desire, and he found himself gritting his teeth over the idea that their interaction would be the stuff of pleasure for the horde—only to have that concern whisper away like smoke.

They fought and bickered, they drew closer to each other, then jerked away, until the moment built toward their first kiss. For anyone else watching it though, they only appeared to be entrenched enemies. And then the moment of the kiss approached, a memory etched into his mind, seared into his very bones. It would be seared into the everlasting record of all who watched too, slavering and hooting, growling and urging him on and...

But the moment passed as if it had never happened. In the account shown to the horde, Delia sailed out of her office without a backward glance, unmolested, untouched, and Lucian could barely keep his face straight as Asmodaea watched him keenly, somehow knowing that something was off but having no idea what.

"Is this it?" she challenged. "This pitiful human is the reason why you destroyed one of our own?"

"She's the first interesting creature I've met in millennia," he shot back, gaining the laughter of the gallery.

"You're protecting her," Asmodaea accused, and Lucian stood again, then threw up his hands, once more shattering the chains that supposedly bound him, making sure everybody realized that he was standing still out of choice, not necessity.

He could feel Belial's gaze upon him, approving, which drove Asmodaea to even greater irritation.

Let her rage, Lucian thought, as she ordered new bonds down upon him, an order that Belial negated with a bored flick of his finger. The saga continued, all the way up to their assault on Kieran Walsh's office in the Prometheus building, and the confrontation he had with Mirr, through him consigning Mirr to the ends of existence, shattered and broken, bare scraps of him left to confront his maker, a confrontation no demon had ever survived. A confrontation no demon ever desired. For even if the Lord of all Hosts forgave them, it meant they would give up the thing that had driven them out of the embrace of All-That-Is in the first place. Their freedom.

When the best possible option was still to be enslaved, obliteration took on even more harrowing meaning.

The images spooled on, and he saw Delia again, when she had come to him in the Oak Park building, after he had amused himself by teaching yoga. That night, she'd stood in front of him, and it was clear to him, if not to anyone else, that she saw more in him than he deserved. More than he dared speak aloud. But nothing else was revealed, other than that stare. Somehow, she had managed to shield him when he had been his most vulnerable, wiping the record clean from the view of the horde.

She'd protected him.

He had never been protected, not since before the Fall, and yet here she stood, impossibly willing to stand in the breach for a creature that had blighted her existence for fifteen years.

She was a fool, and he was manipulating her. Or perhaps he was the fool.

A commotion at the top of the gallery broke across his consciousness, and he turned to see Delia dragged in, wearing chains not unlike his own. Fury rippled through him, and he only barely kept it in check as Asmodaea stared at him, her smile stretching her face wide.

"This little demonstration reminded me that you are not the only criminal who needs to be put to justice, or did you forget that she too, was summoned—and by Leviathan, not me?" Asmodaea gestured to the general of the Indolent Court, who finally roused himself to interest.

"Here we have an exorcist blessed by the Creator, sanctified by All-That-Is," Asmodaea said. "She has a job on this earth, but she hasn't followed the rules, have you, Delia Thompson?" She eased around Delia like a stain, but Delia fought and thrashed, unable to truly see, Lucian thought. "She will be held accountable."

Asmodaea glanced back at Lucian. "Or you will be, take your pick. It's up to Belial to decide her fate and for the generals to judge it worthy."

"Not exactly, Asmodaea," Belial said, holding up a thin finger. "It's up to me to decide her fate, and for you to abide by it, unless and until there is a challenge by Leviathan—or perhaps Samael, since you're lodging the complaint. But I note your own general couldn't trouble himself to be here. He, at least, has a grasp of how pointless this exercise is. But I have seen enough."

He turned to the other generals in the room. "Have you decided how he shall atone for his crime of unsanctioned death? Because I tire of this. There are other entertainments to be had."

"He must pay!" snarled Asmodaea, but Lucian was only half paying attention, his gaze fixated on Delia as the demons around her draped shadows and darkness over her shoulders, weighing her down, gouging her skin, grinding against her bones. She wouldn't know what was happening, he thought. Her dreams would just thicken, darken, and she would feel heavier and heavier until the darkness smothered her whole.

"Name the price," he said, finally deigning to glance Belial's way, and infusing his voice with as much disdain as he could.

As he watched, Belial nodded to the others, gaining their nods in turn. "Since you have a taste for death, you'll serve as the enforcer of the High Court," he said. "Until you, yourself, are killed by a worthier foe."

The gallery went silent. All eyes turned to Belial, who preened beneath the attention. There had not been an enforcer among the demon ranks in millennia. It was a difficult role to fill. First, you had to find a demon willing to consign his brethren to a fate worse than death, knowing that his own life would be forfeit as every other demon in the horde sought to take him down. Then you had to find one who was strong enough to get the job done. It was very rare to find a single demon who could manage both.

Lucian had more than proven he could.

Across the chamber floor, Delia uttered the smallest sigh of distress between her teeth, the only outward expression of the weight bearing her down. How often had he heard her grit through the pain like that, Lucian thought. First because of him, and after to protect everyone else in her charge...even him.

"I will accept the terms," he said.

"Excellent," Belial said, clapping his hands together. "Stay bound, enforcer. And now I call forth Leviathan of the Court of Indolence, to try the human for her crimes."

Immobilized by the will of the High Court, Lucian hissed beneath his breath as Delia was dragged forward.

TWENTY-SIX

I jolted upright in my car seat beside Claire like I'd been seared with a brand, staring around wildly as Sergei's phone buzzed. "What was that?" I demanded.

Claire gaped at me. "What was what?" she asked.

I leaned toward Sergei. "What was that alert? What's going on?"

"Standard protocol," he said. "Descent has been breached by court security."

"No. That's not what I felt." I shook my head. "It was more like something going wrong." I wanted to tell them more, and there was no reason why I couldn't tell them more. But the truth was, what I felt was an absence, not an addition. Like a finger that I'd gotten used to taking my pulse had suddenly lifted away from my wrist.

Lucian, I knew immediately. I no longer felt Lucian. I hadn't realized how solid our connection was, it had simply always been there. Even though it technically had been fading, it hadn't been fading that much, and it strengthened again in the moments after we wrapped our arms around each other—

whether with intimate or intimately murderous intent. But now the ties that bound us had been completely severed.

"The tribunal has started, hasn't it?" I asked. "It was supposed to be days from now, right?"

Sergei shrugged, but he blew through a traffic light as it turned red, the casual action in the middle of the day adding more weight to my concern.

"You work enough with the horde, you give up guessing the reasons behind their actions," he said. "They act when they wish to act, and their calendars are their own. But yes," he said, meeting my gaze in the rearview mirror. "Volkov confirms they have taken Palemerious. The tribunal has begun."

I sat back in my seat, willing my heart to stop pounding. "His name is Lucian," I informed him, and he shrugged again.

"Not as far as they are concerned."

"So, what does this mean?" Claire asked. "Who's judging him?" She gasped as she answered her own question, at least in theory. "Is it the devil?" she whispered.

Sergei shook his head. "The horde polices everything they do on their own level. Which is not to say they cannot be called upon to answer to a higher order. It just doesn't happen. But they don't judge harshly unless their connection to humans is at risk. They need humans to give meaning to their existence."

She peered at him. "Don't tell me you're trying to make me feel sorry for demons."

He snorted. "Never that. But you must understand them so you don't underestimate them."

Something in Sergei's words struck me as important, but I couldn't focus on anything other than the image of Lucian standing before some shadowy accuser, allowing himself to be judged. "How long will it take?"

Sergei shrugged again. "Not long. But time moves differently for a demon. It could already be done."

He pressed on the gas without me asking, and the SUV leaped forward.

As always, approaching the club in daylight felt wrong, out of sync, even though we were finally working toward evening. It didn't help that as we angled around to the back of the building, a man almost as bulky as Sergei stepped out to stand by an access door. Sergei bounced into the lot, saying nothing as he exited the SUV, and we followed. The two men didn't speak, either, communicating only via what I supposed was the international language of eye twitches known by thugs everywhere.

We moved into a remarkably well-appointed hallway, and Claire drew closer to me, clutching her leather tote to her side. "I don't understand what's going on here," she said, her voice low and brisk. "And I don't want to tell you how to do your job, but…"

"Then don't," I suggested.

Another person would have read the room and shut up, but not Claire.

"However, I feel confident in continuing because this is *not* actually your job. This isn't your fight. Lucian has lived and worked with these people…um, these demons, whatever their preferred terms are, for, if we're using their timeline as canon, thousands of years, maybe longer. This isn't his first rodeo. Plus, he's a seventh-level commander. He knows how to defend himself."

"That's not the point," I said. Claire didn't know that I had been summoned to the tribunal, as well. This didn't feel like the best time to point that out.

"Plus," she continued, undeterred. "You don't know what you're doing here. Not here. These aren't demons overtaking humans, or infesting haunted houses, or even hijacking computer infrastructures. These are straight-up demons living their best lives, doing what they do. That is not your area of excellence. It's not even your area of basic competence."

"I don't care." We approached a door at the end of the hallway that seemed indistinguishable from all the others, yet it shimmered slightly as I approached. Something had happened here, I thought. Lucian had been here.

"And for a very specific reason above my personal preference that you don't die and leave me stuck being a pharmacist," Claire said, "there's something I need to say." She grabbed my arm and pulled me roughly around, stopping us abruptly while Sergei went inside the office.

Claire got right up into my face. "If you're not an asset to Lucian in this fight, do you know what that makes you? A liability. You going down there or whatever it is you think you're going to do, insinuating yourself into some private squabble that you know nothing about, is simply going to give them another lever against him. You do understand that, right?"

I stared at her. I wanted to deny her words, throw them back in her face. But I had grown up being unwanted, being the reason why other people's lives sucked. This suddenly felt a lot like that.

"He obliterated Mirr," I said tightly. "He killed him dead because of me."

"He knew what he was doing," she countered, her gaze remaining steely on mine. "And if you think for one God-forsaken moment that after legitimately thousands of years of existence, he's been completely swept away by an accidental exorcist who's made up of more scars than skin and attitude than brains, then maybe you should take a moment to reflect and check your assumptions. Because if you are going to go down there like some ridiculous righteous gerbil in a den of starving hyenas, you should at least stop fooling yourself."

I couldn't help myself, I choked out a laugh. "A righteous gerbil?"

"You know what I mean!" she said. She swung her bag around, shoved her hand in it, and pulled out glass vials of holy water. "Take these," she ordered, handing them to me. "Stick them in your bra, I don't care, but take them and keep them with you until you get out of here. Break them in case of emergency—they break easy. I feel—I just don't feel good about this, Delia, I'm not going to lie."

I blinked at her, taking the vials, one for each hand. "You're right," I sighed. "I don't know what I'm doing here. But I..." I bit my lip, looked away. "This isn't my fight, but it's still my problem."

"I know," Claire sighed, still rooting around in her bag. "It's just—"

"Delia," Volkov's shout rang out from his office, or what I assumed was his office, but something else swept over me at the same time, dimming my eyesight, loosening my focus. At the far end of the hallway, beyond the doors to Volkov's lair, another door swung open.

Twisting oily shadows exploded out of the doorway, sweeping toward us on a scream. I shoved Claire aside, hearing her yelp as she crashed into the wall, but I didn't care. Intellectually, I knew this was a hallucination, knew it was a trap. But it was a trap I'd been waiting for, and I leaned into it. *Let's fucking go.*

My world tilted, and I felt myself pushed over and slammed to the floor. Then something grabbed my feet.

Once again, I knew I couldn't literally be dragged into the pits of Hell by a demonic form. That wasn't how any of this worked. But I also knew the power of the human mind, knew that we could make our reality if we just believed strongly enough, and that we could be influenced to a shockingly effective degree. Hell, Grace had taught me that, if nothing else. And demons had been the original influencers for a very, *very* long time.

I choked on what felt like my last gasp of real oxygen as I was yanked through the doorway into total blackness. My throat constricted and my lungs burned, as if I really was being sucked down into a portal straight to the abyss. I fell—fell some more—fell so long that I was sure I'd blacked out a couple times, but when I crashed to a new floor, it was an actual floor. Made out of wood! How was that...

I looked around wildly, my hands folded tight against my chest, my body still curled into a tight ball. Across an expanse of open flooring was a short wooden wall, and beyond that, stretching up in a circular gallery, I was surrounded by elegantly dressed aristocrats who had something profoundly wrong with their faces, their hands. They were beautiful but also defiled, too long, too pronounced, too big for their bodies and for the space they occupied, like I had landed in the middle of aliens.

"You're dreaming." Lucian's voice ripped across my senses, but he didn't speak like the Lucian I knew. His words were garbled and felt like nails gouging into my ears. This was Palemerious's domain.

"She is dreaming, and what a delightful mind she has," another voice layered over his. "I haven't had the pleasure of seeing her up close, but such an active little mind. And you more than most know how easy it is to lay a finger on such *active* little minds. Have you laid a finger on hers, Palemerious?"

These words washed over me with cold horror, and I could feel my heart shriveling as this new demon approached me. She wasn't a creature of beauty, but I recognized her, even deep within my dream state. I knew her name. And before I could think better of it. My lips parted, and the word breathed out into the dark chamber.

"Ooooo," Asmodaea replied. "She's stronger than most, but then, she would need to be, wouldn't she, to defy the edict from the Creator most high. Not exorcising a demon, but punishing it." She tsked with a nerve-wracking clicking noise of her tongue. "Several steps above your station, wouldn't you say, Delia Thompson?"

She lashed out, and her arms turned into ripping pincers that impaled me to the floor. My fists banged hard, my knuckles splitting open, but I kept my hands tight around my precious vials of holy water. I could feel pain in this dream. I could feel fear. Was this what the victims of demonic hallucinations endured? No wonder so many of them died.

"And now you will be held accountable for Alaria's return to the pits of the horde," Asmodaea said, her accusation followed by the garbled voice of Palemerious.

"She is a human. She's not bound by our rules."

"She is a human, and she *became* bound by our rules the moment she abandoned her own," Asmodaea shot back. "Exorcists don't punish demons, they neither attack them nor diminish them. That's not their role. Exorcists may only *remove* demons from a human or place—any human, any place. They have that authority but only that authority. Not the power of judge and executioner. There must be order, Palemerious, you above all know that. Chaos feeds the weak, and we are not weak. She is *accountable*; now and evermore. She is bound."

I sensed this was a conversation that I should be following more closely, but I could do nothing but track the battering of my pulse through my blood vessels, the freezing of my body. My lungs burned with impossible pain, my heart seemed frozen, and the darkness no longer flowed around me. It was inside me, leeching out like poison from Asmodaea's spikes. And with each inch that it leaked through me, I felt exposed, watched, judged.

Images flashed in front of my eyes, and the gallery roared with delight as those images were apparently projected for their enjoyment. Mordechai in the cemetery, holding forth, his purpling face streaked with sweat, his lips trembling, his eyes wild until finally he clutched his heart and staggered forward, falling as I turned away and ran.

My first attempt at exorcising the demons of the Grahams, releasing the shedim that had infested the long rambling house by the lake. I screamed in agony as I was once again battered by flying chunks of wood. *Shedim, they'd been shedim!* But I hadn't understood the importance of that. Not at first.

I writhed on the floor, hearing Palemerious rage while the chorus of demons behind him crowed with delight. These were not creatures that cared about the injustices to the least of them, I thought. Asmodaea didn't really care that Mirr had died, that Alaria had been shoved back to her beginning place by a human. She cared that protocols had not been met, that the balance of power had been upset. And there could be nothing more concerning than the heart of the human who dared to defy her. I twisted on the floor, losing consciousness inside the dream, but I didn't plan just to survive this test. I couldn't simply black out and wake up on the floor of the hallway upstairs outside of Volkov's office.

I was tired of being everyone's tool. I was done.

I twisted around and forced my hands away from their protective clench across my chest, and cracked my fists on the floor.

Though my hands weren't corporeal, they felt that way as the glass broke, the shards sticking and biting as I squeezed hard. I imagined blood and holy water stinging, the pain rocketing up my arms, and I clenched my eyes shut and began to pray.

I hadn't gotten through the first words when a pit opened up beneath me, and I fell through the floor.

I thought I would go tumbling once more into the abyss, but this fall was short, and it ended abruptly in the steaming lake of oil and fire. I sucked in ashy, thick liquid that coated my mouth and streamed back from my head as I surged up out of the murk once more. My hands, stuck with deeply embedded glass, crashed wildly against other bodies, long sinuous forms that snaked and twisted all around me. Every living thing in this pit was desperately trying to get out, to break free.

I knew what they were. I knew where I was. I was in the lowest pit of beginning in whatever the horde considered Hell. I was in the place I had consigned Alaria, sending her back to this sinkhole of despair, where she wouldn't die but simply expire and be regenerated, expire and be regenerated, over and over again until she built up the strength and fury to move through the other creatures in the muck, breathe in brimstone air, and finally surge forward once again to the far shore, reclaiming her place among the level-two demons.

Unbidden, unwanted, Mordechai's words flowed back to me. "It is not our place to choose the punishment or even to judge. We simply have the power to relieve the suffering where one creature of God afflicts its will upon another without their consent or His. We do not kill. We do not exile. We merely send them on their way, and that is gift enough."

I hadn't done that, though. I'd banished Alaria back to her lowest form.

And I would fucking do it again.

Again!

Twisting my arms around, I slammed my hands down, using the shards and burning holy water as weapons, but I didn't encounter more slithering creatures this time, but hard floor. I pressed my hands down, understanding I was back in the gallery, back among the roaring watchers. I flattened my hands further into the floor, driving the shards of glass and holy water into my palms, mixing with my blood, burning my hands, burning the floor...and setting it on fire.

"She goes!" Lucian's voice radiated with enough fury the hair raised on my arms. "She cannot die here without consequences to the horde. You know that, Belial, even if Asmodaea doesn't. She goes."

Another voice spoke then, low and certain, and filled with... what? Curiosity? Certainly pleasure. "She goes," it repeated. "She goes."

And the smoke swept back over me.

TWENTY-SEVEN

I burst upright, inhaling deep, then nearly blacking out as Claire grabbed my bandaged hands, hard. "Steady!" she hissed, and I didn't miss the fact that she spoke with hushed tones. She glowered at me in the dimly lit room when I could finally peel my eyes open enough to focus on her. I was on some kind of bed in a rudimentary hospital suite of some sort—sink and counter set into the walls, baskets of swabs, and a large and sealed trashcan for...for...

"And three...two...one," she announced grimly, catching me as I lurched forward. She held my hair out of the way while I vomited into a bucket on a low table by the bed—but what came out of my mouth was mostly bile. I was shocked it wasn't the color of motor oil.

"When's the last time you ate, anyway?" Claire asked, easing me upright when I tried to lift myself and failed. I took her proffered towel gratefully. I wasn't surprised it wasn't an ordinary towel, and instead was cool and damp, but I was still amazed at her attention to detail. Which pretty much summed up what I thought about Claire in general.

"Where is everyone?" I asked, wiping my mouth, my face,

and my neck and arms for good measure—as much as I could with bandaged hands. "Man, I shattered the shit out of those vials. That was quick thinking."

"You did, and it was," Claire agreed. "I've got more in the bag, though hopefully you won't need them. And it's ten o'clock. You dropped to the floor in a dead faint, came to long enough to beat your hands on the ground a few times, smearing blood everywhere. Then you blacked out and stayed out, and Nikolai had you moved here. This is a really complete medical suite for a nightclub."

I snorted. "I noticed that." It hurt to breathe, but I tried a few shallow gasps as Claire continued.

"He hovered around off and on for hours, but apparently the club is on fire tonight—not literally, though. At least, not yet. It's busier than it should be, is all."

"Yeah." I wiped my mouth again, straightened more. "Any word from Lucian?"

She shook her head. "Not a peep. Nikolai genuinely seemed worried, which, not going to lie, kind of freaked me out. But as the hours went on, he just started muttering more under his breath, getting angrier and angrier. You know what I mean?"

"I do." I didn't really know what to make of the vibe between Lucian and Nikolai, but the only thing they seemed to agree on was worrying about me. And not even worry in the wholesome "gosh, I hope everything works out for you," way, but possessively, intensely, as if I wasn't just the neighborhood exorcist but some pawn in a game they'd been playing for way too long, even if they hadn't always been partners. A game whose rules they weren't all that eager to share. I didn't love that, frankly.

How well did those two even know each other? Lucian had opted out of Belial's court a solid seventeen years ago. I didn't know how old Volkov was, but he couldn't be more than forty.

How long had he even been the kingpin of Chicago's demon clubs? And if he hadn't been in power when Lucian had been skulking around before he'd possessed me, who had? And had Lucian worked with them? I struggled to remember anything of the incredibly murky dream I'd just endured, but the overriding sense that I'd retained was victory. Whether I'd planned to or not, I'd scored points with the demon world. I was almost sure of it. Given that I ultimately answered to a totally different power, I wasn't sure how well that was going to play on my next performance review.

"We need to get out of here," I muttered.

She snorted. "I couldn't agree more. But Volkov gave me strict instructions that I was to come and get him the moment you woke up."

I hadn't known Claire Bickwell all that long, but I already could recognize the tone in her voice. She wasn't planning on telling Volkov anything.

"So, how are we going to play this?" I asked. "Just walk out the back? As long as Sergei isn't there, we could probably make it to the 'L' in less than ten minutes."

"Or I could call us an Uber," she said. "It's not the greatest neighborhood out there, but this isn't the only nightclub on the street. Plus, it's late, but not too late. We should be able to get a ride."

"And if we don't, we can take the train," I said again. "I kind of don't think anyone from that tribunal is going to be leaving anytime soon. Either they're still fighting it out, or they're partying off all that heavy work."

"Then we're out of here," Claire said, standing. "I don't want to risk running into Jay again, anyway. And where the hell is Storm Court? Please tell me it's nowhere close."

I shook my head, suddenly exhausted. "I have no clue."

She helped me to my feet, and I took a few experimental

steps, nodding to her that I was ready before my brain caught up with her comments. "That's right, Jay," I said, shaking my head to refocus. "How are you doing with all of that?"

Her smile was tight and grim. "Let's get out of here first."

Getting out didn't take as much effort as we'd feared. Nikolai's private enclave of offices was a ghost town, the music from Descent pounding at levels that could be heard all the way to O'Hare. We made it to the back entrance and popped the door experimentally, but nobody stood outside.

"Got to be a one-way lock, you know?" Claire mused. "They don't let anybody back here who's not expected, so there's no reason to guard it."

"Works for me." We headed out, and I shivered, though the night was warm. I glanced down at my arms, catching sight of them in the security lights that bathed the back lot.

"Was I cut by the glass all the way up to my elbows?" I asked, noting the track marks down the length of my forearms. In this light, they looked too symmetrical, not really in keeping with shattered glass, but more like...

"No," Claire said, peering over at me. "But I do see what you mean, those cuts..."

She looked around suddenly, tugging her exorcism supply tote closer to her body. "You know what, why don't we save the physical for after we get home? And by home, I mean my place. Sergei talked a bit about your new digs, and I think I'll take a pass on that for tonight."

"What do you mean?" Despite how crappy I felt, I laughed. "It's nice."

She rolled her eyes. "Oh, I'm sure it's nice. Hill House was nice."

We fell into an easy stride as we moved out onto West Fulton, Claire tapping at her phone and peering at street signs. It was a warm night, and there was good traffic, and she found an Uber driver willing to meet us in fifteen short minutes not three blocks away.

"Closest I could get." She waved the phone at me.

"I don't mind the fresh air." We walked another block, then I tried again. "So...Jay? How are you doing?"

She sighed. "Not great. I never thought about what Lily might do to him after I left. I never gave him another thought, honestly. She was the star, and Jay orbited around her, but they both targeted me. Without me in the mix, maybe she turned on him, or maybe she just ignored him. With his personality, that might have been worse."

"None of this is your fault," I said, echoing what I said earlier, or at least what I'd hoped I'd said. "You couldn't be responsible for anyone but yourself in that scenario. You have to know that."

"Yeah, I guess..." she said. We crossed the street, angling toward the brighter lights nearer to the overpass. You could definitely feel the vibe picking up, the energy. There were more people around, and it all did feel safer. Maybe the Uber driver hadn't been an idiot for having us meet him closer to civilization.

"Well, for fuck's sake," Claire protested, holding up her phone and turning around, as if to find some elusive signal. "I'm suddenly getting that the driver is now twenty minutes away, not five. Who is this joker?"

A chill skated over me. It was too close to my last brush with traffic-related demonic manipulation, and I didn't have it in me to play that game tonight. "You know what? Why don't we just go to the 'L'. It's got to be close."

"Fine," she grumbled and stuffed her phone back in her pocket, as I squinted ahead. The street stretched ahead of us like a concrete river flowing east through the city's industrial bones. Behind us, the warehouse district receded, replaced by the harsh glare of sodium streetlights that painted everything in sickly yellow. The sidewalk narrowed as we walked, forcing us closer to the street, where late-night delivery trucks rumbled past, their headlights cutting temporary slashes through the darkness. In between their newer, more gentrified neighbors, a few abandoned storefronts dotted the north side of the street—roll-up doors tagged with graffiti, windows either boarded or spider-webbed with cracks that caught the streetlight like broken stars.

Finally, the Kennedy Expressway loomed ahead, the overpass rising like the ribs of some massive urban beast, casting deep pools of shadow that the streetlights couldn't penetrate. Above the overpass, an endless stream of red and white lights flowed along the highway—cars and trucks carrying people to somewhere warmer and safer than this strip of no-man's-land between Chicago's glittering downtown and its warehouse blight. The sound grew louder as we approached: the constant white noise of rubber on concrete, engines downshifting, horns and tires screeching. Even the air smelled different here—exhaust and cold concrete, motor oil and something metallic that made the back of my throat itch.

Claire continued to grumble about how Uber was on the way out, while the incidental indignities of my adventure this evening now made themselves known. It wasn't enough that my arms ached and my throat still worked spasmodically, trying to clear the oil slick it seemed permanently lodged at the back of my mouth. In addition to that, words were flowing to me too, accusations and complaints mouthed in the guttural garble of the horde. These miserable, disgusting creatures that God had somehow suffered to live upon this earth, never mind that their entire purpose seemed to be finding ways to plague humans and derive pleasure from their subjugation and misery.

What kind of God would allow such a thing? Mordechai

would've had something to say about that, some comment about understanding our place amid the greater realm of the universe. Understanding that we were meant to serve, not to understand. But Mordechai had lied to me at least once, and given the number of times that his name had flowed from the lips of the creatures who had loomed over me, slavering and whooping, I was pretty sure he'd made more bad decisions than those I even knew about.

Why had he done that? He'd had everything. The support of his community, the dignity of his legacy, and a ten, then fifteen, then twenty, then twenty-five-year-old girl willing to do anything he asked if it meant she could take on another exorcism. Why would he lie?

"This station is close, right?" Claire asked, drawing my attention. I noticed that my head moved slower than it should, my eyes tracking woozily across the industrial landscape. We'd reached the weird pocket between two outposts of civilization in this part of the city. Gentrification didn't expand in neat and even lines, unfortunately. But we were close.

"It's maybe two blocks up," I began, but as we stepped under the overpass, something shifted around us. The sound of the streets suddenly dampened, and the gloom deepened, despite the bright streetlight above us.

Then out of the shadows, Thomas Keegan appeared.

Fury ripped through me, and I held up a hand, bracing my feet wide to keep from falling down. "Stop," I commanded with the confidence of someone who'd just survived the best hallucinations demons could throw at a girl. "I know what you are. You have no business here."

But he didn't stop, he simply laughed. "Leaving so soon after the party?" he asked, in the high, thin voice that reminded me of his tuneless four-note melody. "That's poor manners, but then again, you never did want to see anything to the end, did you? You learned that from Mordechai, didn't you?" He cackled at his own obscure joke. "Ah, Mordechai, how much I longed to meet him again, face to face. But first, I was weak, and then, when I got strong, I was afraid. Don't ever let fear stop you from doing what you need to, Delia. You will always regret it."

"Who are you?" I asked, my voice flat. "You're not Thomas Keegan, are you? And I'm tired of talking at shadows."

I reached for Claire's hand, and she grabbed mine. Not urgently, not in fright, but calm and sure—and I realized she had pulled another vial of holy water out of her bag. She transferred it to me easily, pulling her hand away as I stuffed the vial in my bra. Then I relaced my fingers with Claire.

We started walking again, but Thomas Keegan didn't move, just leered as we passed him and then fell into step behind us. "Do you like this?" he murmured. "Like knowing that I'm following you, knowing that you still *attract* me? That's what the rabbi saw in me that he didn't like, didn't know what to do with. That I *noticed* you, even as I was emerging from the human I'd chosen to get Mordechai's attention. Because you already *had* your admirers. He was one of them—not in a carnal way, perhaps, but there are many ways to use a person. Many ways to be used."

"He exorcised you out of Keegan. What did you do then?"

Keegan pounced on the question. "Did he, though? Did he finish the job?"

I knew the dangers of engaging this creature, that demons loved nothing more than insinuating themselves into your mind, your thoughts, but Claire's heart rate was steadily increasing beside me, her pulse pounding through her clutched fingers. And Keegan wasn't a threat, not really. He was a shedim, sure...and so was Lucian, but...

I picked up the pace slightly.

"I was destined for power—he knew it, I knew it. And so, he proposed a test."

"Bullshit."

Keegan continued as if I hadn't said anything. "You would have been a tasty treat, and I would have learned so much. I would have learned much from him as well. The rabbi, so sure and true. So many secrets he kept. But the inn was full. If I wanted to work with him, I needed to be trustworthy. He suggested I return to the body I'd evacuated, the body of a nobody, a shuffling, scrabbling worker in tattered clothes. A demonstration."

Claire clutched my arm, but I could almost convince myself I could see the archway to an 'L' station up ahead, just a few blocks past the underpass. It wasn't that far now. We just had to get through.

"Yeah? Then what? He sent you on your way?"

"No. He trapped me there."

A sick chill slid through me, and Keegan's laugh chased it down my spine. "You didn't know? Surely you understood that he had the power to take, but also the power to seal. To keep a demon crouched and waiting in walls of bone and blood, desperate and small. He knew how to do it, which means you know how to do it."

"He wouldn't do that," I said, my voice quieter now. "Not—not in the person he'd just released. That's not the job."

"Perhaps, perhaps. But he had to protect you, didn't he? And then he left me—trapped, weak, unable to shake the walking corpse of Thomas Keegan for another eight years...and I was damaged, afterward. Lost, wandering. Mordechai has much to answer for."

"Yeah, well, you're late," I said. "He's dead."

"Such a pity. It took me years to reclaim even the power of my shedim form, but I am stronger than any ordinary shedim now. And I have learned so much. You've learned much too. Perhaps you can teach me...perhaps I can help you."

I heard him shift, then crouch down, heard the scrape of stone on concrete. And in that moment, I realized what had been bothering me.

Keegan was a shedim. Lucian was a shedim. There had been shedim in the lake house on the Graham estate—the only time I'd been actually struck by hurling weapons. Shedim had form and weight, they walked as humans.

They could harm like humans too.

I shoved Claire away from me as Keegan rushed us, stepping into his path, so it was me he took to the ground, me he sent sprawling across the pavement. I was glad for my bandaged hands as I skidded to a stop, digging in my shirt for the vial of holy water, but he bounded toward me, leaping through the shadows with supernatural speed.

Then he covered me with his body—which weighed three times that of a normal man.

"Inn's no longer full, is it," he crooned as he bit down hard on my ear.

"Stop it!" Claire screeched, and she turned away, hunching over her phone, I thought, though I couldn't imagine the Uber driver was going to reach us anytime soon. Meanwhile, I smashed my bandaged hands under Keegan's neck, punching his windpipe. He may be a shedim, but in this form, he needed to be able to breathe to maintain physical form—and he was having way too much fun to just pick up his evil and go home.

Keegan choked and fell to the side. I rolled on top of him, keeping my grip tight on his throat while he pried at my bandaged hands. He glared at me, fire blasting behind his dark irises, and the truth of his identity hit me like one of his hurled bricks.

"Hello, *Zagan*," I taunted, shoving my hands down. "That's

who you are, isn't it? You've been creeping around all this time. You're a shedim, so fourth-level, but not strong enough to get out of the trap that Mordechai set for you, I guess? It must have been so boring for you, living in Thomas Keegan's head."

"Not exactly," Zagan smiled. "Wendy, George, and Barry were entertaining. So were Luke and David."

I went cold. "What about them?" I asked carefully. I remembered those names, of course, five unhoused people who went dead over the course of four years, no one to remember them, no one to stand in sorrow at their graves. Nothing remained of them but Mordechai's careful clippings in a folder.

Zagan smiled at me as he leaned close.

"Why do you think I chose to wear Thomas Keegan's face again? I wanted you to remember. I wanted you to know who was coming for you, and why. And now I can tell you how his victims died, *Delia*. How they smelled. What they screamed."

My sight went red. Ripping the vial out of my shirt, I smashed it between my hands, then drove the ragged glass into his eyes.

"Delia!" Claire screamed.

TWENTY-EIGHT

With a roar, Zagan morphed beneath me, his body expanding outward in all directions until he no longer appeared as the lean, lanky form of Thomas Keegan but somebody built more like Sergei. He shook me off him with a massive shudder, hurling me across the embankment like I was a six-year-old child. I landed in a pile of gravel and trash, skidding several feet before I stopped. I'd barely sucked in a gulp of air when Zagan grabbed me again. He slammed me hard against the concrete base of the underpass, then threw me to the ground. I saw stars and tasted blood.

Claire screamed again, then she charged, swinging her leather exorcist supply bag at Zagan like a cudgel.

The impact should have been minimal. I mean, this was Claire swinging the bag, not the Hulk, but Zagan screamed and twisted away as the contents of her bag spilled over him. I scrambled upright and dove for anything I could grab, coming up with a Crucifix with a pointed base and a heavy, ornate rosary. Even though my hands were bandaged, enough of the wrapping had been ripped away that I winced when the holy objects came into contact with my skin.

Good. I relished the heat. If these things made me feel this bad, Zagan would be damned near crippled by the time I was done with him.

While he pawed at his eyes, I sprang onto his back and locked my knees against him, wrapping the heavy rosary around his neck. He howled again, loud enough to shake the overpass, and I knew that the only reason I'd managed to attach myself to him like a leech was because I had the jump on him. Clearly, he wasn't expecting me to attack. Few humans would be so stupid. Humans were built to run from demons, not confront them.

But all I could see was the march of victims whose stories Mordechai had cut out so carefully and stuffed between the pages of some long-forgotten journal. Wendy Simms, George Roberts, Barry Stone. Wendy had overdosed. Barry had walked into traffic for no apparent reason, straight into the path of an oncoming bus. And George had jumped off an overpass not unlike this one. Jumped, or been pushed. Demons seemed fond of pushing. Then there'd been David Chen and Luke Wilkins—dead by heart failure. Literally scared to death.

"You won't—kill me," Zagan snarled, his fingers ineffectively batting at mine. "Can't."

"Try me, dickhead," I shouted, hauling more heavily on the rosary.

Claire smashed two vials together behind me, then dumped holy water over his legs. "Condemned," Zagan shrieked. "You'll...be..."

"I'll take my fucking chances." I redoubled my grip as I heard the screeching brakes from the road, the slamming of doors. But beneath me, Zagan was starting to lose some of his bulk, his body beginning to shimmer in and out of view.

"Oh, no, you don't, you asshole," I growled. "You stay here until you die."

"*Delia.*" Lucian didn't shout, but the word cracked across my senses, bringing up my chin as he strode toward me, reaching me in what felt like a half-second as someone else jogged up behind him.

I blinked. "Nikolai?"

"Delia," Lucian said again, this time out loud. He stopped now, distracting me from the now-choking Zagan. "You can't do this. It's not your place."

"He is a *murderer*," I shot back, even as I felt hands on my shoulders, pulling at me. Not Lucian's, I realized with some surprise—Volkov's. Lucian took another step forward, positioning himself directly in front of me as Zagan bucked and wheezed beneath me. He was seething with anger, but icy, controlled. The arms around me tugged again, and a new voice sounded over my shoulder.

"Delia," Volkov said, his voice low and steady, like he was dealing with a deranged killer. And maybe he was. "There are rules."

He yanked at me then, hard enough that my concentration cracked. Zagan snarled beneath me, wrenching free. He flipped over, claws slashing, but Lucian was faster. He deflected Zagan's swipe in time for Volkov to fully lift me away. I flailed and kicked in Volkov's arms, fury rekindling.

"What the fuck are you doing?" I demanded. "He's murdered five people—at least five, maybe more!"

Lucian made a cutting movement with his hand. "Demons cannot kill—"

"Oh, fuck that!" I roared, still kicking hard. Lucian had a grip on Zagan's neck now, which seemed to render the demon immobile. I needed to learn that trick. "He was inside a human who *then* killed other humans. That's fucking close enough."

"—It's not your place to pass judgment on him," Lucian finished.

"Then who will? Demons?" I retorted. "Like they give a shit."

Lucian's eyes flashed. "There's a hierarchy of order, as you should know more than anyone, having witnessed it. Demons challenge that order at their own peril. Again, as you have witnessed."

"Well, good thing I'm not a demon," I pointed out, but I stopped kicking, thinking maybe Volkov would let me go if I went still. He didn't.

"And therefore, you can't kill a demon, lest you be judged by them," Lucian pointed out. His argument would have carried more weight if he hadn't trapped me in a Volkov cage.

I jerked against the hold. "Let go of me," I snarled.

"No."

I refocused on Lucian. "Okay, if I can't kill him, then what's the big deal? Let me make him suffer. It's *literally* the least I can do."

Lucian hesitated, and I stiffened in Volkov's arms.

"Oh, so maybe I can do more?" I said. "I *can* still kick him all the way back to his primordial sludge state, right? Even if it pisses off the horde? How long did it take you to crawl out of there the last time, Zagan? A thousand years? Two?"

"You cannot," Zagan shot back, his voice ragged. I had hurt him. Good. "I'm not some second-level screamer. I'm nearly fifth-level."

"But still fourth," Lucian said. "Just because I incapacitated Pruflas, that doesn't move you up in the hierarchy. And what I did to her, I can do to you. Don't forget that."

"No, you can't," Zagan sneered. "You're now bound as Belial's hammer."

Something in my reaction must have caught Zagan's attention, because he turned to me, grinning broadly. "Or didn't you know that? There's always a price to pay, you stupid cunt. Your protector paid yours."

"What is he talking about—and get *off* me," I snapped again at Volkov. This time, he let me go.

Lucian, however, didn't answer me, and instead focused on Zagan. "You're half right. I kill at the will and direction of any general who sanctions the death. But sending you back into the muck, that's still well within my purview."

"Not if I didn't directly challenge you." Zagan shot back. "Your *pet* doesn't qualify."

Lucian's lip curled, and a fresh wave of rage rose up within me. Fucking demons and their loopholes.

Loopholes. Like the loophole Zagan had leveraged to kill straight-up humans.

A new idea flared inside me, white as rage.

"Volkov, you're a Hallow," I hissed under my breath, knowing that Lucian heard me too. "Cover me."

I didn't know if he followed me or not. I didn't care. I rushed again toward Zagan.

The demon's face contorted into a mask of fury as I reached him, but Lucian's hold was implacable, and the creature stayed pinned in place.

I didn't waste the opening.

The broken crucifix felt warm in my hand as I drove it deep into Zagan's chest, just below the sternum. Not to kill, maybe— I couldn't kill him, if Lucian was to be believed, and I couldn't kick him back to the primordial muck without there being some price to pay that maybe I didn't want to pay again or have Lucian pay for me. But I could anchor him. I could hold him in place while I played the last card I had.

"Delia—" Lucian started, but then his eyes met mine. He bore down on Zagan's shoulder. "I can only hold him. No more," he said tightly.

Zagan's mouth opened in a scream that sounded like Keegan's voice, and I almost faltered. Almost. But then I thought of the unhoused men and woman he'd killed. Five of them. Dead because of this creature's impotent rage, and the influence he'd had on a man who hadn't been able to say no.

I leaned closer to him, near enough to see his ruined yellow eyes, to smell the decay of his rotted flesh.

"Listen sharp, Zagan," I gritted through my clenched jaw, my fist driving the crucifix in deeper. "I'm going to offer you something no human has ever offered a demon. A deal."

Zagan's eyes narrowed. "You have nothing to offer me," he croaked. I might not be able to kill the bastard, but I definitely was hurting him. I took solace in that.

"Oh, but I do," I cooed. "You killed like a human. Demons don't kill. You manipulate, you possess, you corrupt—but you don't take human life directly. That's the line you're not supposed to cross. But you *did* cross it. George Roberts, Barry Stone. Remember those names? Wendy Simms. David Chen. Luke Wilkins. Five human souls, all dead by your hand. That makes you accountable."

"Keegan's," he rasped, and I twisted the crucifix deeper. Volkov hovered beside me, strong and sure, while Lucian watched me with flaming eyes. "Keegan killed. Trapped."

"Mordechai trapped you inside Keegan, yes. That was wrong. But he didn't whisper into a sick man's ear. He didn't break a mind already beaten down by the life he'd tried to live." I leaned closer. "Here's your deal, Zagan. God forgives even the worst human depravity. Did you know that? Even murderers can find salvation. But you're not human, you're a demon. And you dared to take the lives of His children. So now He will judge you like a human—or you'll send yourself back to Hell and start over again."

His face contorted. "No—"

"Yes," I said. "You acted as a human, Zagan. You got too close to the fucking sun, and now you'll feel its burn. Protection is available to you, but only if you acknowledge the Lord as your refuge. It's not such a bad deal, is it?" I watched him writhe a minute longer as I quoted Mordechai's favorite psalm. "If you tell the Lord He's your refuge, and you make the Most High your dwelling, no harm will overtake you, no disaster will come near your tent."

I pulled back just enough to see his whole face. "Doesn't that sound like a better option? Will you call on the Lord as your refuge?"

The silence stretched between us, filled only with the distant rumble of traffic above. Zagan's stolen features twisted into something ugly and defiant.

"Never," he spat. "And you have no power over me."

"I don't," I agreed. "But the Lord *is* my refuge, dickfuck. I *make* the Most High my dwelling. He gives power to the faint, and to him who has no might He...increases...strength. And He's coming for you now."

I twisted the crucifix deeper as power flooded through me, not the familiar heat of holy water or the comfortable weight of blessed silver, but something infinite and implacable. Divine strength made manifest.

Zagan's scream rose to match my voice, no longer human.

"I can do all things through Him who strengthens me, you know that?" I leaned in, whispering in Zagan's ear. "He's coming. He's almost here. Answer the call of the Father or take yourself back to the pit of your making. That's your choice. Your only choice. He who dwells in the shelter of the Most High will rest in the shadow of the Almighty. I will say of the Lord, 'He is my refuge and my fortress, my God, in whom I trust. Surely He will save you from the fowler's snare and from the deadly pestilence! He will cover you with His feathers, and under His wings you will find refuge; His faithfulness will be your shield and rampart!'"

Zagan's form began to blur.

"Come to Him, Zagan," I hissed. "For here you will not fear the terror of night, nor the arrow that flies by day, nor the pestilence that stalks in the darkness, nor the plague that destroys at midday. A thousand may fall at your side, ten thousand at your right hand, but it will not come near you...you will only observe with your eyes and see the punishment of the wicked. Say it, Zagan. *Call* on Him."

"*Never.*"

"Then fly back to the pits you sprang from. If I'm accountable to the rules you assholes have, you're accountable to mine. There's no other choice."

I leaned closer then, inhaling his filthy scent, and bit out my next, final words in Hebrew, the tongue that had bound and banished demons since Solomon's time. "For He will command His angels concerning you, to guard you in all your ways."

The explosion of light came from everywhere and nowhere, divine fury made visible. Zagan's scream cut off abruptly as his form came apart, not flesh dissolving but essence unmaking itself. The thing that had worn Keegan's face, that had murdered five innocent humans, that had chosen defiance over salvation, returned to the oily pit from which he'd been birthed millennia ago.

What remained was a splash of black ichor across the concrete pillar, already evaporating in the city air. The stench of burning sulfur and decay lingered for a moment, then was swept away by the exhaust from the expressway above.

I stood there, breathing hard, divine strength still singing in my veins. Around me, the normal sounds of the city resumed—traffic, distant sirens, the hum of streetlights.

"That...was unexpected," Volkov drawled.

TWENTY-NINE

I stared at the oily patch that was all that was left of Zagan for a long moment, dimly aware of Sergei arguing with Claire. Arguing?

I swiveled around, shocked to find Claire on her knees, frantically digging through the trash and rocks. Beside her, her very much battered leather tote lay half open, the heavy rosary now spilling out of it, caked with blood and dirt.

"We will get more. There's no need," Sergei blustered, but Claire jerked away from his helping hand.

"No!" she shouted. "No! We need these artifacts, these tools. They *work*. They're the only thing that does work on a regular basis. We need this. We're not safe!"

Her voice spiraled up, and I stumbled away from the stain of Zagan's memory, heading her way. When she looked at me, her face seemed to dissolve, bright tears sparking in her eyes.

"Oh, Delia," she moaned. "I didn't know what to do. I couldn't protect you. There was so much *blood*."

I swung my gaze toward Lucian, almost desperately, and he moved past me, over to Claire. I couldn't hear what he said, but she started crying harder as Sergei got her to her feet and moved her toward the second vehicle—his SUV. Meanwhile, Lucian dropped to all fours, and with movement I couldn't quite track, he scoured the ground, hissing as he pulled together the religious artifacts.

"I could do that," Nikolai pointed out, as Lucian stood with the bag again.

"You could. But you're too slow." He handed him Claire's tote. "Give this to Sergei. He can take her home."

"And get her car delivered," Nikolai said. "And stay with her as long as she needs. You have my word."

I didn't know if he was saying this to Lucian or me, but I nodded, swaying as he turned away. Lucian was at my side in an instant.

"You're hurt," he said, matter-of-factly. I looked down at my body. My long-sleeve shirt was scorched, the skin of my arms showing bruises and scrapes. "So fourth-level is quite a bit stronger than third," I muttered. "Why do you even move up to the next level if you give up the ability to interact with humans? Why did he ever bother possessing Keegan in the first place, when he could walk around as himself?"

"Let's get you to the car," he said, which I immediately recognized as not an answer, but I couldn't quite figure out why. I allowed him to take me to the long SUV that dwarfed Sergei's vehicle, gleaming with lethal bulk as Sergei's headlights played across it, the bodyguard apparently eager to get Claire away from here. I appreciated the sentiment.

Lucian opened the back door of the larger SUV limo and handed me inside, shutting the door again before I could fully get my bearings. Lights flickered on, and I peered around, trying to make sense of the space. There was a long banquette-style couch of some sort along one side, then two swiveling chairs with a table between them. I moved, not trusting myself to collapse unless I had something sturdy beside me. As it was, I poured myself into the swiveling chair with all the elegance of a sack of flour, groaning as I sagged back. Despite Lucian's assessment of my injuries, I didn't feel any more damaged than usual, though I definitely felt more tired. Like I'd been beaten down instead of beaten up.

The door opened again, and I dully noted Volkov's long, lean body entering the back of the SUV, looking unruffled from his brushed back hair to his barely scuffed shoes. "You look nice," I said, some distant part of my brain acknowledging the vapidity of that statement, but the rest of my brain not caring. I didn't care much about anything right now.

"You don't," he said, his words so light and conversational that it took a second for the barb to land.

"What?" I protested, staring down at myself. "It's not that bad."

Before he could reply, the door of the SUV opened again, and Lucian entered, sliding into the opposing captain's chair. That put me in reach of both of them, which struck me as not ideal, but I didn't have the bandwidth to figure out why.

"What are you hearing?" he asked Volkov as the vehicle started up. I vaguely wondered who was driving it, but once again couldn't hold on to the thought.

"I'm hearing that my club is a revelation for far too many of the horde, and that I can expect increased activity over the coming months." He leveled an amused glance at Lucian. "The betting has begun in earnest on you as well. There's an entire contingent gunning for your demotion, and you've barely started the job."

"Why?" I asked, and both men looked at me, seeming surprised I was still in the room. Car. Whatever this was.

"There hasn't been an enforcer among the horde since the Middle Ages," Nikolai said. "Comparatively recent in demon terms, and yet the world has become a more interesting place in those intervening centuries. Demons take their pleasure in ever more subtle and insidious ways. And they do so largely unchecked, it must be said. The most powerful laws and traditions are observed, of course, but the generals of the various courts don't advance agendas against each other as they once did. They don't scheme or conspire. Because to do so would be to attract the attention of their master, which would serve no one well."

"Assured mutual destruction," I muttered, and Volkov chuckled.

"Exactly so. Now, however, we have an enforcer of impressive pedigree, an individual. And individuals can be bought."

"Really?" I swiveled to Lucian. "You can?"

He didn't bother to answer me, but Volkov did.

"It isn't so difficult to understand. Take Asmodaea, for instance. Should Samael take seriously the whispers that she is planning to forcibly rise through the ranks, challenging him for supremacy, he could make the decision to set an enforcer against her."

"He wouldn't," Lucian said. "He plays a longer game than that."

"Perhaps." Nikolai shrugged. "But perhaps there are others who are less shrewd. Or perhaps some demons fear for their position in some nebulous future not of their choosing. A new enforcer is a benefit to the generals of the horde, but not to the rank and file. As it has ever been."

"So why did you do it?" I asked, slipping closer toward unconsciousness. *Why did I feel so bad?* I should be getting better at exorcisms, not worse, and this time I'd had help. Granted, I'd been swimming in the kiddie pool of Hell not five hours ago, so I suppose I could be excused, but still that memory suddenly connected the dots for me.

I struggled upright in my seat, trying to focus.

"It's my fault, isn't it?" I asked suddenly. "You took the job because I did something wrong."

"Not wrong," Lucian said as Nikolai leaned closer to me.

"Her eyes aren't tracking."

"Answer the question," I said, batting Nikolai away. Then I couldn't remember if I'd asked the question. I shook my head. "Why you? And why now? You've been working with Belial for a billion years, and you were never an enforcer before."

Lucian didn't say anything, but Nikolai turned to him, almost expectantly. As if there *was* an answer to this question, but it wasn't his to share. Which, once again, led me to... "This is because of me."

"No," Lucian repeated, and I looked down at my feet. I was so tired. I didn't think I should be this tired, and there was something wrong with my feet.

I stared. *What the hell had I stepped in?* Something black and viscous was dripping off the bottom of my boot, looking none too healthy. Had I carried some of the primordial ooze back with me? Could I sell it online?

I giggled, all too aware that my thoughts were slightly unhinged, and Nikolai slanted a glance down as well. Lucian's gaze followed.

"Volkov," he barked the name with the urgency of a thrown blade, but Nikolai was already on the move. They both were, actually, dragging me out of my chair and tossing me to the long leather bench that stretched the length of the SUV's cabin. Volkov produced a blade not unlike Sergei's, and I distantly wondered if it was part of their employee uniform, then I blinked as he slashed my shirt from neckline to belly, peeling it wide.

The gashes started right along my rib cage, extending down, welts that oozed black ichor. I stared as Nikolai sliced next through my jeans, peeling them off like the skin of a banana, versus trying to remove my boots first, but then I looked at the boots themselves and grimaced.

"Gross."

"What happened to you, Delia?" Lucian asked, and I looked up to see him directly in front of me, leaning over me as I sagged against the couch cushions. "What did you see when you were attacked in the hallway?"

"Standard tricks," I muttered, my gaze drifting to Volkov as he hacked through the laces of my boots, pulling out the tongue as a new spew of black oil spilled out of them. "Oh, man," I sighed. "Claire is going to be so pissed."

"Delia," Lucian commanded, his voice deeper now, harder. "What did you *see?*"

"Hallucinations," I said, working to get my mouth around the word. "I'm not immune to them, Lucian. I see them too. I may know they're fake, but I see them. I got pulled into a room where you were. I saw you. I saw a lot of you. Not close enough to name, not everyone, but I'd recognize them again." I smiled, wobbly. "Hadn't thought about that. That's good, yeah?"

"Her skin is stained," Nikolai said, and I frowned down at him.

"It'll wash off," I slurred. "It's not even real." Then I swung my gaze back to Lucian, who looked ready to punch a rhino in the head.

"What's your deal?" I grumbled. "I couldn't breathe in that dream. I got angry and I broke the vials of holy water Claire had given me to—"

"*What?*" Both Lucian and Volkov reacted violently to that, their outrage at once overt and hilarious.

"Vials!" I snapped. "Holy water. Claire gave them to me when we could both feel that something was going down, we just didn't know exactly what. Figured better safe than sorry. So I had them, and I smacked them into the floor, and I broke the glass and it cut up my hands pretty good, so I bled and watered your floor and then I sort of fell through."

I frowned. I'd started to shiver. Nikolai drew nearer to me, and I felt the cool touch of his finger beneath my chin, lifting me up.

"What did you see then?" he asked, and I realized he had very pretty eyes. Or, eye, anyway, since he still wore a patch over one of them. I may have mentioned that, or maybe said something about that to him, because I heard Lucian growl.

I looked his way. "There was a pit," I said. "So many things in that pit. Creatures. I got the impression this was where I'd sent Alaria without realizing it. It was pretty bad. I was somehow sturdier, less slippery than everything else around me, though, and they used me to try and...like, climb out."

I shuddered again, and Volkov's hands shifted, reaching out to grasp my shoulders, while Lucian moved to the other side and knelt. He picked up one of my feet.

"How much of you was underwater under the surface?" he asked quietly.

"I don't know. All of me, I guess. It was in my throat at one point. It tasted foul, but then they kept pulling and pulling and I couldn't get a purchase and I just got pissed, and I slammed my hands down against them, fighting them off."

"Your hands," Lucian said, his tone disbelieving. "The ones still holding the vials. You took holy water into Hell."

"I mean, I guess?" I lifted my chin not realizing I'd slumped, only to find them both staring at me. "Look, sorry if I handled my demonic daydream wrong. That place sucked."

"That place is claiming you now," Lucian said. "Drawing you back to bind you anew. Permanently, if it can."

"Wait, what?" That woke me up in a hurry. "No! *Stop* it!"

Volkov hissed out a breath. "You need anchors to this plane, this world, Delia. Human anchors. And shedim anchors wouldn't hurt either."

Lucian nodded, and the look in his eye had gone predatory as he stared at me.

"You're willing?" Lucian asked. "You need to say yes."

"To not go back there? Have you been there? It sucks." I backed deeper into the couches, staring at the shadow twining up my legs, feeling the dampness returning, liquid bubbling out of my pores.

"Are you willing?" Lucian asked again.

"Yes! Yes, for fuck's sake, do anything you need. Yes."

I probably should have been more specific.

In a smooth, sinuous motion, Nikolai lunged forward. He took my face in his hands and yanked me to him, kissing me hard. Lights exploded behind my eyes. Pain, fire, and need. He pulled back, and I gasped.

"What the hell?"

"One of the hazards of being aligned with the Ravening Court," he said with a grim smile, his eyes blazing with heat. "Lust is the most direct line."

I blinked at him. "What?" I said again.

"Delia," Lucian commanded, and then *he* was in front of me, he was kissing me, as Volkov levered himself up onto the couch, the two of them entwining around me. Kissing, touching, exploring, their beautiful clothes now smeared with black goo, their mouths and tongues everywhere. Lucian licked and bit his way up my rib cage, his breath cool over the suppurating wounds, while Volkov drew a wide, powerful hand over my hip, down my thigh, kneading deep as his fingers splayed over the stained-black flesh.

Flesh that wasn't so stained anymore.

"What the hell is going on?" I asked, because I felt I should, but in truth I didn't really care. I'd never felt so alive in all my life.

When Lucian and I had made love, it was hunger, heat and pulsing need, and that was here as well, but this was something more. Cold healing energy burst through me with every kiss and caress, sparking through my blood and waking up parts of my body I didn't know existed. I could feel my feet again, my hands. The deep gashes in my belly no longer ached, and as they nipped and licked and teased, mouths on my breasts, my lips, and down across my belly, I groaned.

Light returned to where I hadn't realized there had been only darkness. Sound filled ears I hadn't realized had gone quiet. I could smell heat, smoke, and heavy spices, honey and wine.

I blinked my eyes open, nestled against Lucian's chest as Volkov broke off a kiss. I jerked to full awareness.

"What?" I managed, then swept my gaze down my body, somehow knowing that it would be pink and whole. Scarred, yes, but no longer bleeding oil. Volkov moved away from me, shuddering with a reaction he couldn't suppress for a few moments. He hunched over, breathing hard, and I stared at him—I'd caused that reaction in him, I'd affected him. Had he expected that? Had he wondered what it would be like to kiss me, to touch me?

Then he turned back to me and his face was smooth again, untroubled, his mouth twisting into a smirk on his face that looked like it might stay there for years.

"Feeling better?" Lucian rumbled above me.

I realized I was still tucked into his embrace. I struggled upright. "And why was that needed again?" I managed.

As I shrugged him off, Lucian backed away but only slightly, while Nikolai opened a cubby beneath the couch and pulled a blanket free, draping it over me with almost clinical detachment. But his face remained flushed, his eyes fiery and dark. And his hands still shook.

"You needed to be anchored to this world, so that another world could not claim you as it clearly wanted to do," Lucian said. "If anyone was paying attention when you returned to the floor of the chamber, they would have realized what you did, what you brought. You broke so many inviolate rules that—"

"Well, nobody was paying attention to me," I snapped. "They were pretty much all focused on you." I turned toward him, wrapping the blanket more closely around me, and flinched. "Oh, my God," I said, reaching out to wipe the blood away from Lucian's mouth. "Did I bite you?"

A tremor of energy passed through the cabin, thick, hot, and full of dark intent.

"No," Volkov said, drawing my gaze again to his face—and his stormy, once-more hungry eyes. "I did."

THIRTY

"You really shouldn't look at me that way. I didn't do anything wrong, and Steve will be right back. I promise."

Despite my earnest tone, the beagle sitting in Steve's chair eyed me reproachfully, ears down, tail not wagging. In the week and a half since he literally burst into our lives, he'd become extremely bossy. Fortunately, Angel the beagle hadn't adhered to me like Velcro, but to Steve, who seemed much more capable of handling his neediness.

"I think he likes you," Claire announced, though I hadn't asked her. She sat at her desk in her perfect summer weight linen suit of soft plum, organizing the day's return calls—requests for services had tapered off since the excitement of last week, but they still were coming in at a strong clip. "And I continue to think we should use him in our promotional material. Everyone loves dogs. Especially rescue dogs."

"He was rescued from demon possession," I pointed out. "In a very messy, stinky, public way. Just check out YouTube."

"All the more reason! At least let him be the mascot for

Darker Truths. Now that Roy has revealed he's the man behind that pod, he needs all the help he can get."

I blinked at her. "Seriously? I thought he was doing well."

"He *is* doing well, but you can always do better," she said. "That's the trap of social media. Yesterday's results are never enough."

"I guess," I said, sinking heavily onto the couch. It had been fully a week since Claire and I had dragged ourselves out of Descent and straight into the altercation with Zagan beneath the overpass. After Lucian and Volkov had driven me to the house that night, I'd slept for three days straight, barely getting up to pee and drink protein water. But my skin had finally lost its ash-gray tint, and I was starting to be able to eat without gagging on the taste of oil. Unfortunately, I had acquired 24/7 surveillance from either Lucian or Volkov, which was already wearing thin.

"Have you heard anything more from Jay Butler?" my demon-shaped security blanket now asked, looking up from one of the overstuffed chairs in our seating area.

Claire shook her head. "No, though of course he knows how to reach me. But I think he's doing okay. Sergei told me that Jay's tip regarding Storm Court earned him an official attaboy from Volkov, and he seems to be doing well as a bartender there. He's a gossip, but he has no problem spreading lies as easily as he does truths. Plus, people like to talk to him. Which is never a bad thing, I guess, when you're running a club like Descent. If he's able to feed real intel to Volkov and lies to everyone else, then he may have found his happy place."

"Did the Storm Court tip pay off?" I asked. "I...I think I missed that."

"Oh, definitely—but you get a pass, that was when you were still in deep recovery." Claire grinned. "But yeah, it was great. Dark Streets dropped their intel to their subscribers right before the rave, and apparently, someone tipped off the police at the same time, so the cops were on hand to crash the rave of all raves and drop the hammer on a black-market sale of what they were loosely calling 'cult paraphernalia.' Apparently, some of it was pretty hinky stuff, all of it was unregulated, and most of it was out of Asia, Africa, even South America. Fortunately, there were enough drugs in the mix as well so that the bust made the police look good. It definitely made Sue Willows look good, and by extension, it made Jay look good, so it was a win all around. The only people that it made look bad were the owners of Storm Court, but, hey. You can't win 'em all."

"That nightclub is run by an entertainment company based out of New York, to my understanding," Lucian said. "Perhaps they'll return there."

"Maybe, or maybe they'll just leverage the publicity to get even bigger." Claire held up her phone. "Their Yelp reviews are off the chain, and the whole thing has inspired a subreddit on alternative entertainment experiences in the city—nightclubs, bars, and even restaurants. Some of the occult-oriented restaurants sound absolutely amazing, by the way, and a couple are gaining serious international notice. So I'm thinking that 'intelligence leak' may simply have been a brilliant marketing strategy."

I squinted at her. "We have occult restaurants in Chicago?"

"Not really occult-occult, but just like, you know, the vibe. Dark and mysterious, here's your taste of delicious evil, that kind of thing."

She burst into giggles as I leveled her a glance. "Oh, come on! We should totally try one of these places. You could pass out a few cards, score some new clients."

I made a face. "New clients aren't really an issue," I said, though I hadn't had the energy to answer any of the messages

Claire had neatly categorized for me. "Speaking of, how's Grace?"

"Grace is doing beautifully, I'll have you know." The voice came from the hallway, and Sandy sailed through the door in a voluminous flurry of lemon yellow, her brown hair up in a messy, corkscrewed topknot. "Her care team is top notch, they've kept me informed every step of the way, and I look forward to working with Grace again once she returns home—which should be in the next few weeks. I'm thrilled to be a part of her recovery."

She paused, gesturing vaguely toward my back office. "There are police in the back parking lot, though, so heads up on that. I can't imagine they're coming for me, and as we know, nobody else works in this building."

"Seriously?" Claire asked, popping up from her desk to cross over to my inner office, where the view to the back parking lot was unrestricted. Sandy smiled at me, smoothing down her caftan as she ambled over to Steve's desk.

"I was actually coming up anyway to talk with you," she said. "Steve is also in the parking lot, on the phone, and he wanted me to check on Angel. But, to get even more specific, Grace has been transferred to an inpatient facility north of the city that specializes in Other Specified Dissociative Disorder, which is what her primary therapist contends Grace is dealing with, and I tend to agree. Since she's in between classes, it's a good time for her to have some really intensive treatment before returning home to continue outpatient care, and her doctors are honestly hopeful that she can work toward true integration of her personalities. It will take some time for them to work backward to the point of trauma, but I think she's in the best possible hands."

"Well, she wouldn't even have made it that far without you," I said, and Sandy smiled.

"Oh, I know my limitations," she said. "Sometimes my best work is done as a launching pad to other therapy. People first need to feel safe, then the path appears. I'm simply the gatekeeper."

She pointed a robin's egg blue fingernail at me. "That said, I am doing a low-key collaging event Friday evening at seven o'clock, and you'd be very welcome to join. You too, Lucian. You might find it rejuvenating to get in touch with your inner child."

Lucian studied her evenly. "I think that would be a questionable experience for all concerned."

"Well, just *think* about it." Sandy laughed. "And you too, Delia. I'm glad to see you up and about again, but you can't work all the time. Not if you're going to sustain." She squinted down at Angel. "And you, good sir, need a bit more sunshine in your life, don't you?"

Angel jumped off the chair at her coo and danced around in a circle.

"I thought so." Sandy grabbed Angel's leash, a bright blue knotted rope with daisies on it, and attached it to his collar. "We have to keep up appearances," she told the dog as the two of them trotted out of the room.

"She's right, there's a cruiser downstairs, and a van behind," said Claire, coming back from the inner office. "But they haven't made a move to do anything yet. I think it's Hernandez, but I can't be sure."

"She knows the way." I shrugged, then glanced toward Lucian. "The police haven't caused Descent any problems, have they? That Storm Court rave didn't bleed over into their territory?"

Lucian shook his head. "Descent has been a part of the Chicago club scene for going on twenty years, and Nikolai Volkov has carried on his predecessors' efforts to ingratiate himself with the leaders of the city. Unless and until a murder takes place within the club, a human murder, that is, there's no reason for the police to get involved. And you could say they are encouraged to actively *not* get involved, if you take my meaning."

"I don't know," I said. "Hernandez said that I'd been noticed there, so somebody's talking."

"Somebody is always talking. What matters is the action that results." He studied me from across the room. "Nikolai said that you didn't sleep much last night."

"What?" Claire bleated from her desk, and I winced. I'd gone five whole days since I'd come back to the office without her getting a whiff of my unusual living arrangement now, courtesy mainly of the fact that the Victorian spooked her.

"It's not like it sounds," I assured her.

"Well, then, tell me what it is like," she said, fluttering her eyelashes. "Is Nikolai, ah…your bodyguard now? Seems like that job's a bit below his pay grade?"

"No, he's not. But apparently, I've inherited babysitter detail, which I said I'd tolerate right up until it got intrusive." I turned to glare at Lucian. "And guess what, it just got intrusive. It stops now. You guys want to see me, you can pay for my dinner."

"I've got just the place," Claire said, holding up her phone again. "Delicto started like six weeks ago as a pop-up, and the right person told the right person who told the right person, and now their chef is opening for real in Madagascar's old space."

"Where?" I asked. "Madagascar, like the country?"

"No, you idiot." Claire laughed. "It was a big deal a few years ago, closed down for whatever reason, and it's just been sitting there, perfect and pristine, but empty. But with enough funding and buzz, all things are possible. And apparently, Delicto's got a super spooky vibe. Perfect first date material."

She bit her lip, glancing at Lucian. "Or double date. Or whatever."

"I'm not...never mind," I said as heavy steps tromping down the hallway broke my concentration.

I looked up to see Officer Hernandez at my front door, her hair swept back into a tight bun, her jaw clenched. She smelled like coffee and adrenaline spikes and a deep, abiding weariness.

"What's wrong?" I asked, quickly standing up. "Did something happen? Did you find something I should—"

"We didn't, and if we did, we wouldn't be able to pursue it, courtesy of a call to our offices yesterday, made by none other than the *mayor*. I don't suppose you would have had anything to do with that?"

I peered at her. "Do I look like I have pull with the mayor?"

She sighed. "No, you don't. Which makes this even more irritating. We digitized everything we could, but we've officially been told this line of inquiry is no longer of interest to the department, and therefore all your materials should be returned to you."

She stood aside, and the same three men who had helped her carry out Mordechai's journals in plain brown boxes a week and a half ago returned the favor and carted them back in.

"You want us to put them back on the shelves?" Hernandez asked drily, and I shook my head.

"No. But do these include the journal you got sent separately?"

"Oh, yeah." She made a face. "He made that point specifically, which, of course, meant that he *knew* about that journal, which not too many people did." She shot me another searching glance. "Twenty years on the force, and I've never been told to drop questions that needed asking. I don't like it, Delia. And even though I don't think you necessarily had anything to do with it, you need to be careful. I've said this before, but if the wrong kind of people start taking too much of an interest in the work you're doing, it could turn out badly for you."

"Understood." I bit my lip as I watched the men bring the boxes in and deposit them in my inner office. I'd found more entries in Roy Granger's version of the journal than I really wanted to, entries about other cases of Mordechai's, details that he hadn't included in the main files.

Even Thomas Keegan had finally shown up in Roy's version of the journal. I had read the rabbi's neat, precise handwriting with a flat, sick feeling. Keegan had died five years ago of heart failure—there'd been no suspicious circumstances indicated. He was a street person who'd managed to hold down a job off and on at the soup kitchen for years after his interaction with Mordechai...but Mordechai hadn't exorcised the demon who afflicted him, Zagan, when he could have because...Zagan was a threat to him? To me? Something about that just didn't wash, but there was no other information I could find in Roy's journal about Keegan other than the fact that Mordechai had purchased a gravesite for him, tended by the same fund he'd established for the graves of five other unhoused people over the years.

George Roberts, Barry Stone. Wendy Simms. David Chen. Luke Wilkins.

Mordechai had even cut out a write-up in his synagogue's newsletter, the publication lauding him for his charity.

He'd written one word down beside the carefully pasted-in article.

Pride.

"I'm definitely happy to have those back," I said to Hernandez, gesturing to the boxes. "But I also appreciate the warning. I don't suppose you were on the detail that caught the rave at Storm Court?"

"No, thank God." she made a face. "But I did catch a glimpse of the evidence intake form. There's some seriously messed-up shit coming through this city. Something else that you'd probably do well to avoid."

The men came back out from their last delivery, giving her the high sign, and she turned to me, hooking her thumbs in her belt in what looked like a habitual move. "Seriously, you'd probably do well to lie low for a minute. It's all well and good that someone shut down this journal thing, but I don't like it. It just feels off."

"Agreed." She nodded to me, then to Claire and Lucian. She exited without saying anything further, but with a kind of preoccupied look on her face that made me think she had already started poking at the problem from a different angle. I didn't feel like Hernandez had it in for me, but she wasn't quite ready to take everything at face value, either. Whether that would hurt me or help me was yet to be seen.

I heard Steve's cheerful acknowledgment of Hernandez as they passed in the hallway, then he returned, scanning the room quickly for the missing Angel.

"Uh-oh," he said. "We got another runner on our hands?"

"Sandy took him," Claire confirmed. "And if you didn't pick up on it, the police returned all of Delia's journals due to some pressure from the higher-ups. Sounds like maybe Roy should look into paranormal interest in local government, you ask me."

"What?" Steve asked as I winced. "No way! And they're looking *out* for us?"

"That's not how I would take this," I started, but Claire cut me off.

"That's exactly how we should take it, or at least that we've caught their attention," she said firmly. "And I don't care what Officer Hernandez says, we should absolutely leverage this attention in the best way possible. I'm not saying that we need to fund their reelection campaign, but if there's an event or a party, or, say, a cooking demonstration at Delicto that we find out that city officials are attending, we would be wise to take part in them."

"Delicto?" Steve asked, furrowing his brow. "What the hell is that?"

"Exactly," I said.

"I'm serious!" Claire countered. "We should be keeping ahead of the supernatural crazy happening in the city, not playing catch-up. And we should know the players involved."

"She's not wrong." I was startled by Lucian's low, quiet voice, and I turned to see him tenting his fingers. "Volkov has taken on additional security, given the horde's heightened interest in Descent, but it's not just his club they're interested in. There's a confluence of energy in the city that he says is unusual. I wouldn't know, because I have been otherwise occupied until very recently." He shifted his gaze to me. "There's more that we need to learn from him, more that he hasn't shared. It's concerning."

"What do you mean, concerning?" I asked, frowning at him. "You've left him alone with me in that house, and you're not sure about him?"

"Wait, what?" Steve asked, startled, and Claire giggled.

I kept my focus on Lucian. "You think he's a threat?"

He smirked, but his manner was charged, almost provocative. "A threat? No. But I think he knows more than he's shared, and while he prides himself on holding himself aloof, we have secured a new leverage with him we didn't have before. It would seem we're more likely to speak freely among each other...wouldn't you agree?"

Irritation and something that felt a lot like horror zipped through me as I stared at him. "You pulled him into this on purpose—into, uh, this tighter relationship with us?" I didn't know how else to put it, not with Claire and Steve staring at me, flat out confused. Hell, I was confused too. Confused and... uneasy. "This is all some kind of game to you?"

I didn't know if I believed it. I definitely didn't know if Volkov believed it, and I absolutely wasn't sure what I would do if I discovered that everything that I'd experienced with Lucian and Volkov in the back of Volkov's stretch SUV...was all a lie.

"Not a lie," Lucian corrected, though I hadn't said that part out loud. "But everything in this world is a game, wouldn't you say?" He smiled, and his next words skated across my mind, clearly intended for me alone.

"And it's your move, sweet Delia."

AUTHOR'S NOTE

This is a work of fiction featuring demons, possession, and exorcism practices pulled from multiple faith traditions—then thoroughly mixed, bent, and occasionally broken to serve the story.

I've taken creative liberties with theology. Many of them. On purpose. Nothing in this book should be taken as a fully accurate representation of any genuine faith tradition, religious practice, or theological belief system.

All characters, events, and circumstances are fictional. Any resemblance to actual persons, living or dead, or real events is coincidental. Any errors are mine—whether from research gaps or deliberate creative choice, it simply depends.

If you're looking for canonically accurate demonology, please consult a theologian. If you're here for a dark demon romance, welcome aboard.

ACKNOWLEDGMENTS

When it comes to being grateful for the opportunity to share these books with you, I'm guilty as charged. These are the people who make it possible, and whom I appreciate so much.

To my publisher, Tanya Anne Crosby of Oliver Heber Books: thank you for standing in the gap for so many authors, and for seeing the far horizon so clearly. You are extraordinary.

To my editor, Sally O'Keef: Your ongoing support and insights make these books a pleasure to write and refine.

To my cover designer, Kim Killion: Another fabulous work... and I'm so excited for what's to come!

To Judi Soderberg and Sabra Harp: You not only help me tell a cleaner tale, you inspire me to keep you on your toes. Thank you!

To my proofreader, Kesha Young: Not only were your catches brilliant, but your reaction to this book made me tear up. Thank you for your passion and your skill. (Any errors are simply diabolical anomalies.)

To my readers: Thank you for walking willingly into the dark with me. For exploring the dangerous, the twisted, and the beautifully broken. You make stories like this possible.

And to Geoffrey: You made this story richer. As you always do.

ALSO BY JENNIFER CHANCE

The Accidental Exorcist

Wicked As Sin

Sexy As Sin

Guilty As Sin

Hungry As Sin

Fang & Fire

Court of Talons

Crown of Wings

Gatekeepers of the Gods

Courted

Captured

Claimed

Crowned

Boston Magic Academies

Touch of the Mage

Blood of the Mage

Heart of the Mage

Soul of the Mage

The Hunter's Call

The Hunter's Curse

The Hunter's Snare

The Hunter's Vow

Witchling Academy

Teaching the King

Tempting the King

Taming the King

ABOUT THE AUTHOR

Jennifer Chance is an award-winning author of magical modern romance and romantic fantasy. She is also the urban fantasy and paranormal romance author Jenn Stark. For free reads, news, and a magical escape from the ordinary, connect with her at jenniferchance.com (linked).

link: https://www.jenniferchance.com

fb: https://www.facebook.com/authorJenniferChance/

A small press bound by the belief that every voice matters.

Sign up for our newsletter to learn about new releases and more.

Buy directly from us to save on ebooks, book bundles, and special editions.

Follow us on social media:

facebook.com/oliverheberbooks

instagram.com/oliverheberbooks

tiktok.com/@oliverheberbooks

bsky.app/profile/oliverheberbooks.bsky.social

youtube.com/@OliverHeberBooksPublisher

oliverheberbooks.substack.com

amazon.com/oliverheberbooks